The Chosen Book 3

Crown of Embers

Meg Anne

For our furbabies…
Thank you for showing us the meaning of unconditional love.
You make us better humans.

CROWN
OF
EMBERS

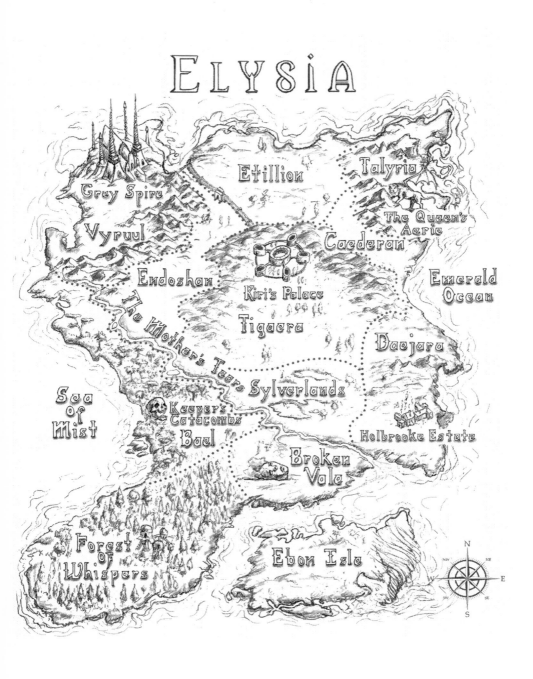

CHAPTER 1

"*T*hat traitorous bitch!" Helena seethed as she slammed her hands onto the top of the worn wooden table. "If it's a war she wants, I'll damn well give her one!"

Von rested his hand on top of hers, working his fingers beneath her palm in an attempt to pry it off the now smoking wood. His sharp hiss of pain caught her attention.

In surprise, Helena looked down and noticed the imprint of her hand where it had been seared into the wood. Her temper was flaring out of control, ping-ponging between grief and anger and causing her magic to react. Bolstered by Von's presence, it was more potent than ever and did not require her conscious thought before flaring to life. Her power was taking cues from her emotions; a dangerous, and potentially deadly, combination.

Balling her hands into fists, she stepped back from the table and continued her restless pacing. "She mur-murd—" Helena choked on the word, unable to say it out loud, to let it be real. Murdered. Rowena had *murdered* him. Anderson. The man who had loved and protected her for as long as she could remember. Every hurt—small, imaginary, or otherwise—garnered the same loving attention and care.

And now he was dead. All because of her and how much his death would hurt her. She hadn't seen it coming, hadn't even thought of needing to protect him. She'd failed him.

Bile rose up as the image of his face bloomed in her mind: mouth frozen open in an eternal scream, two gaping red holes where kind green eyes had once been. Like a rubber band, Helena snapped back from tears into anger. Spinning to face the men standing around her she growled, "I will destroy her."

"We," Von corrected, moving into her line of sight, "*we* will destroy her. Together."

Iridescent eyes collided with molten gray and she could feel him willing her to step back from the murderous edge on which she was teetering. Helena was trembling as her emotions raged within her; her heart was pounding, beating erratically like a bird trying to escape its cage.

She was not the only one affected. Around her, the Circle shifted restlessly, the intensity of her rage seeping into them. Kragen was the first to lose control, slamming his fist into the wall with a roar. Ronan wrapped an arm around him and pulled him back, whispering harshly into his ear. Kragen gnashed his teeth, and with a nod from Von, Ronan pulled him from the Chambers. Helena stared at the hole Kragen's fist had left in the otherwise unblemished stone.

"We need to be rational, Kiri," Joquil said in a low voice.

Sparkling iridescent eyes flew to where he was standing beside Timmins. Joquil straightened under her scrutiny, but did not back down from her withering gaze.

"Fuck rational," she snarled dangerously.

Joquil swallowed back his response when he saw her thunderous expression. Before he could try again, his warm amber eyes began to show flickers of iridescence. A dark smile curled his lips and he purred in a voice filled with malice, "Shall I bring you her head, Kiri?"

Timmins gave a start at the words which were so out of character for the Master. He looked with growing horror between Joquil and Helena. When his eyes met hers, his posture relaxed and the same eerie smile grew on his face.

"Out!" bellowed Von.

2

Timmins and Joquil blinked, their eyes returning to normal. Without delay, the two men rushed for the door and away from the woman whose power threatened to overtake them.

"Helena," Von said in a low, measured voice, trying to pull her attention back to him.

Her eyes went to his as Darrin cried out, "Don't you dare tell me to leave the only person who understands what I've lost."

Von growled, irritation flickering in his gray eyes. As one, Helena and Von pinned Darrin with their gazes.

Darrin was the picture of grief, his bright green eyes bleak and red-rimmed. "That man raised me, and that evil bitch just sent me his head," he fumed. "Perhaps you should be the one to leave! Let me grieve with the only person who is capable of feeling the same loss that is tearing me apart."

"Shield, get. The. Fuck. Out!" Von roared.

Instead of moving toward the door, Darrin stalked toward Von. "Make me."

"Wrong answer." Von slammed his palm out, shoving Darrin with all of his considerable strength. Darrin flew back, falling into the table before crashing to the floor. Von grabbed Darrin by the front of his shirt and lifted him up, pushing him out the doorway before kicking the door shut.

There was a crash as Darrin slammed his fist into the door, causing it to shake. Still staring at the door Von replied almost conversationally, "You might be grieving, puppy, and I'm sorry for that, but not even the Mother will save you if you come back into this room."

There was no response. Von, the only one able to resist the seductive pull of her magic, slowly turned back to face his Mate.

"*Mira*," he said, brushing his fingers along her tear-stained cheek.

Her lips pulled back in a silent snarl, but she did not speak.

"Helena," he tried again. When she still did not respond, he demanded, "Mate." The order echoed along the length of their bond, startling her out of her fury.

Helena glanced around the room, surprised to see it was empty. "Where did everyone go?" she asked, her voice hoarse.

"I asked them to leave," he said with a wry twist to his lips.

She blinked up at him, confused, before asking warily, "What did I do?"

He wrapped her in a hug, pressing a kiss to her forehead. "It doesn't matter."

"Von..."

"Shhh," he murmured.

"Don't shush me," she protested weakly.

He just held her tighter, asking softly, "Are you all right?"

Taking a deep, shuddering breath, she admitted baldly, "No."

Von held her, giving her the time and space she needed before she could speak further.

"She killed him, Von. He was..." Helena trailed off, unable to think of a way to describe everything Anderson had been to her. "Family," she said finally. "Anderson was my family, and he never did anything in his life to deserve what she did to him." Helena's voice faded toward the end, the threat of tears making it hard for her to speak.

"We will put an end to Rowena. Trust me; no one wants that more than I do, Helena. But we need to be smart. She did this, knowing it would provoke you. She wants you to strike while you are unprepared to face her. You saw her army; we need far greater numbers if we are going to face that again."

Helena nodded. "I know, but—"

Von's voice was warm but firm as he interjected, "Do not mistake preparation for a sign of weakness. She landed a great blow today, but this is just one battle of what will surely be many. You will be the one still standing at the end of this. Let us call on our allies and gather our forces. Then we will face her, on our terms and when we are the ones with the upper hand."

His words made sense, and yet they grated. "You speak like you've done this before," she muttered petulantly.

"Maybe once or twice," he affirmed.

There was comfort in knowing she would not be facing this alone. "I want to give him a proper burial," she said suddenly.

"Whatever you want, *Mira*."

4

"Can you bury just a," she grimaced, "head?"

"You are the Kiri, you can do whatever you damn well please."

"Except rush into battle," she countered.

"Except put your life in danger," he amended.

The small smile that rose in response to his words did not last long, her pain outweighing all other emotion. "I don't know what to do," she confessed in a small voice, her head still tucked into his chest.

Von's hand moved comfortingly over her back, "Tonight you grieve the man you have lost. Tomorrow we will celebrate his life and then we can worry about the rest."

"Okay," she agreed, lower lip trembling as her emotions bubbled up again. She sobbed until her tears ran dry and the sky went dark. Von held her the entire time.

"Will you tell me about him?" he asked once she started to pull back from him.

The pain in her aqua eyes shot through him but she was smiling softly as she said, "Yes."

HELENA WAS CURLED up in her favorite cushioned chair, a blanket draped over her lap as she stared silently across the room. A soft snore had her eyes moving to her Mate and a tired smile rose at the sight of him. Von was splayed across the settee beside her, entirely too large and masculine for the dainty piece of furniture. He couldn't help but radiate strength and presence, even when he was all but unconscious.

Von had urged her to come to bed with him hours ago, but she could not quiet her mind enough to drift to sleep. Finally he'd relented, seeing that she needed time to process her loss now that the initial wave of grief had passed. That didn't mean he'd gone far. She'd rolled her eyes when he'd stretched out muttering under his breath about furniture that was too small, while trying, unsuccessfully, to make himself comfortable. Her heart had swelled a little, appreciating how he was giving her space while also letting her know that he was there for her.

As his grumbling gave way to deep, steady breathing, she had thanked the Great Mother once again that it was not his head she had found in that box. There was no question in Helena's mind about whether or not she would have survived that particular loss. If the last few months were any indication, *no one* would have survived that reaction, especially since she'd nearly come undone by mere separation.

Not that it made her heart hurt any less for having lost Anderson. A numbness had settled over her since she left the Chambers cradled in Von's arms. It allowed her to spend the twilight hours lovingly flipping through long-forgotten memories of the man that helped raise her. While there were still a few tears, they were silent, quietly slipping through her swollen eyes as she allowed herself to relive their time together. Helena was also accompanied by the steady ache of grief, but the memories were more bittersweet than painful: a tender bruise being accidentally brushed instead of a dagger twisting through her heart.

She knew that this was not a pain that would quietly fade. Its ache would always remain to some degree. It was the kind of pain that would rear up unexpectedly, as strong and fierce as if it had just happened, in the days and years to come.

Helena couldn't believe that he was gone, that he would never know her children. Never meet the man who held the other half of her soul. Never again hold her in his stooped embrace as he pressed paper-dry lips to her forehead and wished her goodnight. So many moments had been stolen from them, but there was one that she would miss more than any other: the sound of his gruff voice uttering her name with exasperation, even as his eyes twinkled with pleasure, whenever she tried to take care of him.

She let out a low, sad sigh. Anderson's loss would stay with her, but she would not let it change the woman he'd helped shape. He'd already made her promise as much just over a year ago.

The memory of that day surged forth, unbidden. The details that sprang up surprised her with their intensity. It was not a time she cared to dwell on. She had not let herself think of it at all since it had passed. Helena had considered it the darkest time of her life until Gillian's betrayal had shown her just what kind of darkness truly existed in the world, and in her.

Yet, as the recollection of that afternoon swirled into focus within her mind, Helena realized that perhaps what she most needed right now was to remember the words that had provided comfort and a glimmer of hope when she had been lost in darkness.

HELENA SCOWLED at the bright cerulean sky, irritated that the world did not see fit to mirror her mourning with storm clouds and icy rain. There was something about a cheerful spring day that did not feel appropriate for a funeral. Especially not when it was her mother's. Her shoulders sagged at the reminder. Even as she brushed and braided her hair, readying herself for the day, she had not wanted to think about what awaited her outside her small cottage.

Moving to the large wooden armoire that held both hers and her mother's clothes, Helena wilted further. *How in the Great Mother's name were you supposed to select the outfit you wore to bury someone you loved?*

Ignoring the wet blur that rapidly filled her eyes, Helena randomly selected and pulled out a dress, deciding that choosing would be an impossible task. Whatever she chose would end up being remembered as what she wore to her mother's funeral. The only way to avoid it would be if she just attended the funeral naked.

The irreverent thought made her lips twitch. Her mother had always been pragmatic, and she probably wouldn't have bat an eye, noting that it was exactly what Helena had worn the first time they'd met anyway. Helena pushed the silly thought away. It was an amusing diversion, but certainly not the way she wanted to go say goodbye to her mother.

Glancing down at the soft purple fabric clenched in her hands, Helena went still. She'd grabbed her mother's dress; the one she saved for special occasions and holidays. Helena had always thought her mother looked as beautiful as a Kiri when she wore it, with her chocolate brown hair falling in contrasting waves against the vibrant fabric. She stroked trembling fingers along its length, smoothing out the wrinkles she'd caused.

Closing her eyes, Helena pulled the dress to her nose and inhaled deeply. The faint scent of roses still clung to the material. She stood breathing in the familiar and comforting scent of her mother's favorite perfume for a few silent seconds. With a pang, she forced herself to lower the dress. If she didn't hurry, she would miss the entire ceremony. Spurred into action, Helena let out a shuddering breath and quickly pulled the dress over her head, letting it fall loosely around her. When she opened her eyes, a soft gasp left her lips.

While she lacked some of her mother's more generous curves, and her hair was several shades lighter, wearing that dress it was as though her mother was standing before her. Helena traced her reflection on the cool glass, not noticing that her aqua eyes were red-rimmed and watery or that her eyelashes were dark spikes from a night spent crying. Her nose was bright red and her face puffy, but all of those details faded. As she gazed into the mirror, all she could see were her mother's eyes.

A sob bubbled up but Helena pushed it back. *How can she be gone, when she's staring back at me?* A sharp knock had her jumping and stepping back. With a final, lingering glance at the mirror, Helena left the small bedroom and went to open the door.

Looking grimmer than she had ever seen him, Anderson stood waiting for her. He had combed and parted his white hair, and made sure to wash and press his best clothes. His gnarled hands were spinning his faded work hat in a distracted manner while he waited for her to answer. At the sight of her in the doorway, his hands faltered, and his mouth fell open before a wide grin stretched across his face.

"Well, look at you. If you ain't the spitting image of your mother..." his words trailed off at her flinch. Understanding filled his green eyes and he pulled her into a bear hug. "No need to be sad, little bug. Your mama may have returned to the Great Mother, but just because she's not here with you and me, doesn't mean she's gone. She's just watching you from above now. Besides, Old Anderson here has it on good authority that your mama wouldn't want you to be sad.

Not when she is at peace without a single care in the world. Don't give her a reason to linger here, worrying about you."

Helena made a face at his words. They were soothing, but she was feeling selfish and in no mood to be understanding.

Anderson chuckled at her dubious expression. "It's just like when you were little, 'member? Your mama went away, but she ain't gone forever. You'll be with her again one day. In the meantime, Old Anderson will keep you company."

Tears filled her throat, but Helena fought them back. She squeezed Anderson as hard as she dared, trying to ignore how frail he felt in her embrace. Frail was not a word she wanted to associate with the man who always seemed larger than life.

His voice was gruff as he asked, "Would you do this old man the honor of accompanying him to say his goodbyes to the daughter of his heart?"

Warmth spread through her at his words. She had always thought of Anderson as her grandfather, and hearing that he had considered them part of his family as well made her feel less alone. Shared grief somehow seemed easier to face.

Her heart too full for words, Helena merely nodded and wove her arm through his. With a soft click, the door shut behind her and they made their slow way to the large oak tree that divided their two properties. It was, or had been, her mother's favorite place to come and relax after a particularly grueling day. Helena could think of no better place for her to be now. Anderson had hired some men from town to dig the grave and take care of the details. All that was left to do was say a proper goodbye.

As they cleared the last rise, tears began to fall from her eyes in earnest. It was not the sight of the tree, but the beautifully carved wooden bench that Anderson had crafted and placed there.

"Somewhere for you to sit when you come to visit her," he'd said gently, as he watched her reaction to his gift.

She squeezed his hand, trying to suffuse her thanks into the action.

He gestured toward the bench. "Go on now; go say your words. I'll give you two some time alone before I come and join you."

Nodding, Helena stepped away and swiftly crossed the distance. Once she reached the bench, she lovingly traced the words Anderson had carved into its sun-warmed wood: *So too, shall I love.* It was her mother's favorite expression. One she had uttered often when reminding Helena that the Mother loved all her Chosen equally, and it was up to them to do the same. It had become a personal motto that embodied the kind of life Miriam wanted to lead, and the kind of person she hoped her daughter would become: selfless, loving, compassionate.

It was too much. Helena broke down, sobs causing her shoulders to shake. Her knees gave out, and she collapsed on the bench, wrapping her arms around the back of it as though through it she could actually hug her mother. In reality, it was all that was keeping her upright.

After a few moments, Anderson was there, pulling her up and wiping the tears that were still streaming down her face. He didn't say anything, just settled himself down next to her and held her as she allowed her tears to wash away the pain of her loss.

Helena hiccupped as her tears finally subsided.

"Feeling better, little bug?"

She wiped at her nose, not surprised when Anderson held out a faded piece of cloth. "A little," she admitted, after she cleaned up her face.

"There's nothing harder than having to say goodbye to someone you love," he said somberly.

Helena stayed quiet, knowing that he was referring to his wife, whom Helena had never met.

"I wish I had the words to take away your pain, Helena, but there is nothing anyone can say to soften that blow. The body may be gone, but never the spirit. Never the memories. Hold those close when you miss her most and she will never truly leave you."

Helena swallowed and nodded, the use of her given name adding weight to his words.

"She was so proud of the woman you've become. That is how you honor her, bug. You hear me? You stay true to yourself and you will never let her down."

10

She nodded again, this time taking a shaky breath to try to combat the threat of fresh tears. "Yes," she rasped.

Anderson nodded, as if it was settled, and then pulled her back so that her head fell onto his shoulder.

"What about the ceremony?" she asked.

Anderson shrugged. "Fancy words aren't going to change anything. You just let your heart speak for you. That is more than good enough."

"Okay," she whispered, settling back into him. That, at least, Helena knew she could do.

As they quietly said goodbye to one who had been an essential part of their world for so long, they sat like two puzzle pieces learning how to fit together now that the piece that had held them together was lost.

As THE MEMORY FADED, the soft light of dawn began to streak the sky with pale shades of pink. Thus began a day for goodbye but also remembrance. Helena had shed enough tears. It was time to remember what Anderson had taught her and celebrate his legacy; to honor his life with her memories and to be the woman he had helped raise. Perhaps she no longer had Anderson, but she would always have his words.

It would have to be enough.

CHAPTER 2

$\mathcal{T}$he men of Helena's Circle surrounded her. Darrin's fingers had gone white from tightly grasping her right hand, while Von was a steady presence at her left side. Kragen, Joquil and Timmins stood just behind them. The others had also come to pay their respects to the man their Kiri had loved. They may not have known him, but they still grieved his loss because of the effect it had on the woman they served.

Ronan's ice-blue gaze caught hers from across the courtyard as he looked up from the small garden. Helena had spent the early hours of the morning planting it in Anderson's honor. She'd done so using a combination of actual gardening and her power to help the cascade of flowers grow outside of their normal season. Ronan did not smile, but his gaze radiated warmth and support.

A bit away from him, Serena and Nial wore matching somber expressions, their fingers interlaced as they waited for Helena to speak. Miranda and Effie, along with Alina and the rest of the household staff, all filled in the space behind her friends. A few people from neighboring villages had also made the trip, traveling throughout the night to pay their respects to the new Kiri's loved one. Helena was not sure who had spread the word, but she could only assume Timmins played a part.

It was a large group, much larger than Anderson had probably ever expected, given that he had spent the whole of his life tucked away on his small piece of land. She hoped, despite so few of the people that came to pay their respects actually knowing the man, it was clear that he had been deeply loved.

The weather was mild, only a few fluffy clouds moving through the clear sky while a soft breeze made the leaves dance on their branches. It was a beautiful day, but this time Helena was not nearly as bothered by the realization. She wanted Anderson to have peace and gentleness now, when it was clear that his passing had been anything but.

"It's time, my love." Von's voice was gentle as it filled her mind.

Helena gave a barely discernable nod to indicate that she heard him. She knew that the others were waiting for her to say something. There were formal words that needed to be spoken. Words which were supposed to help speed Anderson's journey back to the Great Mother, but Helena was not going to say those words today. Instead, she would follow Anderson's advice and allow her heart to speak for her. It seemed important not to stand on formality; not for the man who had taught her how to see dragons in the clouds and find the best worms in the dirt.

"The Mother brings people into our lives for a number of reasons. Some are sent to challenge us, some to love and shape us. For me, Anderson was all of those things." Helena's voice was steady, although a bit thicker than usual. "Those of us that knew him would agree on that point. You could not help but be a better person for his guidance. He was patient and fair, and knew how to talk you into doing just about anything whether you originally intended to or not. I can't count the number of times he talked me into doing chores by simply making me believe we were playing a game."

She broke off as a few in the crowd chuckled appreciatively. Beside her, Darrin let out his own watery laugh, having experienced the exact same thing himself.

"But as with all of her Chosen, the Mother only lets us borrow them for a while before calling them back home to her. Anderson has been called home. In my heart I do not believe it was time for him to go. Then again, I don't think I could ever truly believe it was time, not today and not twenty years from now. None of us wish to say goodbye to someone who has been a fixture throughout our life."

Murmurs of agreement met her words. Helena let the silence grow, forcing herself to take a deep breath. As she fought to remain present and not get lost in her emotions, a bright flash of orange caught her eye. A giant butterfly, easily the size of her fist, fluttered delicately above the newly planted flowers, hovering for a second before coming to rest on a large purple bloom. *Anderson.*

Helena could not say what brought the thought, so certain and absolute, to her mind, but she knew it to be true. This was his way of showing her that he had not truly left her after all. The words he had spoken came to her again, *"just because she's not here with you and me doesn't mean that she's gone."* Neither was he.

Feeling stronger, she allowed herself a small smile as the butterfly flitted back up into the sky before becoming an orange speck that faded completely.

"No one is ever truly gone. Not so long as you remember the lessons they have taught you during your time together. I choose to focus on that, the time we had, instead of the time we have lost. Anger and hatred can make the world a cold and dark place. But even in the darkness, there is always the chance for light, for hope. We are that hope. It is our choices, the ones we are faced with every day, that will bring color into the world or leave it in darkness. I choose to bring light. I will not let Anderson's death be the foothold that allows darkness to overtake Tigaera." Her voice had changed during her speech, and the gentle wind picked up speed causing her hair to lift and flow around her shoulders. The murmurs grew louder as her power began to transform her.

"Rowena thought to cripple me with her blow, and that cannot go unanswered. She sought to weaken me, but she has only made me stronger. Rowena clings to darkness, using fear and isolation to take down her enemies. But there is something she has forgotten. I am not alone." Von's love swelled within her, and she thought she heard a firm *never* whisper through her, but she was still speaking and could not be

15

sure. "Tigaera has many allies; allies we will call on now. More than that, nothing can remain hidden in the light. No matter where she goes, Rowena cannot escape the combined force of Elysia. She. Will. Not. Win."

Helena's words were a promise that reverberated throughout the crowd. There was a period of stunned silence as those gathered realized what she had said; what very few in the crowd had actually known. Rowena was alive and this man's death had been a declaration of war.

A few hesitant claps sounded before the entirety of the crowd erupted into cheers.

"For the light!"

"For our Kiri!"

"For Elysia!"

There was more to say, more to do, but for now Helena was done. With a formal nod, she spun from the crowd and began to take slow, measured steps back toward the Palace.

"I did not realize that his funeral would become a war rally," Darrin said mildly.

"Neither did I," she replied tartly.

"Do you think this is what he would have wanted? For his death to be used as a call to battle?"

Helena's brows lowered over sparkling eyes. "I think Anderson would have wanted us to remember who he raised us to be. I do not have the luxury of mourning by closing myself away from my responsibilities, Darrin. Anderson knew who I was, who I was destined to be. He would expect me to be nothing less."

Darrin's shoulders fell. "I know."

She placed her hand on his shoulder, forcing him to stop and meet her gaze. "I wish that I could undo this. That I had the power to call a spirit back to its body, or that I could have at least protected him from *her*," Helena all but snarled as she spat out the word.

"You could not have known where Rowena would strike," Darrin reminded her. She heard his forgiveness and knew that he did not blame her, but Helena was not ready to absolve herself. If she had not been the Vessel, the one prophesied to bring down the Corruptor, Rowena would never have had reason to kill Anderson. His death had been unnecessary, but she would not, could not, allow it to be meaningless.

Darrin saw her thoughts in her eyes and nodded his understanding. Changing the subject, he added, "Thank you for speaking today, for being strong when I could not. He was all the family I had left. Losing him…" Darrin trailed off, letting out a harsh breath.

She took his hand in hers, squeezing hard. "You still have family, Darrin."

He smiled appreciatively, although his eyes were still dull with grief.

"We will honor his memory the way he taught us," she said firmly, her eyes finding a small orange speck darting through the sky just above them.

Shaking off the weight of his pain, Darrin straightened and met her gaze head on. "Where do we start?"

Helena's smile was warm, and slightly fierce, as she replied, "We live."

"THAT WAS SOME SPEECH TODAY," Von murmured as he stroked Helena's hair. They were curled up in bed, her head resting on his shoulder as she stared into the dancing flames of their fire.

Her smile was wry as she replied, "It wasn't exactly what I had pictured, but I suppose that's what happens when you improvise."

His chuckle vibrated beneath her cheek. "Perhaps the words were not exactly what you intended, but that does not make them any less true."

Helena sighed. Word had already spread far and wide about her declaration that morning. Missives had begun pouring in from every corner of Elysia. Some offered support while others minced no words indicating their displeasure with their Kiri for throwing them headlong into a war they were sure they could not win. How anyone could get all

17

of that out of a ten minute, impromptu speech was beyond her, but she would deal with it. The one thing that remained clear was that they needed to rally their allies, and fast.

Rowena would not wait long before striking again. She would continue to chip away at Helena, in increasingly inventive and twisted ways, until she finally provoked the Kiri into action. Helena wanted to be ready so that they could make their move on her own terms. Right now Rowena had the upper hand, she had already amassed an army, had been doing so for the better part of a year right under everyone's nose. Helena was starting from scratch. Sort of. At least she was Kiri. That had to count for something. Helena did not feel comforted by the reminder.

Sensing her wandering thoughts, Von brushed a finger beneath her chin and pulled her face up toward him. His gray eyes assessed her face, a small frown forming at what he saw. He pressed a kiss between her eyebrows, trying to smooth the crease that had taken up residence there.

"Timmins has already sent out the call. Tigaera's allies are on their way."

"It will not be enough to only call on those we know to be loyal. If we are going to defeat her, we will need to seek out those that have not yet chosen a side."

It was Von's turn to look worried. "You seek the aid of the tribes?"

Helena nodded.

Von straightened, his eyes widening with surprise as he asked, "How do you expect to find, let alone entice, them?"

"By any means necessary," she said grimly. "I cannot afford to let Rowena get to them first."

Von let out a low whistle.

Helena's concern colored her voice. "I know that I do not have much to show for myself, let alone enough to give them a reason to align their fate with mine—"

Von cut her off, "Helena, within your first handful of weeks as Kiri, you lifted the ban on Daejara that had been in place for thousands of years— something no one else bothered to even attempt. Then, with the assistance of less than a dozen people, you saved all of the Chosen."

She rolled her eyes. "I would hardly equate rescuing you to saving an entire race of people."

"Helena," he said firmly, his tone brooking no argument, "you know as well as I do what would have happened if the Fracturing occurred. It would have been the destruction of the Chosen. Rescuing me was your only option."

Her lips twisted in amusement, even as his words pushed back the wave of doubt that had been threatening to drown her. "You sure think highly of yourself, Mate."

It was his turn to grin. "Not of myself, of you. You have already faced insurmountable odds."

"Just barely…"

"You are capable of more than you know."

She sighed, struggling to sit up, but he held her tight.

"Helena, you are only just beginning to understand your power. Imagine what you can do now that we are together; now that our power is once again feeding off and strengthening the other's. Do not doubt yourself, my love. The fate of the Chosen may rest on your shoulders, but it is not a burden you bear alone. You have already proven yourself to be a formidable enemy. Rowena was not prepared for you. That is what causes her to lash out. She seeks to use your compassion against you, seeing your greatest strength as a weakness she can exploit. Your silence will only enrage and confuse her."

"She will not stop until she gets what she wants," Helena said quietly.

"I know."

"More will die."

Von tightened his arms around her. "I know."

Her voice was small as she whispered, "I do not think that I can say goodbye to anyone else that I love."

As much as he wished he could tell her she wouldn't have to, Von refused to lie. Instead, he pressed another kiss to her forehead and held on to her.

CHAPTER 3

"*More* than half of the Daejaran forces have refused to come."

Helena's head whipped to face Timmins so fast her hair lashed her face.

Before she could speak, Von snapped, "What?"

Timmins shrugged apologetically, holding a piece of parchment up for Von to see. "According to my letter from the newly appointed ambassador, there are those that feel—" he paused searching for a politically correct phrase.

Ronan interjected, sparing Timmins the indignity of failing to find a tactful response. "Tigaera ignored Daejara for centuries. There are many that cannot be bothered to care about the fate of the Chosen here, when none could find it within themselves to spare that same concern for them."

Helena frowned, but did not speak. When phrased that way, she could not fault their logic.

Von scowled darkly. "Ungrateful, small-minded—"

She placed a hand on his arm, cutting him off with a rueful shake of her head. "What of the others?" she asked Timmins.

He lowered the stack of papers clutched in his hand and met her gaze with a pained expression. "Many have replied, but they are not sending the forces we've requested. They wish to meet with you before committing."

"They do not believe me," she clarified, her voice hollow.

Timmins winced. "They find it hard to imagine the army you've described, having never experienced anything like Shadows themselves."

"The fools," Kragen snarled.

"They have forgotten what it means to serve," Von muttered.

"Can we blame them?" Joquil asked. They all turned toward him, varying degrees of surprise on their faces as he continued, "They are not the only ones who have forgotten. The Chosen have known nothing but peace, unless they are familiar with the stories of their ancestors. The kind of war you are describing... it is the stuff of legends, not reality. They do not understand that kind of power as they hold barely a sliver of it themselves." Joquil shrugged as he concluded, "You are asking them to imagine something they cannot begin to comprehend."

"So we show them; we make them believe," Darrin said, crossing his arms.

Joquil lifted a brow. "You think it will be that easy?"

Darrin gestured toward Helena. "You doubt her?"

"Never!" he snapped, offended by the implication.

Helena rolled her eyes at their childish bickering before asking, "Timmins, how many are coming?"

He cleared his throat. "Two representatives per realm."

Her jaw dropped. "Per realm? Out of all of the hundreds of territories and villages, only four are sending representatives?"

Timmins nodded, causing the rest of the men to begin shouting in outrage. Helena's eyes met Von's; it was as she had feared. They could not expect others to follow her blindly, not with the lives of so many at stake. She would have to convince them and find the tribes; those long forgotten or ignored by the Chosen.

Von dipped his head, indicating she should share her plan with the rest of the Circle.

"We will need Miranda," she stated.

22

Timmins' brows flew up in surprise. "What do we need the Keeper for?"

"If the Chosen have forgotten who they are, it is time they remember. Who better to help them than a Keeper?" she countered.

Timmins frowned but said nothing.

"We will hold a banquet in two days' time."

"Kiri, they will not be here by then," he protested.

Helena ignored him. "Miranda will be our esteemed guest, as well as our entertainment. After dinner we will call upon her to share tales of the Chosen's past. All will be invited, even though many will be unable to make the journey in time. We will need to *persuade*," she emphasized the word, "every bard we can to be in attendance so that they may pass her stories on to those that cannot make it."

"You think to sway them with stories?" Darrin asked, disbelief heavy in his voice.

Helena shook her head. "When the representatives of the realms are all present, I will meet with them and show them what we are up against. When they return home, they will be greeted by the Keeper's tales which will reinforce what they learned from me. I anticipate it will make a very convincing argument."

"Once they are swayed, others will fall in line," Ronan murmured.

"You will spread fear," Timmins cautioned.

"Not fear, truth," Helena corrected. "We cannot ignore this threat. Ignorance is not a luxury we can afford. To remain ignorant will see us all killed."

It was clear her Advisor did not like the plan, mainly because of its reliance upon a woman he could hardly tolerate.

Von squeezed her hand, urging her to continue.

"After they leave, the rest of us will need to be ready to travel."

Kragen groaned. "No more tents, Kiri. I beg of you."

She chuckled despite herself, "I am weary of the road as well, Sword. This time, we will employ faster methods." Her stomach rolled at the thought of the Kaelpas stone, but a little discomfort was well worth the time that could be saved with the purple stones.

23

"Do we even know how to recharge the stones?" Darrin asked, following her line of thought.

Joquil nodded. "I was able to find the spell in the archives."

"After looking it over, I think I might have found a shortcut," Helena added, referring to the amount of time required to charge the Kaelpas stones.

"Okay, so say we have an unlimited supply of stones. That doesn't help with traveling to places you've never been," Darrin reminded her.

Helena was sorely tempted to stick her tongue out at him but checked the impulse. "We will start by traveling to places that we *have* been, seeking out others that can get us close to where we need to be as we search for allies."

Her intention became clear, the men going still around her. Joquil looked stricken, his face bleaching of all color. Helena was about to ask him what was wrong when Ronan burst out, "You cannot be serious."

"Helena, no. We are not willingly seeking out the Triumvirate. Or calling on the lost tribes. That is a suicide mission. They are called the Forsaken for a reason. They have no allegiance to the Chosen!" Timmins sputtered.

She did not back down, shrugging as she said, "They are gifted, which means they have been blessed by the Mother; that makes them Her children. So what if their power is different than ours? We cannot be blind enough to believe that we win this fight on our own."

There was more that he wanted to say, but Timmins bit back the words.

Beside her Von remained quiet, letting the others come to realize the value of her plan. He understood their fear and had already had time to process his own. "It's a brilliant strategy," he said quietly. Despite its lack of volume, his voice carried.

"Rowena will not see it coming," Ronan said slowly.

"You are assuming that the Forsaken will agree," Timmins started.

Darrin picked up the argument, "They have no reason to side with us."

"They have just as much to lose if Rowena wins," Joquil pointed out.

Helena sat back, arms crossed while the men continued to debate. Around and around they went, until finally Von interjected, "No one has dared to approach them before."

"Because no one knows where to find them," Darrin snapped. "Or do you not know what the word lost means?"

Von glared at him but ignored the barb. "The Chosen have long been afraid of powers that we do not understand. Do you not think that the appearance of a Talyrian is a sign that it is time to get over that fear?"

The other men faltered, not understanding.

"The Talyrian pride is considered one of the lost tribes, according to the archives," Helena informed them, clasping her hands in front of her on the table.

"Been doing some light reading?" Ronan queried with an amused lift of his brow. Helena's lips raised in a small smile.

Joquil sat back, amber eyes glowing brightly as the meaning of her words took root in his mind.

Timmins mouth fell open. "You think the appearance of Starshine is a sign that the others might also be willing to come forth? And not just the Talyrians but the rest of the Forsaken?"

"The old man finally figured it out," Von snarked along the bond. *"You would think for one that spent his life face down in a book he would have arrived at the point more quickly."*

Helena snickered. *"It's not like you realized the Talyrians were one of the lost tribes either."*

She could feel his shrug as he said, *"But I am the Mate, not the Advisor. My qualification for the position is not reliant upon my ability to retain useless pieces of information found in old books."*

"I didn't realize that you had any qualifications..." Her teasing smile faltered as his silver eyes blazed.

"Oh, Helena. I think you'll find that I am more than qualified." The voice that whispered through her mind was all seductive purr and

it caused a bright blush to bloom on her cheeks. Von chuckled, his point made.

Ronan's eye caught Helena's and she blushed harder at her friend's knowing smile. *How had Von distracted her so easily?* With everything else going on, it was indeed a testament to his *qualifications* that he could pull her thoughts from the matter at hand. The rest of the Circle was looking at her, waiting for her to elaborate now that they were on the same page.

"If we cannot convince the Chosen to join us, we will need to recruit other allies. Where else should we look, if not the tribes? It only takes a few people to commit before others willingly join. What's the expression?" Helena paused, trying to recall it before snapping her fingers. "Wisdom of the crowd! And what better way to inspire confidence than with the aid of the Talyrians?"

A collective sigh went around the room. She had a point. None of them could deny the awe the first sight of Starshine had stirred.

"So first we try to convince the Chosen, then we seek to do the impossible and find the lost tribes," Timmins concluded warily.

"What else is new?" Ronan asked with a grin. "Pretty much everything we've accomplished up to this point should have been impossible."

"Exactly. It's just another Moonsday for us," Kragen quipped.

Helena laughed, relieved to see the others following suit. No one said her plan would be easy, but at least they had one. Helena's smile wobbled as a thought took root in her mind, *but so does Rowena.*

CHAPTER 4

*H*elena grew increasingly restless as the hours slowly passed. It was the morning of the banquet and guests had begun to pour into the Palace immediately following her announcement. All were eager to take part in the first formal event hosted by their Kiri since her trial many months ago.

Von didn't need their bond to determine that his Mate was on edge. "Helena," he called, trying to pull her attention back to him.

She blinked, turning away from their window and toward where he was standing just behind her. "Yes?"

He chuckled and shook his head. "This was your idea, *Mira*. Why are you so nervous?"

She wrinkled her nose. "Just because it was my idea, doesn't mean I'm not allowed to be terrified of the outcome."

Von threw her a skeptical glance. "You're eager to face Rowena one-on-one but afraid of your people's reaction to free food and entertainment?"

Helena threw her hands up in exasperation. "It's not the party I'm worried about! It's the backlash from the stories. It's the realms' response to learning about the depths of Rowena's corruption and what that means for the Chosen. It's the fact that everything hinges on garnering the help of people that were shunned by the Chosen for centuries."

He placed his finger to her lips to stop the torrent of words that were spilling forth with increasing frequency. "Shhh," he murmured.

She frowned, not appreciating being silenced. *"That only works if I let it,"* she reminded him via the bond.

He smirked and responded in kind, *"It wasn't you I was silencing, darling. It was your unfounded fears."*

"Unfounded! Von—"

"Shhh," he said again, his gray eyes growing serious. "There is no reason for you to borrow trouble, Helena. Worry about the things you can control. Take them as they come. You have enough to deal with, without worrying about things that have not even gone wrong yet."

Helena pouted, she wasn't sure if she was more annoyed that he had shushed her, twice, or that he had a point. She let out a breath and her shoulders fell, a small bit of tension ebbing away.

"I'm just feeling a little stressed," she muttered.

Von's eyes strayed meaningfully toward their bed. He knew exactly what they could do to let off some steam. Seeing the distracted expression on Helena's face, any thought of getting her in bed fled. Well if that was off the table, there was one other surefire way to help her work it off. "You haven't trained with Ronan since we've returned. Let's go down and join the others for his workout."

She looked up at him appraisingly, her words measured as she said, "I suppose it would help kill some time."

He smiled indulgently, purposely taunting her. "You keep bragging about how you've bested all the men of the Circle, but there's still one you've yet to take down."

Her eyes glowed at his challenge. "Do you really want me to beat you in front of your men?"

"I would love to see you try," he laughed, clearly unconcerned.

Her grin turned feral. Without another word she turned toward the door, making her way to the training field, not needing to look to know that he was following close behind.

IF RONAN WAS SURPRISED to see his friends stalking toward him, he did not let on. He nodded by way of greeting, continuing his demonstration without missing a beat. The others were not so unaffected by the sight of the Kiri and her Mate.

Von and Helena moved to the back of the group; their long, easy strides in perfect time with the other's. It was a large, sprawling mix of people comprised predominately of the Rasmiri and Daejaran forces. Also in attendance were Kragen, Darrin, Serena, Nial and Effie. A couple of months ago, Helena would not have expected the small, flaxen-haired girl to pick up a weapon. After watching her more than hold her own against an unrelenting swarm of Shadows, Effie's desire to train only made sense. No one could afford to be caught unaware.

Ronan pulled one of the warriors forward. "Watch closely to see how versatile this block is," he called to the crowd, moving himself into a defensive stance. With laser-like focus, he indicated the warrior should attack.

The dark-skinned man launched himself at Ronan without question, using a series of moves that on anyone else would have rendered their opponent unconscious. But Ronan was not any opponent. Red hair glinting like fire in the sun, he lunged, neatly dodging the other man's flying fists to spin and land his own blow. Now behind his student, Ronan used his hands and knee to knock the man down before acting out a killing blow. Only mildly chagrinned, the man picked himself up off the ground and moved back into formation.

"What did you see?" Ronan asked.

"Demetrius attempted an obvious attack that you saw coming from miles away," someone shouted with derision.

There were a few chuckles but Ronan merely scowled until the murmuring faded back to silence.

"His body position telegraphed where he was moving first, which allowed you to counter the movement and side-step the attack," Nial answered smoothly.

"Exactly. Had I not known what to look for, a shift of weight in the feet, the slight lifting of his right arm, I would have missed it and my opponent would have been successful. However, since I knew exactly what to look for, I was able to use his momentum against him, using it to disable him quickly and efficiently. Now, break off into pairs and practice. Each blow landed by the attacker means two laps for the defender!"

There were a few groans, but the men and women were eager to get to practice. Soon the sounds of grunts and punches filled the air around them.

"Shall we?" Von whispered in her ear. Helena's grin was more than answer enough.

Stepping apart they moved into position facing each other, each pulling their hair up into tight knots.

"Pretty," Helena called, allowing herself a moment to appreciate the stark male beauty of her Mate. His obsidian hair, pulled back from his face only enhanced the brilliance of his gray eyes and the sharp angles of his cheeks and nose. There really wasn't anything 'pretty' about him. He was too much of a warrior to be anything but lethal, but when she looked at him, Helena only noticed the seductive curve of his lips and the ways his muscles bunched and shifted as he removed his shirt. She licked her lips, helpless to ignore her primal response to him.

Von winked at her, knowing by the tell-tale blush on her cheeks where her thoughts had wandered.

For those that had stopped to watch the Couple, there was no doubt this was more than mere sparring practice. It was understood that they would not use their power to enhance their combat. This was a full-fledged test of physical skill and strategy. Those in the Circle had already moved in, eager to see them in action.

"It looks like they want a show," Von teased, a small smile on his lips.

"Oh, they'll get one," Helena promised smugly, not hesitating before she attacked.

Von countered the move easily, laughing as he blocked two more rapid-fire blows. *"Is that all you've got?"* he taunted.

"Not even close," she assured him, ducking low and using her

momentum to knock him off-balance. He recovered quickly, which kept him from falling completely.

The crowd continued to grow around them, people beginning to cheer for their champion, but Von and Helena blocked out the distraction, focusing solely on each other. Their bodies became a blur as they moved, each attack and counterattack so perfectly in sync with the other, that their movements appeared choreographed. It was a dance, but a potentially dangerous one.

He had to give her credit. Helena was a masterful fighter, using her size and speed to easily duck and weave around him. His years of experience were all that kept her from easily defeating him.

Von wiped sweat from his brow. "Tired yet?"

"You wish!" Helena took two running steps toward him, launching herself in the air so that her legs wrapped around his neck. Helena rotated in the air, her legs' hold on him causing him to twist and flip with her in the air before pulling him to the ground. She landed on both feet. Von was not so lucky.

The crowd went crazy as Von landed hard on his back, the air flying out of him in a loud whoosh. He was momentarily stunned and not entirely sure how he ended up in the dirt. Helena was still standing, looking down at him with her hands resting on her hips.

"Don't look so proud of yourself," he grit out, reaching out a hand and grasping her around the ankle. One firm tug was all it took to pull her down beside him. She landed on her ass with an undignified grunt.

Von laughed, easing himself up into a sitting position. "Truce?" he asked.

Helena gave him a considering look, the competitive part of her wanting to continue until he admitted that she'd beat him. She took a deep breath. "I suppose it wouldn't look very good if we showed up to the banquet completely covered in bruises. It probably wouldn't hurt to stop while there are still places that have not yet started to swell."

His chuckle was cut off by a groan as he got to his feet. "Mother's tits!"

Helena laughed. He may never admit that she'd won, but the damage she'd caused was more than enough for her ego.

"I'm glad I'm not the only one that sees stars after a sparring match with our Kiri," Ronan boomed, slapping Von hard on the shoulder.

Von grunted, giving Ronan a baleful look. "No need to look so giddy."

Ronan shrugged. "Can't help it brother. The last couple of months I was the one ass to ground. It's a nice change to still be standing at the end of practice."

Helena giggled causing both men to scowl at her. "If I recall correctly, it was only the last couple of weeks of practice when I was able to knock you on your ass consistently."

"Now's not the time to be cute, *Mira*. My pride is wounded enough as it is. No one has defeated me in hand-to-hand combat in ages." Von groaned again as he discovered a new bruise.

"Perhaps you should start training with Serena and Nial," Ronan said. "It never hurts to cover the basics."

Helena laughed harder when Von lashed out, striking Ronan hard enough that he stumbled. "Well played," she said, giving Von a soft kiss on the cheek.

He brushed a stray piece of hair away from her forehead and pressed a quick kiss to her lips. *"It is worth every ache to see you smiling at me like that again."*

The look in his eyes seared through her, but they moved apart as the rest of the Circle joined them.

Nial stepped over to his brother. "I can't lie; it gives me great joy to see I'm not the only Holbrooke that can be bested by a woman."

Serena elbowed him sharply in the ribs. "Nial and I would be more than glad to put you through your paces," Serena teased, grinning at Von's dark look before adding to Helena in a softer voice, "nice job."

Helena returned the smile. "It was a close one."

"As it should be," Kragen said, holding up his fist for her to bump with her own.

Helena touched her fist to his and raised a brow asking, "How do you figure?"

Effie made a dismissive sound, answering for him, "The Mate is supposed to be a perfect match for the Vessel. It would hardly do for either of them to be weaker than the other."

"Well when you put it that way," Helena said.

The others chuckled, happy to have things feeling normal again.

"I guess that's all the time we have for practice today."

Following Ronan's gaze, Helena watched Timmins approach their group.

"Seems you are right," she said to Ronan with a sigh.

"Did you really want to continue rolling around in the dirt?" Darrin asked.

She gave him a cheeky smile, before looking at Von. "With the right incentive, rolling around in the dirt can be quite a bit of fun."

"Aye." Von grinned, his eyes going silver.

Darrin made a puking sound. "I'm sorry I even said anything."

The others laughed, Effie taking Darrin's hand in hers with a shy smile. His expression changed, softening as he looked down at her.

Timmins made a small sound, pulling their attention back to him. "The first of the delegates has arrived," he informed them.

That was all it took for Helena's smile to fall and the easy comradery of the morning to fade. It was time for her to be Kiri once more.

CHAPTER 5

*E*verywhere she looked there was an exquisite exhibition of magic with each Branch represented in stunning detail. Massive hearths set in each of the walls were blazing with Fire of every color. The flickering flames were coordinated throughout the room to add to the overall atmosphere. Toward the front, where guests were greeting each other, the flames were the brightest. As you moved back into the room, the flames turned deep violet and flanked a dance floor that was currently empty.

Spheres of swirling lights were floating throughout the room, shifting colors to match the nearest hearth. Also drifting throughout the room were trays of various delicacies that never went empty. Soft strains of music pulsed throughout the hall, but the swell of voices nearly drowned it out as people laughed and chatted happily.

Those details alone were stunning, coming together to create an atmosphere of festivity that was absolutely unparalleled, but even they paled in comparison to the true centerpiece of the room.

The back wall was gone, replaced by a massive waterfall surrounded by lush plants and flowers. It stretched high above the natural ceiling, which had been made to appear like the night sky. At its base was a deep pool, illuminated by both the blue flames from the nearby hearths as well as submerged balls of light. A few guests splashed in the pool, surrounded by a transparent rainbow mist caused by the churning water. Simply put, the hall had been transformed into an oasis.

Helena let out a small gasp of pleasure, unable to remain unaffected by the beauty before her. It was lavish, a complete study in excess, but it was also a celebration of the power that flowed through each of the Chosen. For that reason, it was glorious.

Feeling the weight of thousands of eyes focused on her, Helena began to fidget, suddenly self-conscious. Before she could try to duck out of sight, the hall erupted into loud cheers of welcome.

Alina had been right, as usual. The hour spent dressing and primping had not only been worth it, but necessary. Tonight, Alina insisted that the Kiri needed to exude power. To that end, she had selected a dress of deep aubergine, the dark purple color a perfect contrast for her eyes. The bodice was snug from shoulders to hips before flaring out and falling in waves to the floor. It was the only color she wore.

Every other sparkling detail served to emphasize the purity of her power. The stitching was a metallic silver that glittered where it was caught by the light. Alina had curled her hair and then pinned it up using small stones that created a similar effect. Not to be outdone, her Kiri pendant seemed to radiate its own inner light, twinkling where it rested just above her breasts. To further enhance the effect and tie everything together, Alina had dusted her skin with a sparkling gold powder. From head to toe, Helena was aglow.

Still uncomfortable under the weight of such scrutiny, Helena forced herself to smile and prayed that it didn't look like a grimace. With another roar of approval, the Chosen began to celebrate in earnest. The party could officially begin now that their Kiri had arrived.

Von's quiet chuckle had her eyeing him. *"You look radiant, Mira. Nothing to worry about on that front."*

Helena smirked; apparently her prayer had been rerouted from the

Mother and sent through the bond. Either way, the reassurance was welcome. *"You look all right, too."*

His only response to her teasing words was a sardonic lift of his brow. Helena tried to bite back her grin but failed miserably.

Von looked absolutely sinful. He'd been dressed to matched, his formal pants and coat a fitted black material doing nothing to disguise the bulk of his muscles. His shirt was the same deep purple as her dress, with the top-most button undone in a classic act of defiance.

He'd also allowed Alina's brother Aemond, Von's personal valet, to talk him into a shave and haircut. The difference was astonishing. The thick black locks that had hung in loose waves past his shoulders had been chopped so that the ends now barely touched his neck. It was still long enough for pieces to fall down into his eyes, but Aemond had styled it in a way that kept it back. The sharp angles of his nose and jaw were more defined without the thick strands of hair obscuring them. His gray eyes appeared bigger and more luminous. Even his lips seemed fuller. He still had the savage aura of a man forged in battle, but where he had once been nothing but warrior, he was now clearly royalty. Helena had had trouble keeping her eyes, and hands, off him ever since.

"You're staring again, darling," he teased.

"It's not very polite of you to point it out. Not when you can feel my reaction to you and there's nothing I can do about it." Helena wasn't entirely sure she kept the pout out of her mental voice.

His eyes went molten. *"They've all seen you, there's no reason we can't escape to a dark room somewhere and help you get more... comfortable."*

Helena was sorely tempted. It felt like it had been ages since she'd lost herself in her Mate's body. He saw the answer in her eyes and some of the heat left his own. Using his phantom fingers, he brushed a finger along her cheek and over her lips. *"Later then."*

"Definitely," she agreed. Forcing herself to look away, she scanned the room again.

Seeing her friends laughing and having a good time helped her relax. Even after all they had been through, they did not get bogged down by what was ahead of them and still knew how to make the most of the small moments of pleasure they were granted.

Kragen and Ronan were talking animatedly beside one of the many bars, each man holding a sloshing mug of amber liquid. Not too far away, Serena and Nial sat, heads bowed toward one another as they shared a plate of food. Even from where she stood some distance away, Helena had no trouble noting the happy blush that stained her friend's cheeks as she laughingly accepted a piece of food that Nial held up to her lips.

Looking toward one of the many open doorways that led out to a balcony, Helena caught sight of Effie's blonde curls. She was looking longingly at the dance floor, while Darrin stared longingly down at her. A small smile played on Helena's lips as she watched the couple that still pretended nothing was between them. Seeing his chance, Darrin tenderly clasped her hand in his as he leaned down to press his lips against her fingers before gesturing toward the dance floor. With an excited squeal, Effie pulled him after her, their joint laughter lost in the dull roar of the crowd.

Still smiling, she let her eyes wander some more until they eventually landed on Miranda, who looked stunning in a dress of crimson. The Keeper's expression was solemn. Curious, Helena followed her gaze to where Miranda's granddaughter spun in Darrin's arms. Sensing her, Miranda caught her eye. The older woman smiled slightly, dipping her head in greeting, but her midnight eyes were unreadable. Before Helena could ponder further, Miranda turned and made her way deeper into the room.

Deciding to let it go for now, Helena's eyes finished their circuit of the hall. The only two of the Circle missing from the jubilant crowd were her Advisor and Master. They were in the Chambers awaiting the arrival of the last delegates. Timmins was going to summon her as soon as they arrived so that the real meeting could begin. But until then, there was no reason she and Von could not enjoy themselves as well.

"I like the way you think," he growled, close to her ear.

"You just enjoy any opportunity that allows you to rub up against me," Helena muttered dryly.

"You say that like it's a bad thing."

She grinned at him and pulled him toward the dance floor. The sea of bodies parted, granting them access to the now crowded space beside the waterfall. The music was fast and pulsing. All around them, partygoers turned into swirls of color as they danced in time to the music. Helena and Von joined in, bodies moving as one. Helena closed her eyes, focusing only on the music. There was no conscious thought, no intent, simply a fusion with the pulsating beat. The weight and sadness of the past few days began to fade with each twist of her body. It was a cleansing. The anger, frustration, and heartache were all washed away.

Opening her eyes, Helena faltered slightly as she met Von's burning gaze. He looked ravenous. She bit her bottom lip, feeling shy and overexposed. He reached for her, running his warm hands along the sides of her body until he grasped her hips and pulled her against him.

She could feel him, warm and solid against her, completely attuned to his desire raging through their bond. It felt like there were words he wanted to say bubbling up within him, but all he managed to get out was a single drawn out word before he slammed his lips down on hers in front of everyone.

"Mine."

Everything faded except for him. Weaving her fingers through his feather-soft hair, she tugged at the strands as she kissed him with all of the pent-up passion that had been pushed aside given the recent turn of events.

They were completely unaware of everything around them, until a sudden roar of water and thousands of small explosions caused them to step apart. Hearts pounding and eyes wide they glanced around. Small gasps of amazement met their ears as colorful bursts of light bloomed across the sky. Von snickered, already realizing what had happened. Helena blushed fiercely, and muttered a fervent curse as understanding dawned. Once again, her power had responded to the intensity of her emotions. At least this time her guests remained unscathed.

In response to the added intensity of the rushing water, the rainbow mist pressed in, growing thicker. Helena lifted bemused eyes back to Von, expecting to find his silvery gaze shining with amusement. Instead she was shocked to see Von looking stricken. His skin had gone pale and his eyes were wide with terror, the black of his pupils almost entirely swallowing up the gray.

Not wanting to draw attention, she shouted down the bond, *"Von!"*

He didn't respond.

Helena reached out a trembling hand, firmly grasping him about the arm and slightly digging her fingers in. *"Mate!"* she shouted again, using her power and his title to reinforce the call.

That grabbed his attention. Von blinked rapidly and took a deep gasping breath, as if he had been drowning and just finally caught a breath of air. Helena studied him with no small amount of concern. *"What just happened?"*

Von looked at her, embarrassment and shame causing his cheeks to pinken. He glanced at the people around them before interlacing his fingers with hers and pulling her to a more secluded spot against one of the walls.

"I got lost," he said, his voice sounding strained even along the bond. It cost him, deeply, to admit it.

"Lost?"

"In the mist."

And suddenly she understood. Months of hellish hallucinations still had their claws in him. Her hand tightened around his, squeezing hard to remind him that he was safe. *"What can I do?"*

He shook his head, smiling wryly. "Nothing, *Mira*. No need to worry."

She gave him a look; it was far too late for that. Anything that caused him to react that way pretty much ensured she was going to worry.

Von pressed a swift kiss to her lips, effectively ending the conversation. He didn't want to talk about it. Not here, not now, and possibly not ever. She let out a frustrated sigh, but before she could press the issue, a flash of color caught her attention. Turning slightly, she noticed Timmins standing in the main entryway staring at her. Following her gaze, Von noted the appearance of her Advisor. "Looks like it's time for the real party to start."

Helena frowned, brows furrowing as she replied, "You and I have very different definitions about what constitutes a party."

Von's deep laugh eased a little of the tightness in her chest.

"Let's get this over with," she huffed.

A LONE MAN pressed the heavy door open and moved into the darkness of the room. His footsteps were silent. After years spent staying out of view, he'd perfected the art of moving without making a sound.

He'd also learned to never assume silence was an indication of solitude. Out of habit, he glanced around to verify that he was, in fact, alone. Confident that he was, he made his way to the corner and pulled a sheet from the mirror it had concealed. Dust filled the air as the sheet fell to the floor. His eyes blurred and the need to sneeze was overwhelming, but he resisted any reaction. For his Queen, there was nothing he couldn't endure.

Remaining unseen by the Circle for years required a willingness to reside in darkness; to live and walk amongst those long forgotten by the glittering excess of the Palace dwellers. All in all, this room was a notable upgrade from his usual residence.

"You're late."

Eyes wide, he found himself staring into the cool blue gaze of his Queen. He dropped to his knees, bowing his head as he knelt before the swirling figure in the mirror. "Apologies, my Queen."

"I will not tolerate mistakes, not even from you."

He remained silent, knowing from experience that was the only correct response.

"Have they arrived?"

"Yes, my Queen. The impostor has already left the party to meet with them. The Keeper hid her exit by calling everyone to the stage to listen to her lies."

Even through the mirror, he could feel Rowena's icy rage. "Then it's time. You know what to do; the Circle must be broken."

"Yes, my Queen," he replied, risking a look upwards, but she was already gone.

CHAPTER 6

*T*he air was thick with tension. Everywhere Helena looked someone was staring back at her, although their reasoning for doing so clearly varied. Some were wary, others curious, and some openly hostile. At least the expressions reflected in their eyes gave Helena some insight into how she should proceed. Thankfully some of the staring eyes were friendly.

She remembered a few faces from her naming ceremony, but most of the representatives were strangers. Also in the room were the rest of her Circle and Ronan. Helena hadn't been comfortable with the thought of leaving him out of the conversation when he'd become such an integral part of their team.

Each of the realms in attendance—Etillion, Endoshan, Sylverland and Caederan—had two delegates present. That meant that Helena and her Circle were outnumbered, but only just. There was very little she knew about their realms, other than a few salient facts Timmins had drilled into her mind over the last couple of days.

Etillion and Endoshan were northern lands that shared a border with Tigaera. There was no love lost between them, despite their shared ancestry. The realm had once been united, but sibling rivalry had caused it to split in half a few hundred years ago. Their delegates, pointedly ignoring each other, were distinguished by the burnished golden color of their eyes and lilting way they spoke.

The two with curious gazes wore robes of forest green. The silver tree embroidered on their chests made it obvious they were the Etillion representatives. The female was thin with an open face that seemed prone to smiles. She had short brown hair that swung just past her pointed chin. Beside her was her male counterpart. His brown hair was thick and curly, hanging in waves down his back. He was tall, but slender, appearing more scholar than warrior. Perhaps that would be a point in Helena's favor.

Helena was not surprised that the delegates from Endoshan were in sharp contrast to their neighbors. Instead of robes, they were swathed with silks of the deepest black. The thick bands that were wrapped around them served as sheathes and usually bristled with weaponry. There was no doubt these were warriors. Both of the men were bearded but had shaved heads. They were two that had no trouble hiding their annoyance at her summons.

Standing just behind them were the two men from Sylverland. Their home was located just to the south of Tigaera and was best known for its series of lakes. The water was so pristine, it was commonly believed to be infused with liquid silver, creating its notable hue and thus its name. Its inhabitants, the Sylvanese, were distinguished by their pale blonde hair and silver eyes. The two before her were adorned in various shades of blue, their attire comprised of thick, expensive fabrics. These were men of means who were more familiar with a life of luxury than war. Something about the way the two men stood beside each other alluded to a familiarity that surpassed mere friendship. Helena couldn't put her finger on what exactly it was, but she couldn't help but be reminded of the way Nial and Serena positioned themselves when the other was near.

Last were the pair from Caederan, a realm that was situated between Daejara, which was to its south, and Talyria, which was to the north. Not knowing much about them, Helena found herself sharing the same wary expression they wore. The female looked familiar, with black curls framing a round face with interesting reddish-brown eyes. She was short, shorter than any other person in the room, and plump. The combination served to make her appear all the more curvaceously feminine. Standing next to her was a man of similar build. Rather than appearing feminine he exuded brute strength. The width of his chest and arms, and the scars that covered him, were warnings to tread carefully in his presence. His beard was long and braided, small bells woven into the thick strands. They both wore colors of the sunset, deep oranges and reds that complimented their dark hair and complexions.

Helena forced herself to meet each of their gazes. Despite the nerves that had her stomach twisting inside of her, she exuded confidence and control. She was their Kiri, chosen by the Mother as her Vessel; she would not back down.

"Greetings brothers and sisters," she said formally.

Kragen and Ronan's faces darkened like twin storm clouds when no one returned her greeting. She caught their eyes and allowed herself a small smile. Their stances relaxed, but Kragen crossed his arms, ensuring that everyone got an eyeful of his impressive strength. As far as warnings went, it was subtle, but effective.

"Mother's blessings, Kiri," the woman from Caederan said in a sweet, high-pitched voice.

"To you as well," Helena replied, letting some warmth infuse her voice. "Thank you all for traveling here under such short notice. I—"

"Why *have* you called us here?" one of the men from Endoshan demanded. His lips were pulled down in a severe frown and his golden eyes flashed with something that felt like disdain.

Helena could feel Von bristle behind her, not appreciating the way the delegate dared to address her. *"Relax."* She sent the thought along the bond while lifting an amused brow at the man who'd spoken. "If you'd let me finish, I was just getting to that part."

The delegates from Etillion snickered, enjoying the fact that they'd just witnessed a rival being summarily dismissed. The man scowled and gestured with his hand that she should continue.

"Oh thank you, if you insist," Helena said with mock graciousness, unable to keep the comment contained. She was fairly certain her Circle could feel her mental eye roll. *Who does this guy think he is?* Apparently, the thought had been transmitted, because Von answered.

"I believe he is the Endoshan heir."

"More like a royal jackass."

Von's laugh rumbled through the room, startling the delegates and causing them to look around uneasily. The Endoshan heir's frown deepened. He did not appreciate being the butt of some unknown joke.

"The Corruptor has risen," she said finally, using the title from the prophecy to ensure they knew of whom, and what, she spoke. The comment was the equivalent of lighting a match before tossing it into a barrel of oil. There was a shocked hiss, the sounds of gasps echoing throughout the room, before eight different voices rose into a roaring cacophony.

"That is impossible!" the heir countered.

"You would believe that," the female Etillion snapped, her eyes wide and frightened as her skin was leeched of all its color. Her companion placed a comforting hand on her shoulder, and the two shared a long silent look before turning back toward Helena.

"How do you know this?" the taller of the Sylvanese men asked, his voice deep and melodious.

"She captured my Mate."

Eight pairs of eyes turned to Von, using his presence to silently contradict her statement.

"I got him back," Helena stated dryly. "In the process, I was introduced to her army..." she paused, ensuring she had their complete attention before adding, "of Shadows."

The room erupted once more. The Caederan woman shrieked and the man she was with reached for a weapon that was not there. The Endoshans and Sylvanese had similarly violent reactions. Only the Etillions remained calm, their golden eyes serious as they processed her words.

"So the prophecy is true. The Corruptor seeks to eradicate the Chosen."

The words were spoken so softly it took Helena a moment to realize who had uttered them. She finally nodded to the man from Etillion. "Yes."

"That would make you the Vessel?"

Helena nodded again.

"That. Is. Impossible!" the Endoshan heir seethed.

She studied him, her head tilting as she did. "Why are you so determined to believe that? Will it keep you or your people safe if you deny it?"

His partner stopped him with a hand on his arm before he could respond further. While his mouth remained closed, it did nothing to stop the rapid rise and fall of his chest or the fiery anger that burned in his eyes.

Knowing that the only way to maintain control of the room was by remaining calm, Helena met and held the gazes of each delegate before speaking further. Once all murmurings had ceased she said matter-of-factly, "Rowena is real, whether you want to believe it or not. The threat she poses cannot be ignored. It is not merely my court she stands against; it is the entirety of the Chosen. Nothing is sacred to her. She did not hesitate to damn her own child by turning her into an abomination. The other she murdered in cold blood."

Their shock was palpable.

"Ro-Rowena? B-but she is dead..." the Caederan female stuttered, her hand clenching the arm of the man standing next to her.

"She faked her own death," Timmins said gently, not wanting to upset the woman further.

Her eyes moved from him back to Helena. "You are sure?"

"Unequivocally."

The woman's eyes shuttered. "Then we are doomed."

Von snarled behind Helena. "Will you give up before you fight? Do you think so little of the one blessed by the Mother or are your people simply not worth fighting for?"

"Shut your traitorous mouth, Daejaran," the Endoshan heir hissed. Fury and power rose within Helena. How dare he speak to her Mate that way. There was a surge of wind that caused the shutters to fly open. Nearest to the window, the Caederan woman squeaked and jumped away.

This time it was Von that reached through the bond. *"Let it go, Mira. You cannot combat centuries of prejudice in a single night."* There was a tenderness in his voice that conveyed how much it meant to him that she wanted to try.

"The man is rude and ignorant. I am growing increasingly alarmed by the thought of him overseeing or leading any realm."

"As am I," Von murmured.

"Please, Tinka meant no offense," the Caederan man said, mistakenly believing the surge of power was in response to his companion. He held out a hand as if that would prevent further insult, "but we know nothing of the Vessel's power. What you are asking—"

"I did not realize a Kiri had to prove herself. Did I not pass the Mother's trial already?"

The question was met with uncomfortable silence, many of the delegates dropping their eyes or glancing around at the others uneasily.

"I'm not here to perform parlor tricks for you," Helena snapped, her eyes flashing iridescent. Ronan let his eyes slowly travel from Helena to where the window now gaped open; she bit back a smile as he winked.

"We are not asking for them," the Sylvanese man interjected, "but do you not think we deserve to know more about the woman who is asking us to put our lives, and the lives of those we love, on the line?"

"That is the case whether you choose to believe me or not. Your realms have been allied with Tigaera for centuries. We've been blessed that they have been years filled with peace and prosperity. But now we are on the cusp of war and you want to abandon us to face our greatest threat alone?" Helena's words were harsh, but she refused to hold back. She had already lost people she loved, would likely lose others, she didn't have time to dance around egos or fear.

The words struck home. Helena could tell by the way their shoulders slumped and they looked to their partners. She was almost afraid to hope, was actually holding her breath, when the first of them spoke again.

"Etillion will stand with Tigaera," the pair said in unison. "We do not require proof. Your words and request alone are more than enough. We are allies as you say. It is our duty to stand for the Chosen and to protect our people."

Helena forced herself to release her breath slowly. "Thank you."

The others were not so quick to make promises of support. The silence swelled until finally, the Caederans, still looking peaky, stepped forward. "If things are as you say, then there is no choice. Caederan will stand with Tigaera."

"This is not a decision we can make for Sylverland. We will take your words back to our people and discuss the best course of action."

Helena wanted to shout at their short sightedness, but she forced herself to keep from reacting. The Circle was feeling less diplomatic. All around the room, anger and disapproving stares were leveled on the two men in blue.

"I'm glad I've never given the lot of you cause to look at me like that," Helena said to Von.

"To be fair, there have been moments of extreme exasperation, but you have more sense than to do or say anything stupid enough to make us."

His response made her smile slightly, even as she turned to the men from Endoshan and saw their answer reflected in their eyes.

"They still do not believe me," she said a bit dejectedly.

"They are too arrogant by half."

The heir opened his mouth, likely to formalize his refusal, but no words escaped. Instead, a large, thundering boom shook the room. Dust and debris fell to the floor as the room continued to shake.

"Mother's tits!" Kragen swore as a piece of wall fell and smacked his head.

Just as quickly as it started the room stilled. Looking around, Helena asked, "Is everyone all right?" There were soft murmurs of assent.

The overwhelming scent of smoke began to permeate the room through the open window. Taking a step toward it to see what was happening, Helena went cold as the first of the terrified screams reached her ears.

They were under attack.

CHAPTER 7

*H*elena flew through the halls, the sound of her thundering footsteps echoing loudly. Kragen and Ronan were barking orders at the Rasmiri guards. Darrin and Von were close by, neither man wanting her to barge into a situation they knew precious little about. Timmins and Joquil had helped arm the delegates so that no one was unprepared for whatever they were about to face. Helena had the feeling it wasn't going to be that simple. Knowing Rowena, nothing would prepare them for whatever trap she had set.

"How did they get in?" Helena snapped, the voice of her power amplifying the fury she was feeling.

"It's too soon to say, Kiri," Timmins responded.

"I want you to find out who is responsible for this, and I want you to bring them to me. Alive," she ordered. Timmins nodded.

"The rest of you, with me," she shouted as they rounded the last corner before stepping into a world of chaos.

It was impossible to forget the horror of the Shadows, but seeing them here, in her home, was devastating. They swarmed like ants, their gray skeletal bodies relentlessly pursuing the guests that had only moments before been laughing and dancing. There were already hundreds of corpses littering the floor as a small contingent of Shadows cut a path through the partygoers.

There was little time to process what was happening. Helena could only just make out Miranda helping frantic guests escape the slaughter. Serena and Effie were already covered in blood, both fighting as best they could in their formal clothes to provide cover and distraction for Miranda. Nial and the few Rasmiri already present were holding their own but could not seem to bring down the Shadows. No one had been prepared. Not for a fight in the heart of the Palace, and certainly not for facing off against the Shadows.

Gasps of shock sounded behind her as the delegates came face to face with the nightmare few believed to be real. She heard a few uttered prayers to the Mother before one of the Sylvanese asked, "What do we do?"

"Help get the others out of here," Helena ordered, seeing from the horrified faces of the Etillions and Caederans that they would not be much help on the battlefield. With quick nods they moved away, helping pull people off the ground and supporting them as they limped, or dragging them when they couldn't manage that, into the hallway they had just left.

"But how do we stop them?" the Sylvanese man asked. His pointed demand for clarification was laced with steel; he had no intention of sitting out this fight.

"Magically, they are immune to everything but Fire. Barring that, nothing short of removing the heads will keep them down," Von informed him.

There were a few answering war cries as blurred figures rushed into the mass of bodies. Helena was startled; it was a blur of black and blue. The Endoshans had decided to fight after all.

Around her, the Circle was braced for battle. Grim faces and weapons emanating with power were only waiting for her final command before adding themselves to the fray. Helena was at a loss; no one saw this coming. They should have; *she* should have, but she had mistakenly believed they would be safe.

Sensing her struggle, Von spoke for her, easily stepping into the role of Commander, "Draw them away from the guests. Work together, no one should be facing one of these dickless corpses on their own."

"Should be easy enough to do. I only count ten," Darrin called, surprise coloring his voice.

"Pity, that doesn't leave any for you to kill," Kragen grinned as he lunged into the fray, his weapon flying as he began to swing for their necks. Darrin was right behind him, not about to be left behind.

Only ten had done this? Helena felt sick. Rowena was toying with her, showing her how easily she could sneak in and wreak havoc; how little effort it took to destroy her people. Helena called on her power, feeling it rise to the surface, eager to eliminate those that dared to invade her home. Just as she was about to lash out, she hesitated, not wanting any of her Fire to harm one of the innocents still making their way out of the room. There were simply too many moving bodies between her and the Shadows.

"There, to the left," Von shouted, pointing to a figure standing slightly apart from the others.

Helena's stomach knotted with revulsion as she saw the figure Von had indicated. It was a Shadow, marked with the same snaking black lines writhing in its eyes and rotting gray flesh as the others. But while they could do little more than mindlessly attack, this one still retained the ability to call on its power. Helena flashed back to Vyruul, riding on Starshine and seeing Rowena standing on a balcony flanked by six figures. This creature was one of her generals.

As if he could feel her eyes on him, he twisted in a slow, serpentine fashion. He tilted his head as he observed her before letting his mouth fall open in the sinister imitation of a grin. "Kiri," he rasped.

Helena was stunned to hear him speak, although given his use of power it probably shouldn't have been so unexpected. Before she could recover, he launched a liquid green orb in her direction.

Snapping to attention, she reinforced her personal shield as she dodged it and let her own ball of Fire fly. Where the general's orb made contact, the floor began to smoke and dissolve. *Acid*, she realized with growing horror. Just as Rowena had twisted her magic, so too had her general. Instead of the pure form of Water, this monster was able to conjure acid. No wonder Rowena only felt the need to send ten Shadows; the sheer amount of destruction he could cause with just a single ball of his acid made him a one-man killing machine.

Letting the others deal with the handful of Shadows that were still standing, Helena focused solely on him. Around her wind began to whip past, thunder growling in the sky as a storm of power began to rage. The sounds of battle were quickly drowned out by the roar of thunder. The Chosen began to scream in earnest, not realizing it was Helena who was feeding the storm. Bodies pressed against one another, frantic to escape the fury they felt building in the room.

The general continued to smile as he lazily lobbed ball after ball of acid at Helena. He was not threatened by her display of power. Maybe he needed a little more convincing. Fire had been Helena's go-to since she'd inherited her power, its scorching heat and ability to destroy a perfect complement to the extreme emotions that usually fed into it. But with the amount of people in the room, she didn't feel confident she'd be able to control it completely, even with Von's return.

Helena felt a feral smile of her own begin to grow. She couldn't burn, but she could bury. Channeling the energy of the storm, Helena funneled its power through her body to blast the raised dais on which Rowena's general was standing. There was a loud crack as the wood splintered and rocked before it came crashing down. The general snarled in outrage as he lost his balance, collapsing with the wood. Helena wasn't finished; she needed to keep him out of the fight long enough to give her Circle an advantage.

The power of the lightning continued to crackle along her skin and pulse in her blood. She released it into the ground again, feeling the earth shake from the force. Try as he might, the general could not stand back up. He was too off-balance from the quaking beneath his feet.

The earthquake was the distraction her people needed. They were down to just a few remaining Shadows. Darrin slammed his shield into a Shadow, stunning it long enough that Kragen's sword was able to swing true. Ronan and Serena had another cornered. It was still coming after them even though one of its arms and most of its left leg had been removed. In a move only possible due to the years of experience between them, Serena swung her blade up while Ronan swung his ax around. The Shadow did not know which blow to dodge. Serena's blade, reinforced with her power, rent the Shadow in half, while Ronan's ax made easy work of his head. It crashed to the ground with a sickening thud and dark spurts of blood.

Since the general was still struggling to get free of the rubble, Helena released her hold on the lightning, allowing the room to settle. Von was beside her, swinging a flaming sword to dispatch the only one still standing. The air sizzled where the flames made contact with its rotting skin. With a final, gurgling cry, the last of the Shadows fell.

The general broke free from the wood, bellowing as he watched his final man fall. He glanced around as the Circle and their allies closed in. Ronan was spinning his ax in his hand, while Von and Helena held swirling orbs of power in their palms. The Sylvanese were bouncing on their feet and the two Endoshans wiping foul black ichor from their curved blades. Every one of them staring intently at the vile creature.

He tried to find an escape route but there was none; members of her Circle had every possible exit blocked. Finally, he let out a laugh that sounded like the crackle of leaves. Raising both emaciated arms into the air, he threw back his head and let his tainted power arc out of him. Ronan charged, looking to tackle the general, but the horrified gasps of the others had him spinning around.

Where the massive waterfall had once burbled there was now a rush of acid-green water burning a path through everything it touched. Helena's mouth fell open. There was no time to think, she had to act. Diving deep into the pool of her power she cast a shield that surrounded her people just before the acid could make contact. It hit the invisible barrier and Helena screamed. She could feel the searing burn of acid as if it was touching her skin.

Von growled in rage, feeling Helena's pain as if it was his own. The rest of her Circle roared, desperate to protect and defend their Kiri. There was nothing they could do against such power and they lacked the time necessary to coordinate the complex blend of power required to diffuse the acidfall.

Acting on instinct, Helena connected to the heart of her power. Her hair flew up around her, and her pupils contracted, disappearing completely beneath the iridescence of her eyes. The men that comprised her Circle transformed, turning into pulsing pillars of light. Von shone the brightest, the depth of their bond strengthening any power he held on his own.

She plucked at each glimmering strand of their power, now illuminated by her un-dampened state, and wove them with her own substantial thread. With her power now liberally reinforced by her Circle, Helena called on Earth. There was a thunderous groan and then the world shook violently as a massive sinkhole began to grow where the waterfall had once stood. The roiling mass of acid began to slide into the gaping hole.

Pushing more of her power into the earth, thick brown mud bubbled up, entirely replacing the dance floor. The mud, heavy with liquid, began to pour into the sinkhole, covering and eventually containing, the acid.

The startled shouts of the delegates pulled Helena back. Banking some of her power and releasing her hold on the others who had started to look a bit pale, Helena turned once more to the general.

He was gone.

CHAPTER 8

*H*elena screamed in outrage. It was a feral, inarticulate sound that had the others wincing and covering their ears. There was an answering roar in the distance as Starshine and the Daejaran pack added their voices to the chorus. Seething, she spun, needing something, anything, to unleash on.

"Mira," Von called, feeling the desperation building within her.

It was too late; she was too far gone for reason. She was balanced on a knife's edge, the sheer intensity of her power combined with all of the emotional extremes of the last few days pulling her toward violence. She hadn't been this out of control since under the effects of the Fracturing. That it was happening now, within the presence of her Mate, was terrifying.

"We have to stop her before she brings the rest of the place down and kills us all!" Darrin shouted.

"Is that your way of helping?" Ronan snapped.

"This cannot be the Mother's blessing. This is her curse!" Tinka wailed. The Caederan woman looked a child standing next to the warrior. Her entire body was trembling as her companion wrapped his arm around her and murmured softly.

Serena, disheveled and covered in sticky black ichor, gave the woman a disgusted glance. "Get them out of here!" she ordered. It was unclear who she was speaking to, but Effie, the most used to taking orders among them, reacted first.

"Here now," she said, her sweet voice entirely unexpected after the horrors of the past few minutes.

Tinka flinched when Effie held a hand out to her, and Darrin's green eyes went flinty.

"You either go with her, or you can go with me," he snapped.

"Let's go, Tink," the Caederan man said in his deep voice, eyeing Darrin warily.

"But Khouman—" she whispered, fear still thick in her high-pitched voice.

"None of that, Tinka. This is our Kiri. You cannot doubt the Mother's choice when she just saved all of us."

With a slow nod and an apologetic glance, the Caederans carefully made their way out of the still smoking ruins of the room.

"That goes for all of you!" Darrin boomed when the other six stayed behind. There were a few uttered curses and protests as the rest of the delegates fell into line behind Effie. Darrin stepped back.

"There, that was much more helpful," Ronan murmured.

"Is everything a joke to you?" he asked, irritation giving his voice an edge.

"Puppy, the day I stop taking the piss out of you is the day I die. Life's too short to be a miserable bastard."

"What's that supposed to mean?" he bristled, chest expanding as he took a step toward Ronan.

Kragen moved quickly, grabbing Darrin by the back of his shirt. "There now, let's not go and do something stupid while we're still in the middle of dealing with our first crisis."

"You may want to consider calming the fuck down. We already have one out of control person on our hands. Let's not add you to the list." Ronan sounded downright reasonable as he spoke. If it wasn't for the way his worried eyes kept moving to stare at Helena, he would have seemed almost chipper.

Darrin struggled to break free of Kragen's grip, his cheeks and ears turning bright red with his embarrassment.

"Do you promise to behave?" Kragen asked.

"Yes," Darrin bit out.

Kragen released him and Darrin stumbled forward. Straightening, he looked to Von, "Help her, damn it. You're her Mate, use that bond of yours and fucking do something."

Von lifted a dark brow, having mostly ignored the other men until now. "What exactly did you think I was over here trying to do? Egg her on?"

Joquil stepped forward, "She needs a way to safely release the power. She pulled too much and has started to lose control of it."

Looking around Von tried to find something that she wouldn't utterly destroy. As it was the room was almost completely done for, but the structure was still sound. If it collapsed it wouldn't just be the people inside the room that were lost. Short of getting her out of the Palace entirely, Von was at a loss.

Darrin's words came back to him. *Use that bond of yours.*

An idea sparked. Von turned back toward the fuming woman who held his blackened heart in the palm of her currently clawed hand. If ever there was a reason to risk annihilation… The thought drew out, loosely forming into a plan. The land could not handle the brunt of her power, but he could.

Years of battle allowed him to remain calm, despite his growing concern. Placing a hand on either side of her face, Von called her again, infusing his voice with every ounce of love and wonder he'd experienced since he first met her. *"Helena."* Her name was a prayer, reverently uttered and full of unspoken hope.

Power exploded through him as her shimmering eyes focused on his, unable to ignore his plea. Von's back arched from the force of it, everything she had been holding onto slamming into him. Her power was an inferno, burning him from the inside out. Gritting his teeth, he pressed his forehead to hers. He began to pant, his eyes turning molten silver as their joint power filled him.

"Vessel," he rumbled down their bond, his voice echoing with the harmonious voice-of-many generally associated with Helena's power.

Helena blinked. *"Mate?"* The word was a question, as if she was not entirely sure who was speaking.

Her power was intoxicating. Von had never felt anything like its seductive pull and could easily understand how it could take over completely. As it continued to flow into him, Helena's eyes began to return to normal, although flickers of iridescence remained.

Unable to contain all of this power on his own, Von's hands began to tremble. *"I need you to take it back now, Mira. Not all at once; just a little at a time."*

Her eyes widened as she realized what was happening. Refocusing, she placed a hand over his racing heart. Helena closed her eyes, drawing the power back into herself and through her, back into the room. Von braced himself, half-expecting what was left of the room to come crashing down around them. But instead of destruction, Helena chose transformation.

He could still feel her need for violence, her power throbbed with it, but it was not all-consuming. Her priorities had shifted, righting themselves as the part of her that was compassion and light came back into control. At least for now.

THE ROOM WAS SUFFOCATING. Helena felt as if each one of the souls of the fallen was trapped and screaming at her to release them. Peace; they all needed peace. It was too soon to feel this much grief and loss again. *When will I get a break from burying people that I love?*

Von's heart continued its steady, if rapid, beat against the palm of her hand. It grounded her, giving her something tangible to focus on. He was holding onto her excess power, but he would not be able to contain it for much longer. She needed to release it as quickly as possible.

There were too many bodies for her to individually carry them, as she had done for the villages they'd come across during their trek to Daejara. Not to mention the fact that simply sifting the earth to make graves was far too delicate a task when she had so much power requiring immediate release. That didn't mean she wouldn't honor them.

Helena refused to allow this room to be a haunted, feared place. She would not allow it to be a blight for her or her people. The Palace had been erected as a testament to the power and glory of the Chosen. It would continue to serve that purpose, albeit in a new way. With that determination in mind, Helena's power flowed into the room.

The others looked on in rapt fascination as all around them objects began to lift up off the ground before flying through the air. It was happening faster than any of them could track. The room that had started off the evening as a lush, glittering oasis and then quickly descended into chaos and carnage, was amidst yet another transformation. The mounds of smoking dirt and piles of bodies disappeared. In their place, trees and flowers bloomed. Helena was creating a forest right in the heart of the Palace.

Let their blood bring new life. One for every one lost, Helena thought, not feeling the tears as they fell from her eyes. She had probably only met a small handful of the dead, but that was not the point. None would be forgotten. Even though she could not tell you each of their names, the trees could. If one was to place their hand upon the bark of the tree, they would hear the name of the one they represented whispered amongst its leaves.

By the time she was done they were surrounded with life. The trees ranged in size and age, each reflective of the one whose name they now carried. A gentle breeze tickled the leaves, making them dance on their branches. Helena tipped her face up, enjoying the sparkling night sky, even though they were on the bottom floor of the Palace. At least there could be beauty in magic, as well as destruction.

"It is a beautiful memorial, Kiri," Timmins said in a hushed tone.

Overwhelmed by the events of the day, Helena could only nod. She let her eyes wander around the forest. While she was pleased with the result, it didn't lessen the pain of losing so many of those she was supposed to protect.

Guilt ate at her. She had known, on some level, this would happen. There had been a moment in Vyruul when Rowena had taunted her from the balcony. She'd had a choice, go for Rowena or get her Circle out. She'd chosen to save the people she knew, the ones that had grown to mean more to her than all others. In doing so, she'd put every single one of the remaining Chosen at risk. These deaths were on her.

The Keepers had warned her about this. Their words haunting her as she stood in this place made from the bodies of the dead:

'The path you choose will decide our fate.'

'The fate of all the Chosen.'

A shudder racked her body. One thing was becoming increasingly clear. There might be peace for the dead, but until Rowena was stopped, Helena would have none.

CHAPTER 9

*I*t was either very late or very early. Either way, Helena couldn't sleep. Every time her eyes fell closed, the piles of bodies were there to greet her. The weight of all that death, and knowing that she was the reason for it… that she was asking people to willingly place themselves in situations that guaranteed even more of it, was too much for her to handle.

"Helena, you are not the only ruler to ever be faced with this," Von murmured, using his thumb to gently free the lip she had been unconsciously biting. She looked up and the devastation in her eyes nearly undid him. She was in pain; he could feel it resonating through him. It was the kind of pain that gnawed at your soul until it incapacitated you completely.

"Darling, you have to be kinder to yourself," he said, moving to pull her into his arms.

"It's my fault."

"No more than it is mine."

"They are my people, my responsibility—"

"Is it my fault every time one of my men dies in battle?" Von cut in.

"Well, no, but—"

"Do you blame or look at me differently because I have had to kill men in battle?"

"Of course not!" she protested, twisting to stare at him.

"Then why are you doing it to yourself?"

The question threw her. Her brows furrowed as she tried to find an answer.

Von gently stroked her face, running his calloused fingers lovingly over her skin. "You cannot keep holding yourself to a higher standard. It will cripple you. As a leader you need to make decisions. Those decisions will protect some, and they will lead to the deaths of others. Your people follow you by choice. They know what awaits them on the battlefield, and *they fight anyway*. Do not be so arrogant as to think you can control every outcome. Not only do you rob your people of their heroics, but you place such a burden on yourself. You need to be able to be decisive and defend your decision no matter the outcome. If it does not go the way you intended, you learn from it, and from your enemies, and then you *move on*. You have to, because there will always be another battle or decision waiting for you."

Helena sat a bit dumbfounded, his words a balm for the raw edges of her soul. Von was not one for long speeches or declarations, but her warrior had known with only a look exactly what kinds of thoughts were tormenting her and he'd just slain them all.

"I love you," she said simply, wrapping her arms around him and snuggling close.

"And I you," he whispered against the top of her head. "You should try to rest now. There will not be much opportunity for it in the days to come."

"I don't think I'll ever sleep again," she sighed.

"Yes, you will. And you will laugh, and make love," he punctuated that with a squeeze that made her squirm, "and you will be happy again. I promise you, *Mira*."

"When did you get so smart?"

Von chuckled, "It's just experience. There are moments in life that always stay with us, they may give us purpose or direction, but they do not determine the entire course of our lives. The only thing that determines that are the choices we make each and every day. Think about it. I may have never met you if I hadn't decided to ignore the ban and plead for the case of Daejara and my brother."

"I don't believe that," Helena murmured sleepily. "The Mother would have found a way to bring us together."

"Likely so," he agreed, not wanting to dwell on the thought of a life spent never knowing the woman curled up in his arms. "I'm just saying, each choice we make opens up new opportunities. Nothing is definite except that our lives are comprised of millions of choices."

"Mmm," she murmured, her body going lax against his.

"Sleep now, my love. I will keep watch."

Von settled in, content to hold his mate in his arms while she slept. After months spent without the simple luxury of being beside her, there was nowhere else he'd rather be.

THE LIGHT KNOCKS on the door startled him, and Von jumped before looking down to ensure that Helena still slept soundly.

"Enter," he called softly, his fingers playing with the soft ends of hair that ran down Helena's back. Other than a few whimpers, Helena had remained asleep. Each time she'd started to grow restless, he'd press his lips against her forehead and whisper that all was well. Upon hearing his voice, she would immediately settle. Even in her sleep she needed reassurance that he was still with her.

If he was surprised to see Nial standing in the doorway, Von did not show it. "Brother," he said, his tone no less warm despite its low volume. He still couldn't quite believe that his brother was healthy and whole once more. Seeing him walking, let alone fighting, took his breath away every time he saw it.

"How is she doing?" Nial asked, concern shining in his stormy blue-gray eyes.

"She is stronger than she gives herself credit for, she will be fine."

"It cannot be easy."

"No, but she will manage. What brings you?" Von asked.

"They were worried," he said, meaning the Circle, "but none felt comfortable interrupting you two."

"And they sent you?" Von asked, amused.

"They figured I was least likely to be harmed, given that you are fondest of me."

Von chuckled. "They do not know me very well. You more than any of the others, save perhaps Ronan, should know better than to interrupt us when we are alone."

"That's what I said."

The brothers laughed.

The easy smile started to fade from Nial's face as he sobered, remembering what else he had come to share. "The delegates have already started their journey's home." At Von's lifted brow Nial continued, "They were eager to get back to their people and warn them about what was coming."

Von nodded, it only made sense. "They are not the only ones with such a trip ahead of them."

"Do you know when we leave?" Nial asked.

"Tomorrow."

"And where do we head?"

Von hesitated, it was not that he didn't trust his brother, but there was still the matter of how Rowena was able to get her people inside unbeknownst to the rest of them. If there was a spy on the loose, he did not feel comfortable giving away any information that could be used against them, not even under the protection of sight or audio shields.

Nial sensed his train of thought and said, "It doesn't matter, I will tell the others to pack for all possible scenarios. Can you tell me how long we'll be gone?"

Von shrugged. "As long as it takes."

Nial sighed, nodding as if that was what he had expected. He laughed suddenly, "Did you ever think that not just one, but two Holbrookes would be part of the force fighting *for* a Kiri?"

As a son of the realm that still bore the scars of a centuries-long ban, established due to a rebellion led by his ancestors, the thought hadn't even been a possibility.

"I cannot say that I did," Von confessed with a wry smile.

"It suits you."

"What does?" Von asked, not following his brother's train of thought.

"Happiness. I have not seen you like this since before..." Nial trailed off, not wanting to say the words that had always brought such pain in their wake.

"Since before your accident."

Nial nodded.

Von took a deep breath, trying to steady himself as the old ghosts came back to haunt him. "Watching your future stripped away from you in a heartbeat was unbearable for me. I would not accept that one with such passion for life could be content to remain locked away in his rooms."

"I would not be here without you," Nial admitted, the depth of love he had for his brother embedded in the words.

"Nor I," Von said with a rueful smile.

That made his brother grin. "You're welcome then!" With another soft laugh, Nial started to step back toward the door.

"It suits you as well," Von called after him.

Grinning over his shoulder, Nial replied, "I never believed happiness like this was in the cards for me. But here we are, two Holbrookes, both mated and preparing to defend the world. Sounds pretty perfect, if you ask me."

"Getting a little ahead of yourself, aren't you?" Von asked, referring to Serena. "Last I checked, you two haven't taken the vows."

"A mere formality. It's only a matter of time, brother. We Holbrookes are irresistible."

Von shook his head, seeing the little boy his brother had once been in the man's shining eyes. "Good night, brother."

"Night!" Nial whispered, softly shutting the door behind him.

Adventure, love, and purpose; it was all Nial had ever wanted, and because of the amazing woman in his arms, now they both had it. Von would never be able to thank her for the gift she'd given him. Running his fingers along her hair again, Von had to admit, it was more than he had ever allowed himself to hope for. They might be on the brink of the bloodiest war in history, but he was still the happiest he'd ever been in his life. That alone was worth fighting, and dying, for. More than worth it.

Whatever he had to do to protect the woman he loved, he'd do without question. He'd been a harbinger of death and destruction before, and had done it for infinitely less noble reasons. Von would gladly step into that role again if it would spare Helena the heartache of experiencing it herself.

Let their enemies come. He'd be waiting.

CHAPTER 10

*W*hen Helena woke, she felt more rested than she had in weeks. It was surprising, all things considered, but welcome. True to his word, Von hadn't left her side until she'd woken up to the sound of birdsong. The steady thump of his heart had been the perfect lullaby.

All of the insecurity and doubt he'd kept away started to bubble up within her again in his absence. There was much to do, and so little time. *How am I supposed to know if I am focusing on the right things?*

As if he could feel her troubled thoughts, Von sent a lingering caress along their bond. There were no words; he must have been talking to one of the others, but the phantom touch was reinforced with his message from last night. Blocking out the niggling doubts, she took two slow breaths and made her way to the clothes Alina had laid out sometime the night before. The fact that the woman had the foresight to do so, even after the chaos, was impressive.

She dressed quickly, lacing up the travel leathers and soft cotton tunic with practiced fingers. Her thoughts began to wander again as she moved to lace her boots. She couldn't help but think about what lay ahead of them. Nothing was straightforward. Not their direction, and certainly not her plans.

Originally, she'd thought that a visit to the Triumvirate was in order, seeking their knowledge of potential futures to help inform and guide their movements. But if last night's events were any indication, there was no time to spare. They needed allies now, which certainly pushed the timeline up. They would have to proceed blindly, but that was all right. It was no more than she'd had to do for most of her life anyway. So, they would head toward the lost tribes first.

Helena fought back a shudder at the thought. There was nothing specific that she was afraid of, although the hushed stories whispered about them in every corner of Tigaera certainly didn't endear them to her. But stories were stories. At most there was perhaps a sliver of truth to be found there. She could not imagine that the Forsaken would deny their aid after learning of Rowena's army. Then again, many would call her a fool. It was hard to say what, exactly, would happen when they reached out to those who so many had routinely ignored.

She wanted to sigh but pushed back the impulse. It was too easy to imagine defeat. Not wanting to give the possibility any more power, Helena decided to only consider a more positive alternative. If they could get all of the lost tribes to join them, they'd have a force that would vastly outnumber Rowena's.

Smoothing her hands along the supple leather, she ensured everything was in order before standing and snatching her deep amber cloak from its resting place on the chair. She was already moving when she twisted it around her shoulders. Leaving her room, with all of its comforts, was easier than she would have imagined. Her future, and that of all the Chosen, was waiting for her to determine its outcome.

Helena took the stairs at a run, eager to be outside amidst her friends. Already she could hear the hum of their voices, along with the flickers of their power. She smiled, enjoying their connection. It reminded her that no matter what they discovered, they'd do so together. She might be the one to make the hardest decisions but they would help her face the consequences, whatever they may be. There was a certain peace in that.

When a small voice in her mind warned her that she might also have to say goodbye to them, Helena immediately silenced it. It was too painful to contemplate, no matter how true it might be.

Moving quickly through the colorful halls of the Palace, Helena forced herself to meet the gazes and match the hopeful smiles of the Chosen. The closer she got to the stables, the more desperately hopeful the gazes she encountered. She was their Kiri; they believed she would protect them. Helena would not give them any reason to doubt their beliefs, even though she doubted herself.

Stepping out of the last hallway and into the brilliant sunlight, Helena took a deep breath, filling her lungs with the sweetness of the morning. Last evening had been filled with death and bloodshed, but the morning still greeted her all the same. The simple truth of it rocked her. Life went on, and so would she. *Hadn't Von said the same?*

As if her thoughts had conjured the man, Von's smoky eyes caught hers from across the field. His hand was buried in the thick fur of his wolf Karma as he checked to make sure that all of the necessities were properly stored. They would not be making this trip on wolf-back, or even Talyrian back for that matter. As promised, Helena had worked with Joquil to find a way to escalate the creation of Kaelpas stones.

They took a notoriously long time to charge, but given the strength of Helena's power, combined with her control of all five Branches of the Mother's power, she was able to imbue the small purple stones with enough strength that she could circumvent the full timeline. Not only circumvent, but entirely replace. Helena had spent the better part of a morning making dozens of the stones. She would likely spend countless more keeping them charged in the days to come. Especially given that they were the primary means of transportation for the foreseeable future.

That did not, as Darrin had pointed out, get them past the need to have a guide to help them reach unknown locations. They were limited to traveling only to those places in which at least one amongst them had already been. Luckily, they had a Keeper in their ranks.

Miranda had traveled much of Elysia in her time as a Keeper. It was because of her, that they were even able to travel directly into the lands of one of the forgotten realms. Their first stop would be the Ebon Isle. It was notorious for its storms, which were caused due to the massive maelstrom always present just off its coast. That was also how its people inherited their affinity for water and air. They were said to be created from the storm's fury itself, the ability to channel its power innate in each of them.

Helena could not help but feel a kinship with the people who could command the sky and sea. She only hoped they felt that same connection. Their power would do much to strengthen their forces.

She crossed the distance between her and her Mate quickly. Heat and approval flared hot in his eyes as he took her in, and she could feel his desire for her throb through their bond. Her lips twisted, of course he would think now was an appropriate time for such intimacy.

"There is never not a good time," he countered, his own lips twisting in a sensual grin.

"Yes there is. Like right now, when we are mere minutes away from entering an unknown land to try to garner the aid of its people who do not recognize the Kiri as the Mother's Vessel."

He frowned. *"Well, when you go and put it that way…"*

"What other way is there to put it, Mate? I only speak the truth." Her eyes were bright with mirth.

"I cannot help it if I hunger for you. I've only just gotten you back. Would you deny your Mate his pleasure at the sight of you? Especially when for a time you were only a vision he imagined during the worst of his nightmares?"

Helena's smile fell completely. *"Never."* Her mental voice shook a bit as she delivered the promise, but his smile was understanding as he responded.

"There is much time we need to make up for, my love. But we will have the rest of our lives together to do so. For now, we will focus on ensuring that such a future exists. Then we can ignore the rest of the world and lose ourselves in each other."

Her stomach tightened at the sexual promise in his words, even as she mourned the fact that such luxuries would have to be on hold for the foreseeable future. *"And how long do you think the world would let us ignore it?"*

"I don't give a fuck what the world wants. After this business with

Rowena concludes, Mate, you and I have some things to take care of. Far away from here."

The smile that she gave him was radiant. *"I can't wait."*

His eyes were molten as he replied, *"Nor I."*

She shook her head, pushing away thoughts of uninterrupted time with her Mate, and all that would entail, to focus on the growing number of people standing in front of her. *How in the name of the Great Mother am I supposed to travel with all of these people without Rowena knowing exactly where we are?* It was going to be impossible. A full army would also put their potential allies on edge. Helena sighed, already knowing that her Circle was going to be very unhappy with her newest request.

Kragen sidled up, seeing the calculating look in her eyes. "What are you thinking?"

"That we cannot travel with these numbers."

He frowned, deep brackets etching themselves in his face. "We cannot be unprotected."

Sighing again she agreed, "I know."

"What do you propose?"

"Dividing our numbers."

Helena could see that he wanted to argue, and what it cost him to push back that instinctive response.

Darrin had no such trouble. "Do you truly wish to make it that easy for her to murder you then?"

She shot him a dirty look. "Yes. That's exactly what I have in mind."

Darrin scowled, not appreciating her sarcasm.

"What do you have in mind, *Mira*?" Von asked in a carefully neutral voice.

"A series of go-betweens. Soldiers that make the initial jump with us, to become familiar with the surroundings, before coming back to the bulk of the force here. That way, if we come upon Rowena or any of her army, our reinforcements will not be far behind. We could have several of them, that way the majority of the army could appear almost instantly."

The men considered her words carefully. "If we scheduled regular check-ins we could help them become familiar with the landscape and any new locations. It would mitigate the distance the rest of the army would need to travel to meet up with us," Von said.

Kragen mulled the suggestion over. "It could work."

Darrin frowned, as usual. "I do not like the idea of us being unprepared."

"I cannot show up on their doorsteps with an entire army at my back. It would be as good as declaring an outright war. They are not our enemies, and we do not want to give them the impression that we believe them to be," Helena countered.

"I know, but I still don't like it."

"Fair enough, but we will all be there to protect her," Von reminded him.

Helena quickly agreed, "Yes, of course. The full Circle, Ronan, Serena, Nial, and Miranda." At Darrin's deepening scowl, she added, "Effie, of course is welcome if she'd like to come with us."

"And the Talyrian?" Ronan asked, having been listening the entire time.

"Obviously," Helena agreed.

"What of the wolves? And a handful of other guards."

When Helena hesitated, Von said, "It would be odd for a Kiri to travel without at least some of the Rasmiri in attendance."

"And for the Daejaran Commander to be without his men," Ronan pointed out.

Exasperated, Helena rolled her eyes. "How many men are you suggesting?"

The two men commented without thought.

"Twenty," Von said.

"At least forty," Ronan stated.

They shared a glance, their lips lifting in amusement.

"Forty?! The entire point is *not* to seem like we are marching on them," Helena nearly shouted.

"Anything less may indicate weakness."

Helena threw up her hands. "Are you all unable to defend me then?

Or yourselves? How weak I must seem, to require so many men to protect me!"

"When has that ever been the point?" Ronan asked, his eyes glacial.

"It's not about protection. It is about appearances, Kiri. These are the men that follow you. You must be a force to be reckoned with, not someone they can easily dismiss."

The sky turned black and wind whipped through the air. "Let them try," she said, her voice harmonious and filled with the threat of violence as her eye shone with iridescence.

Darrin paled and swallowed audibly. "Hellion."

Helena blinked, and the storm instantly subsided. "Forty then. No more. And that number includes the Circle and the other's I've mentioned."

"Forty plus mounts."

Helena crossed her arms, but she didn't argue further. The Daejaran pack was fierce and would make traveling once they arrived much easier. "Fine," she agreed.

The men of her Circle nodded. "I will select the Rasmiri who will join us," Darrin announced.

Helena's spared a glance for Ronan and Von. "Which of you will select the men from Daejara?"

Von smirked. "For all that he pretends to be in charge, I am their Commander. That said, I would not question anyone that Ronan put forth as an appropriate guard."

Ronan's eyes seemed to glow with the compliment, but he said nothing.

"Choose wisely," Helena said, before turning her back on both of them.

"Of course, Kiri," Ronan murmured.

"We will get through this," Von promised, sensing the swelling tide of anxiety in her.

"So you say."

"Helena." Her name was both question and protest.

"I do not want to lose more good men and women. I hate that I

place so many in danger."

"You cannot control that."

Thunder growled and shook the sky. Helena watched her Mate glance up before adding ruefully, *"If any of us could control the future, I would put every last gold piece on you. But, Helena, you cannot. These men and women serve because it is their wish. They believe in this cause, in Elysia, as much as you do. You are their hope."*

Helena shuddered. *"And that is why I fear."*

"Because you are wise and compassionate. Do you think Rowena mourns the loss of her Shadows?"

"Only in as much as it affects her own power."

"Exactly. And that is why you will win. You put the needs of others before yourself. Your compassion is your greatest strength."

She wanted to argue further, but his words swelled within her, giving her hope. With one last breath, Helena turned back toward Von and the Chosen that were already moving into place behind him. *"Let us hope you are right, Mate."*

CHAPTER 11

*E*yeing Miranda, Helena broke off from the others and approached the older woman. "Keeper?"

Turning midnight eyes on her, Miranda responded, "Kiri."

"Thank you for your assistance," she started awkwardly.

"Why do I get the impression you didn't come over to review our itinerary?"

Helena sighed. "Because I didn't."

"What's on your mind, Kiri?" Miranda asked, not unkindly.

"Last night..." Helena trailed off, uncertain of what exactly she was trying to say.

Nothing if not patient, the Keeper waited for her to continue.

"There was a moment where it felt like I was still under the effects of the Fracturing," Helena confessed, confusion and fear making her voice small. "How is that possible?"

Miranda laid a hand upon her arm. "Your Mate has returned, but the bond is not fully complete and so your power continues to overwhelm you."

Helena's brows furrowed. She could vaguely remember Effie referencing something similar when she'd spoken of the prophecy so many months ago, but the meaning of the words had been forgotten.

Seeing the question on her face, Miranda elaborated, "The Vessel is a conduit of the Mother's own power. The depth of it surpasses comprehension and it is too much for anyone to hold on their own. Your Mate helps reinforce the barriers within you that contain and hold that power in check. He is the tether that binds you to the world, to your innermost self. And it is the bond between you that allows you to maintain control over your power instead of being overtaken by it. With the bond incomplete there are..." she paused, searching for the right word, "cracks, that allow the power to leak out."

"How—why—" Helena broke off as frustration ate at her. After everything, she still was not free from the effects of the Fracturing, although the bulk of the side effects had been thwarted simply by Von's presence. But what the Keeper was saying could not be denied.

Von had already proven in the last handful of days that he was the only one who could help her rein in her power. He'd done it once when she'd been lost inside her grief over discovering Anderson's mutilated remains, and then again just last night when he'd taken the full force of her power inside himself for her to draw back out at a more manageable level. *What happens when even he cannot withstand the next explosion of power?*

Fear snaked up her spine, causing her to shiver despite the mild weather. This was the absolute last thing she wanted to have to worry about with the looming threat of Rowena's next ambush.

The Keeper shrugged. "I cannot begin to understand the intricacies of your bond, Helena. I can only offer the answer to the first question you posed. Once the bond is fully accepted, you will control your power absolutely."

"But I have accepted it!" she burst out. "Our souls recognized each other. We spoke the vows. I can feel him, even now, in the depths of my mind. What's left for me to do?"

Miranda's eyes were as apologetic as her words. "I am sorry, Kiri. Truly. I wish I could tell you."

"Helena? Is everything all right?"

She found him without needing to search. Von was staring at her, dark brows lowered over concerned gray eyes; his lips were set in a deep frown.

Offering a small smile, she replied, *"Everything is fine. Just more cryptic warnings from the Keeper."*

He crossed his arms, expression dubious. *"What aren't you telling me?"*

Helena made a face, annoyed that he could sense the omission, even as it underscored her point. How could their bond possibly be incomplete when they were so in tune with one another?

"Keeper?" Helena asked softly, eyes still focused on her Mate.

"Yes, Kiri," Miranda responded warily, as if already knowing what Helena was about to ask.

"How much longer do I have before I lose control completely?"

The silence expanded between them until Helena finally twisted back toward her. The woman's face was pale, her eyes wide and unseeing. When she spoke, her voice sounded from far away.

"The mist stalks its prey, unwilling to release its hold. It sinks its claws in deeper with every swipe. You must find where its hold is deepest and reclaim the final piece. If you fail, all will be lost. The sky will glow red with flame, the air will fill with ash, and the Mother's Tears will run with blood." Miranda blinked, her eyes coming back into focus as she swayed where she stood.

Helena grasped her, keeping Miranda upright as they shared a look of mute horror. Both women were stricken by the prophecy she'd just shared. Helena swallowed, throat suddenly dry. Once again, she was presented with the warning from her trial, albeit from a new avenue. The words were meant to be enigmatic, but Helena knew enough to make out the gist of their meaning. A part of Von was still being held hostage by the mist. Helena frowned, silently berating herself. The warning signs had been there all along, she just hadn't understood them. A vision of Von, ashen and wide eyed when he saw the mist surrounding them in Vyruul, filled her mind, while his broken words from the night before echoed back like an eerie soundtrack: *'I got lost.'*

She had already searched him, had pulled out every lingering piece of the *Bellamorte* she'd found, but she must have missed one. In doing so, it seemed that she'd inadvertently kept them from being able to complete the bond. Aqua eyes moved back to her Mate, running over his body as if it would reveal the part of him that was still under silent attack. Helena knew it wouldn't be that simple. If it had been obvious, she'd have already dealt with it.

Von met her gaze, his own eyes clouding as he tried to decipher her troubled expression. Before he could inquire, Timmins broke through the moment with a bellowed, "Kiri! It is time!"

Blinking, Helena and Miranda shared a final look of trepidation. Helena sighed and pushed the Keeper's warning aside to refocus on the task at hand. She would have to address the issue, and soon, but for now her attention was required elsewhere.

Reaching for Helena with a trembling hand, her nails digging in where they made contact with Helena's arms, Miranda whispered, "You cannot fail."

The unspoken message behind the Keeper's words was clear. Von's life was not the only one at stake if she failed. But when hadn't that been the case since she'd ascended? This was just another thing for her to add to her increasingly long list of impossible things to do.

MIRANDA, looking for all the world like nothing had just happened, stepped forward with a Kaelpas stone glittering in her outstretched palm. "Are you ready, Kiri?"

Helena nodded, scooting in closer to the older woman. She would be making the initial jump with her Circle and their friends, along with one designated runner who would be coming straight back to collect the next group. With each new group, a new runner would step in so that no one person had to make the leap more than twice, which would also leave almost a handful of people remaining in Tigaera that already knew how to reach the others if necessary.

Von moved into position beside her, weaving his fingers through hers. She squeezed once, enjoying the way his warmth tingled up her arm, before reaching out her other hand to rest it on Miranda's shoulder. There was a bump at her hip, and Helena twisted, chuckling when she saw Starshine's turquoise eyes balefully glaring at her.

"I'm sorry, girl. I know you'd rather fly."

There was an annoyed huff and a small bit of smoke curled in the air. Helena bit her lip, not entirely sure how the Talyrian would react to travel via Kaelpas stone, but the wolves had made the jump from Vyruul last time. She could only hope it wouldn't affect Starshine too badly.

There was another feline grunt, but Starshine pressed herself against Helena. The rumbling purr she felt everywhere they connected made her grin. Starshine wasn't happy about their means of travel, but she still enjoyed being near her mistress. Helena definitely reciprocated both sentiments; her stomach was already knotting in anticipation of using the stone.

"Brace yourselves," Miranda murmured. Helena thought the Keeper sounded a little too amused for her liking, but the feeling of being squeezed through space made any further thoughts impossible.

When the ground steadied, Helena grasped her knees and took several gasping breaths. "Will it ever stop being terrible?" she panted.

There were a few grunts of agreement from beside her, where the others were in more or less the same state. Von and Miranda alone appeared mostly unaffected. Helena shot him an annoyed glance. It wasn't fair that she had to suffer while he still looked entirely unruffled.

Feeling her ire, he grinned at her and shrugged.

"Bastard. You could at least pretend," she said without heat.

He coughed half-heartedly. *"Better?"*

Helena rolled her eyes, amused despite herself. Finally able to stand, and breathe, she pushed herself upright. As she took in their surroundings, her mouth fell open in awe. They were poised on the edge of a dock that was surrounded on all sides by angry waves. There must have been a shield keeping the worst of the water from touching them or the dock, although her hair was entirely at the mercy of the wind and had already ripped free of her neat braid.

The feeling of being suspended in the middle of the sea was intimidating, but it paled in comparison to the mass of churning wind and water rising up and towering above them. She'd heard that the

Ebon Isle was known for its storms. Now that she was face-to-face with one she certainly understood why, although that didn't make the greeting-by-cyclone any less surprising. The tempest twisted on top of the inky sea, dancing with the edges of the maelstrom. It was surreal to watch wind and water mate in the sky, while just beside it there was a massive whirlpool that seemed to drop all the way to the center of the world. The juxtaposition was hard to comprehend.

A grumpy roar had Helena pulling her gaze from the storm to her Talyrian. Starshine shook out her wings, pacing along the edges of the dock and whining. Eyeing the sky, Helena imagined that the Talyrian was not overly fond of the torrential downpour. One-by-one the Circle moved toward her, and together they made their way carefully to the place where the dock met the land.

Lightning split the sky and Helena swore she could feel an answering throb within her. Nothing was natural about this storm, and her power was humming with the need to answer its call.

Darrin eyed the sky, his frown deepening as the storm seemed to worsen. "I can't say I'm impressed with what I've seen of the mysterious Ebon Isle," he muttered.

Ronan bumped his shoulder. "Unmanned by a little rain?"

"A little rain? Are you blind?"

Ronan chuckled. "Let us hope the Storm Forged are feeling hospitable."

Darrin grimaced at the thought of having to spend the night in the rain. The others laughed. Effie took pity on him, and put her small hand in his, offering silent comfort.

Timmins had just smoothed away his own grin when he asked, "Should we start making for the keep?"

"It would be best to wait for the others to arrive," Kragen said, but after a quick look back at the dock, he saw that they already had. Letting out a low whistle he shook his head. "It's almost worth feeling like a wrung-out tunic for the convenience of that kind of travel."

"Almost," Helena emphasized dryly.

Von was considerate enough not to laugh out loud, but she snarled at him anyway due to the flickers of mirth shooting along their bond.

The group made their way toward a stone keep sitting precariously atop a hill of rocks. The keep had obviously been crafted with magic. There was no other way it would have been able to withstand the assault of the water, or the crumbling bed of rocks it rested upon.

They must have been quite a sight, trudging through the wind and rain, with the Daejaran pack loping beside them and one very annoyed Talyrian prowling at their side. Miranda walked just beside Helena and Von, being the one that had the connections to the Storm Forged and the only one who had been to the isle before. Unfortunately, there had not been time to send word they'd be coming, nor did Helena or the Circle feel comfortable announcing their plans.

"Halt!" a disembodied voice rang out. The storm grew in intensity, the howl of the wind eclipsed only by a crack of thunder.

They came to a sudden and complete stop, their eyes warily searching for the speaker.

A man separated himself from the wall of rock he'd used for camouflage. His face was as hard as the stone behind him. With only a quick glance, Helena could tell this was not a regular Chosen. He was tall, very tall. She had to crane her neck back to meet his eyes. His skin was a dusky blue while his hair was the color of the sea during a storm. The power of the storm raged in his eyes, which were a deep, glowing sapphire. Now she understood why the people of Ebon Isle were referred to as the Storm Forged.

"Mother's blessings to you!" Miranda called, stepping forward.

The man glowered at her, lifting his twisted driftwood staff threateningly in his hand.

"We seek an audience with the Stormbringer," Miranda continued.

"And you are?" the man asked, the thunder in his voice echoing in the sky.

"The Keeper Miranda Ikusimón. I am joined by the Mother's Vessel and her Circle."

If the man was impressed by her answer, or her companions, he did not show it.

Helena could feel the men of her Circle growing impatient behind her. None of them were used to being the ones on the defensive.

"We seek his aid!" Timmins added from his place just behind Miranda. The Keeper scowled, not appreciating his assistance.

That caused a reaction. The man threw his head back and laughed. "And why would the Stormbringer wish to ally himself with the likes of you, Chosen." He bit off the word, slinging it at them like an insult. "The Mother has no place here. The Storm Forged do not recognize her divinity."

"You may not recognize the Mother, but that does not mean she has abandoned you. I can feel her in the air even now. The threads of your power tie you to her whether you wish it or not." Helena did not need to shout for her words to carry. The air itself amplified and carried them on its currents.

The man was impressed by her manipulation of his power. He was the one behind the storm and had not anticipated one in their ranks being powerful enough to do so. The wind began to die down as the man considered the group before him.

"If you prove yourself untrustworthy, you will taste the wrath of the Storm Forged. There will be no mercy."

Starshine growled menacingly in response to the thinly veiled threat being aimed at her mistress. The man, finally noticing the Talyrian, seemed to lose a bit of haughtiness. He blinked a few times, not convinced he was seeing things correctly.

"Then it is a good thing we do not seek to harm," Helena countered.

The man nodded and the storm died completely. In the distance, the cyclone continued to make its way across the horizon but the clouds cleared, and the sun began to shine.

"Welcome to Ebon Isle, Mother of Spirit," the man said when Helena made it to his side.

"Thank you for agreeing to speak with us, Stormbringer," she replied, making no move to hide her smile when his eyes widened at her use of his title. He had thought to hide it awhile longer and had not anticipated being found out before he was ready.

A moment of stunned silence passed and he laughed again. "Well met, lady. I should expect nothing less from the Mother's Vessel. Nor from one with the power to command a Talyrian."

A deep growl emanated from Starshine and Helena's smile turned feral. "You don't know much of the Talyrians nor their queen if you think I have any control over her."

From where she stood, Helena watched his throat bob as her words sank in. He looked unnerved as he hazarded another glance at Starshine who was now openly snarling at him. In an attempt to divert further insult he said hurriedly, "Please, make yourselves comfortable in my home. You are the welcome guests of Anduin Stormbringer."

For now. The unspoken words echoed loudly in her mind, reminding her that his extension of friendship was tentative at best, and that they would need to proceed with extreme caution.

Helena smiled her thanks, looking back to convey the need for continued caution with the others. There were a few nods, the warning received, before she turned back to face the man with glowing eyes.

Without another word, Helena and her people followed Anduin as he led them up the hill and into his keep.

CHAPTER 12

he keep was a celebration of the sea and sky, or perhaps it was simply a reflection of the people who lived on the Ebon Isle. Decorated in every shade of blue and green, it felt as though she was moving through the water while the air teased her skin. Helena found it thrilling; her power was eager to come out and play with the magic she could feel surrounding her.

Curious stares met them as they filed one at a time into the massive hall. It was a circular room; the entirety of it comprised of windows, save for where it connected to the hallway they just exited. The room was filled with the Storm Forged. They had the same glowing eyes as their leader, although the shades were every variation of the sea. Some had skin or hair the color of sea foam, others appeared as though they had been painted the deepest shade of indigo. It was both startling and breathtaking. The Storm Forged were every bit as fierce and lovely as the cyclone making its way across the horizon.

Von took his place beside her, his steady gaze reinforcing her calm. Joquil, who had been even more reticent than usual, moved to stand at her other side. Surprised to see him there instead of Darrin or Ronan, she gave him a curious look. His amber eyes were wild, as if he was having a strong emotional reaction that he was trying unsuccessfully to contain.

She placed a hand on his arm, not wanting to voice her concern in the midst of strangers. Joquil continued to meet her gaze, silently conveying a message she did not understand. With a final searching glance, Helena dropped her hand. She would need to make time to speak with him as soon as they were done here.

Ronan and Nial stood beside Von with Serena not far behind them. Darrin and Kragen were behind Helena, Effie almost hidden between them. Timmins stood next to Miranda, both a bit ahead and apart from the rest of the Chosen. It was the traditional spot of the Advisor, or rather, the one who would speak for the group. Not that Helena had any intention of letting someone speak for her. She was mostly just amused by the continued posturing between them. Both of them were trying to take the lead, and neither wanted to concede ground.

The rest of their force had been tasked with finding a place for the wolves, after which they were sent to the barracks to find rooms and rest for the evening. Once the storm had cleared, Starshine had taken to the sky, intent on exploring this new territory.

Knowing that there were none in this room incapable of protecting themselves, Helena released her stranglehold on her power, finally allowing it to rise to the surface as it had been clamoring to do since they'd first set foot on the Isle.

"You have come a great distance to seek an audience, Kiri," Anduin said, his voice booming throughout the room. "Especially given that the Chosen have no love of those they call the Forsaken." The silence that followed his words was heavy as the Storm Forged waited for her to tell them what required her to seek out their aid.

"I have. It is time for the Chosen to remember who and what they are. That includes the Storm Forged."

There were a few outraged hisses; none in this room wanted to be compared to the pampered children of the Mother.

"We have a common enemy, Stormbringer."

He took a seat, moving like liquid as he slid into it, greatly amused by her words. "And who would dare make an enemy of me?"

"The Corruptor," Miranda supplied, once again using the title from the prophecy known to all of Elysia's inhabitants.

His smile fell and his sapphire eyes blazed. "You came all this way to tell me bedtime stories? I have to say, I'm disappointed." If it weren't for the way the Stormbringer's fingers gripped the arms of his chair, Helena would have believed him unaffected.

"I would not waste my time with so foolish a reason, Stormbringer."

He waved away her words, eyes seeking out his court as he replied, "The Corruptor is no more than a boogeyman. A myth."

"She has already amassed an army of Shadows."

Anduin's laugh was incredulous, but Helena thought she detected a note of hysteria. Whispers rose around them like the shrieking of the wind.

"The only thing Anduin will respect is power, Helena. You have to show him that you are a bigger threat to him and his people than she is." Von sent her the thought, having already assessed the opponent before them.

"I do not wish to anger him..."

"Trust me, Mira. Show him who you are."

With that, Helena allowed her magic to run free. Her eyes sparkled with iridescence and her hair fell in long waves down her back before lifting in a breeze no one else could feel. When she spoke again, her voice was layered and harmonious. "Stormbringer."

Anduin sat up in his chair, startled by the change in the woman before him.

"How did you obtain your title?"

He tilted his head, not expecting the question. "There is no other that can match my power." There was no arrogance in the answer; he was stating a fact.

"Let us strike a bargain, Stormbringer."

Intrigued he leaned forward. "What kind of bargain?"

"A test of our power, mine against yours. If I best you, you will ally your people to my cause. If I do not, my people and I will leave here without any ill will or further request."

The Storm Forged broke into surprised laughter. None of the

Chosen reacted; this was not a game to them. They knew Helena was deadly serious.

Seeing that she was not kidding, Anduin's eyes glowed more brightly. "What you speak of is not done lightly, Kiri. The only time a reigning Stormbringer will fight is to defend their title when a challenge has been placed on the throne. It is a fight to the death. If you were to defeat me, you would obtain the title." His words clearly conveyed how unlikely such an outcome would be.

"So be it."

Tension swelled as her words were whispered and repeated throughout the room.

"You seek to challenge me?" he scoffed. "Do you even know what you ask?"

"Do we have a bargain?" she countered, not wanting to admit that she had absolutely no idea what the hell she was doing. Instinct and Von's words were all that guided her.

The smile on his face was predatory. "We do, Mother of Spirit. But not tonight. If we are to do this, we will follow as tradition mandates. It will be a true challenge."

Helena nodded her assent. Excited whispers filled the room.

Rising from his seat, Anduin addressed his people. "A challenger has stepped forward. Tomorrow Aegaeon's Challenge will commence. Tonight we will feast!"

Cheers erupted around the room, but they were bloodthirsty and frightening. Whatever Aegaeon's Challenge entailed, it would not be easy. Sensing their dismissal, at least until the feast, Helena and her Circle made their way out of the hall and back toward the suite of rooms that had been set aside for them.

"How was that for power?" Helena asked, her heart racing in her chest. *Mother's tits, what have I just gotten myself into?*

"I don't think it's exactly what I had in mind," came the uncertain reply.

Helena spun, causing the others to halt in surprise. "Perhaps you could be a bit more specific next time, Mate!"

Von looked chagrined, which caused Ronan to snicker. Soon Kragen and Serena joined in, the others following suit not long after.

"You think this is funny? All right wise guy, you are in charge of discovering what the hell I just signed up for, and then figuring out how I avoid getting us all killed tomorrow."

Ronan nodded, but his eyes were still full of laughter.

"Only you would be laughing at the threat of execution," she muttered.

He shook his head. "You misunderstand, Hellion. It's just amusing to see that no matter the situation, some things never change."

She waved him off, too worried to appreciate his levity. "It doesn't matter. See what you can find out."

Still chuckling, he nodded and made for the barracks.

As soon as the door shut behind them and an auditory shield was placed around the room, Helena spun on her Master. "Joquil!" she shouted, causing him to flinch.

His amber eyes lifted from the floor, seeming to shine from the shadow of the alcove he was perched in. Swallowing he asked, "Yes, Kiri?"

"Did you know?"

He paled. "Yes," he admitted, bowing his head.

"And you didn't think to warn me?"

"Kiri, I—"

Von moved beside her, scowling while he crossed his arms. Even Timmins looked uneasy as he eyed her Master.

Joquil cleared his throat, unaccustomed to, and uncomfortable with, the attention. "I did extensive research into the lost tribes during my —" he paused for a long moment, seeming to be at a loss for words, "training. I was curious about their magical abilities, and how they differed from those of the Chosen."

"Wolfshit," Von said, not buying it. Joquil gave him an assessing glance but did not have a chance to comment before Timmins spoke up.

"Where did you even find any information about the tribes?" he sputtered. "No such texts exist in the archives." He was beyond displeased that there was yet another person that had more information than he did.

Joquil coughed, an internal debate warring within him.

"What aren't you telling us, Master?" Helena demanded, her voice layered.

Joquil deflated, his eyes sliding away from hers as he stared at the floor. "When I was younger, a Keeper who was traveling through the Forsaken Territories found my village."

Helena went entirely still as she processed his words. Joquil was from one of the lost tribes. There was a sharp intake of breath from behind her as one of the others deciphered his words as well, but no one spoke.

"When they found me playing in the back of my father's market stall, the Keeper stopped in the middle of his conversation with one of the tribe elders to study me. He stepped over and grasped my arm, his touch burning me like a brand." Joquil's usually honeyed voice was hoarse as he continued, "I will never forget the way his eyes went out of focus, or the peculiar milky-white hue they turned as they bore into my own. When he spoke, his voice cut like a knife."

Joquil's hands were trembling as they ran over his face. "I still remember his words:

'The Vessel comes. You must help her bear the Crown of Embers if she has any hope of becoming the Queen of Light. When it's time, you must submit, giving in to her power completely.

Your training begins now, young Master, for your prowess will be her guide, and without you she will not find her way. To serve, you must leave the life you know behind. There can be no ties, save the one you have to her.

Your destiny awaits.'"

There was a moment of tense silence before Joquil continued, "I left with him that day, arriving in Tigaera to begin my apprenticeship with the retired Circle members. My family saw it as a great honor to be discovered by the Keeper; there were no tears when they said goodbye. It is simply not the way of those born to the twilight."

"You are from the Forest of Whispers," Timmins said, recognizing the phrase.

"A Night Stalker!" Darrin whispered in shock.

Joquil looked up, amber eyes burning as he solemnly confirmed, "Yes."

As the admission left his lips, he held himself stiffly, as if braced for a blow. He was a Master in all four of the five Branches of magic available to him; a rare and considerable accomplishment throughout all of Elysia. There were perhaps only a handful of others that could say the same. The amount of power he could command was astounding, and yet, this confession stripped him of it all. To see him brought so low, all of his quiet dignity laying in tatters at his feet, made Helena's heart ache and her anger at his omission ebb.

"Why keep it from us?" Helena asked gently.

His laugh was short and brittle. "Never would one of the Forsaken be allowed to enter into the service of a Circle. We are savages not fit to be near any of the Chosen, let alone the Kiri."

Each bitter word landed like an arrow through Helena's heart.

"The only way to serve, the only way to fulfill my destiny, was to hide my past. And so I buried it." His eyes burned with defiant pride. Even after all they had been through together, a part of him still expected to be cast aside with the admission.

Helena was startled by the tear that rolled down her cheek. Joquil's story was unexpected to say the least. Although, discovering that he was one of the Night Stalkers explained much. His penchant for silence and his ability to quietly fade into the background were two of the most notable.

Speaking over the emotionally charged silence Von asked dryly, "All right, so you are one of the Stalkers, what does that have to do with the Stormbringer's challenge?"

Joquil blinked, not expecting the revelation of his lifelong secret to be brushed aside so quickly. Sitting a little straighter he answered, "When I traveled with the Keeper, he told me many things. One night during our journey, we received word about a new Stormbringer ascending. The Keeper explained how the title was earned and told me that a time would come when I would witness it for myself. I had forgotten all about it until we stood before him." As he said the last he looked again toward Helena, remorse shining in the depths of his eyes.

That explains what happened in the hall then, Helena thought with a sigh. "Do you remember what he told you of the challenge?"

Joquil nodded, his panic flaring again. "I do."

"And?" Von drawled.

Joquil lifted a brow, matching Von's bland tone perfectly, "Do you recall the maelstrom just off the coast?"

"No... I must have missed it," Von replied, deadpan.

Helena shot him a look, but he stared unblinkingly at the Master.

Kragen and Darrin snickered, both enjoying someone else being at the end of one of Von's barbed statements, had Ronan been there he would have joined them.

Joquil's eyes narrowed but the left side of his lip began to curl in amusement. His shoulders relaxed and he crossed his arms mirroring Von's stance. "Your lack of observation is impressive. I had higher hopes for the Commander of the Daejaran mercenaries."

Von smirked and Joquil grinned. Helena frowned, her eyes zipping between the two men. *What in the Mother...* she thought, and then it clicked. By treating him as if he had not just shared his most closely guarded secret, Von had shown Joquil that nothing had changed. Helena snorted with disbelief, *Men*.

"Okay, now that whatever that was is out of the way..." Helena started.

Joquil cleared his throat, "Right. The maelstrom is the answer."

Helena blinked and looked at the others thinking she'd missed something. "Remind me of the question."

"In order to defeat the reigning Stormbringer, and to beat Aegaeon's Challenge, the one who declared the challenge must summon a storm from the depths of the maelstrom. The cyclone that you saw when we arrived, that was created by Anduin when he ascended."

"His power has kept it going all this time?" Timmins asked.

"Yes."

Helena could feel her skin leeching of all color but forced herself not to give in to her panic. "So we must both draw a cyclone from the depths of Aegaeon's maelstrom?"

"He said that it's a death match," Darrin pointed out.

Joquil's face was grave as he confirmed, "The winner is only declared when their storm overpowers the other. The loser is always swallowed by the storm."

"Oh."

Adrenaline sent her pulse roaring in her ears. Feeling her rising panic, Von sent waves of calm and support through their bond.

In theory it seemed simple: call forth a storm more powerful than the other. But having felt the magic pulsing through the air, Helena knew it would require considerable skill to manipulate and then control the forces already at play. She had enough trouble controlling her own power on a good day and now she was supposed to handle someone else's? Not only that, she was supposed to use it to murder them? Here she was trying to stop people from dying and she'd just inadvertently walked right onto another kind of killing field. The thought was so absurd she wanted to laugh.

Kragen's booming laugh startled her out of her thoughts.

"Oh, not you too," she moaned, thinking back to Ronan's earlier laughter.

Kragen shrugged. "I just couldn't help but think *Battle of the Storms* seems a much more fitting name than *Aegaeon's Challenge*. At the very least it's more straightforward when it comes to what's expected."

Helena's lips quirked. At least one of them didn't appear worried about tomorrow's outcome.

"Aegaeon was the first master of Air and Water. He is the one that created the maelstrom," Joquil informed them.

Timmins gave him a startled look, before sighing deeply. Miranda would have been highly amused to see that she was not the only cause of those sighs.

Helena lifted her brow, smirking. "See. When you know what it means, it's abundantly clear."

Kragen grinned. "You really think you would have pieced it all together with only that information?"

She shrugged. "Maybe not, but if I could, why would I need you lot?" His knowing smile grew, causing her to add, "In any event, I still would have figured it out before you!"

Kragen winked and the other men laughed.

There was a loud crash as the door flew open, smashing into the wall.

"Helena!" Ronan roared, rushing inside.

"*Mother's tits!*" Von swore, releasing the power he'd already pulled up and had aimed at the door.

Earlier joking aside, they were all still very much on edge.

"I-I know what the challenge entails," he panted, out of breath from his full sprint back to her.

"So do I," she informed him.

His rush of words stopped as he stared at her, mouth agape. "How?"

Helena's eyes slid toward Joquil, but the guarded look he wore halted her words. She would tell Ronan what they'd learned, but not while the wounds were still raw.

"My Circle is cleverer than they appear."

"Do you think you'll be able to do it?"

Helena was unsure which of the men had asked the question. Each of them were staring at her intently as they waited for her answer. Except for Von, he alone seemed entirely confident in her ability.

She opened her mouth to respond, but stopped, faltering as she recalled the roiling mass of water and the endless black hole it encircled. Could she? Helena wasn't so sure. At least, not entirely on her own. The night before she had performed powerful magic, but it was only after she'd woven the threads of their individual power together that she was able to make the earth open up and swallow the acidfall.

Helena forced herself to stand tall before them, pushing all of her fear and doubt away. There was only one answer she could give them, so she did.

"Yes."

Whether it was true or not remained to be seen.

CHAPTER 13

*T*hey strategized for a while longer, agreeing that Joquil would be their key to soliciting help from the rest of the Night Stalkers, given his inside knowledge. Assuming, of course, they made it through tomorrow unscathed. That much finalized, the others left to find their own rooms and get ready for the evening's festivities. They'd spoken much longer than she'd thought, leaving her with barely enough time to bathe and get dressed before they were expected downstairs. In fact, Helena was certain they were already late.

She finished brushing her hair and looked longingly at the bed. The last thing she wanted to do the night before facing-off against Anduin was go to another party. Especially considering how the last one had ended. Unfortunately, Helena the woman's wishes lost out to Helena the Kiri's duties almost every time. Tonight was no exception.

She sighed, trying to work out the tightness in her shoulders. Knowing what was expected of her tomorrow had her stomach in knots. There was very little, if anything, that she was enjoying about her current predicament. She was here to forge alliances and remind the Storm Forged that they were part of the Chosen. Somehow, destroying their leader didn't seem to be the best way to go about creating that partnership. It went against everything she believed in and was fighting for in the first place.

Hearing the door to the bathing chamber open, Helena made to turn toward her Mate when she felt him at her back. Von swept her tangle of curls aside and brushed a lingering kiss on the base of her neck. His fingers trailed softly down the side of it before continuing their journey down her shoulder.

Helena shivered, eyes falling closed as she leaned into him. *"You're starting something we don't have time to finish, Mate,"* she protested weakly, loving the feel of him against her. She craved his touch, which was nothing new, but there was something infinitely more desperate about her current need for him. Ever since she'd gotten him back, they'd been thrown into Rowena's chaos and barely had a chance to enjoy being reunited.

She missed him. Missed the quiet moments when they would curl up together whispering in the darkness, and the way she could surprise him into laughter. But more than anything, Helena missed the feel of him sliding inside her and the way he'd hold her close as she fell apart beneath him. She wanted those moments with him more than she wanted her next breath.

Being with her Mate was easy. It didn't require effort or complicated decisions like everything else in her life. She was exhausted and overwhelmed by the emotional weight she'd been carrying these last few months. When she was with Von, all she had to do was let go. Right now, Helena was desperate to let everything go.

"That doesn't mean I can't take advantage of the time we do have," he whispered hotly against her skin before biting down on the muscle between her neck and shoulder.

Helena sucked in a breath and arched into Von as he wrapped his other arm around her, pressing his palm flat against her belly. His heat surrounded her and all thoughts of responsibility and politics fled, leaving only Von in their wake.

He continued trailing kisses along the skin exposed by her dress, his fingers working their way down her body. She could feel his fingers resting just above the growing ache between her legs and let out a soft groan. The hand at her shoulder moved across her chest, his hand palming and kneading her breast.

"V-von," she stuttered in weak protest.

"Helena," he murmured in her ear before lightly licking the outer shell.

She shivered, his gentle assault making her need for him all-consuming. The fingers splayed over her belly began to flex and slowly gather her skirt. The air felt cool as it kissed the skin of her legs. He worked quickly, until the skirt was bunched about her waist and his warm fingers were pressed directly against her.

Helena had the distant realization that he was using his power to keep her skirt up, but then he began to stroke along her center and there were no conscious thoughts, only need. How he could do this to her, steal her focus and become the center of her world, even on the eve of battle, amazed her. Then again, if these stolen moments were the last they'd have, was there a better way to spend them?

"Von," she moaned again, arm lifting to wrap around his head and hold him closer; her hips moving desperately in response to his teasing fingers. He was stroking the skin between her legs lightly, never quite hitting the spot that ached to feel him.

The hand at her breast dipped down under the dress, his fingers plucking and twisting her pert nipple. The sensation set off little fireworks behind her eyes and a gasp left her parted lips.

"I love how responsive you are, *Mira*," he said.

"O-only for you," she panted.

She could feel his answering grin, even though she could not see it.

"Do you want me to touch you here," he asked pressing a slick finger down her center, "or here?" With that he slid his fingers further down and up inside of her.

Helena gasped and arched into him. "Wh-why not both?"

"Good answer," he chuckled, beginning to work her in earnest.

Her need began to spiral tight inside of her, an arrow flying toward its target.

There was a loud knock at the door and a voice called, "The Stormbringer requests your presence downstairs, Kiri."

Helena's eyes flew open and she tried to squirm away, with a strangled, "Be right there!"

But Von held her tight, growling, "You're not going anywhere until you come for me, Helena."

"O-oh," she moaned, torn between not wanting to be caught and her body's need.

"Now, Helena," he demanded, fingers hitting the perfect tempo.

She shattered around him, body clamping down on the fingers that were still moving inside of her.

"That's it. I want all of it."

"V-von," she whispered brokenly as her climax continued.

Another knock sounded at the door. "Kiri?"

Spent and languid, Helena forced her eyes open. "I'll be right down; I just need a few more minutes."

"Very well, Kiri. I'll let the Stormbringer know you are on your way," the muffled voice replied before the sound of receding footsteps met her ears.

Helena twisted in Von's arms, her heart still pounding in her chest.

He grinned at her wickedly, taking in her flushed state with satisfaction shining in his gray eyes. "And you said we didn't have time."

"It appears I was wrong," she said breathlessly.

Still grinning, he lifted his fingers to his lips, his eyes never leaving hers. "Mmm," he murmured as he licked them.

Helena blushed, the erotic sight enough to make her ready for him again. She ran nervous fingers down her unbound hair while simultaneously trying to smooth out her now-rumpled dress.

Von gave her one last, knowing grin before declaring, "All right, now we can go downstairs."

"Hopefully it's not too obvious what made us late. Or was that your intention?" she half-heartedly accused.

"Oh, it was."

Her eyes flew to his. Von shrugged, entirely unapologetic. "You looked tense. Now you don't." He smirked and she felt it throughout her body. "I couldn't let you go in there looking like you were worried about tomorrow. That's practically rule number one. Your opponent should never see you doubting yourself. It gives them an advantage and that is the last thing you ever want."

She studied him for a moment. There was definitely a special kind of logic he was using, but her brain was still too fuzzy for her to pinpoint the flaws in it. Besides, she had to admit she appreciated the results.

"I suppose I can't argue with that. I certainly feel less tense," she admitted before adding wryly, "actually, I'm not even sure I remember my name."

His answering chuckle followed her the entire way downstairs.

HELENA HAD BEEN ANTICIPATING an opulent affair in line with the kind of events thrown at the Palace. She could not have been more wrong. The Storm Forged were not an extravagant people. The room was filled with their crowing laughs and the clinking of glasses as they drank deeply, but there were no special adornments or displays of magic. The large stone hall with its wall of windows overlooking the sea, was exactly the same as it had been when they were in there earlier. The only differences were the vibrant splash of color added by the sun as it completed its descent and the additional tables which had been brought in to hold the food and people. Overall the atmosphere was merry but completely relaxed.

Spotting the Circle, Helena and Von went to join them. "Not what you were expecting?" he asked in a subdued tone as he walked beside her.

"Not in the least. With all his talk of ceremony and tradition, I had expected something a bit more..." she trailed off.

"Stuffy?" he provided.

Helena laughed, that was exactly what she had expected: austere expressions, barbed threats hidden behind saccharine smiles, and a lot of posturing. Instead the atmosphere was warm and inviting, and the people around her couldn't care less about who she was and why she was there. After their welcome this morning, it was a drastic change to say the least.

"Well, you won't hear me complain about the difference," she replied.

"Nor I," he agreed just as they reached the others.

"Now this is my kind of gathering," Ronan commented, his words echoing their sentiments and making Helena chuckle.

"And mine," Kragen agreed, slapping him on the back. The two men grinned at each other before sauntering over to a nearby table laden with ale.

The two men were completely oblivious to the female heads which turned to stare at them in their wake. Helena couldn't fault the women for noticing that they were attractive, well-built warriors. When those same eyes began to ogle Von, however, Helena found herself feeling less understanding. She frowned and forced herself to look away before she caused a scene.

As she did, Helena caught Serena glaring menacingly at one particularly obvious group of admirers. The women had hailed Ronan and Kragen, waylaying them before they made it back to their friends, and were now flirting shamelessly. Kragen was eating up the attention, flexing at the request of a couple women. Ronan looked more uncomfortable, shrugging off one dark-haired woman's wandering hands.

Feeling her friend's stare, Serena met her eyes before grinning sheepishly. "Just because he's not mine, doesn't mean I'm not allowed to feel protective."

"Mmhmm," Helena murmured, wondering if she should intervene on Ronan's behalf when he excused himself from the group and joined Timmins and Joquil on the other side of the hall.

Nial walked over then and Serena's entire face lit up. While the blonde beauty still felt a little possessive of her ex-lover, she was very much in love and committed to the younger Holbrooke. Helena couldn't fault her for that. Mated or not, she was also fiercely protective of those she counted as hers.

Needing to touch Von, she wove her fingers through his.

"Feeling a little territorial yourself?" he asked, not missing the way she had scowled when female eyes turned his way.

Helena bared her teeth in a feral smile that made him laugh. He pulled her toward him, brushing his lips against her forehead. *"Have you already forgotten what happened upstairs?"*

She blushed, her insides going liquid at the memory. When she looked up at him her aqua eyes were shining. *"Why do you think I am feeling the need to gnash my teeth and snarl 'Mine!'?"*

Von brushed a stray curl from her face, his expression tender. *"If it makes you feel better, I share the urge."*

It did. They shared a heated look, all others forgotten.

"I wouldn't mind more parties like this," Darrin remarked, breaking their moment.

Helena found herself in silent agreement. There was something beautiful in the simplicity of the gathering. At the Palace, the parties were a celebration of the Mother's magic; here it was a celebration of life.

"There's nothing stopping us from having our own gatherings like this," she replied.

"Except for a raging psychopath currently on the loose and slaughtering your people," Darrin pointed out.

With his words, all of Von's work to distract her was undone and the full burden of her responsibility returned. Helena frowned, "You know exactly how to kill a mood. Have I ever mentioned that?"

Darrin gave her a sidelong glance, assessing how much of her words were temper versus truth. "If by 'kill a mood' you mean remind you that we're surrounded by danger and cannot afford to lower our guard, then what you're really saying is I'm good at my job and I thank you for noticing. I did vow to shield you from harm, Helena. Not throw you headlong into it."

"Where in your job description does it say you get to be a smug bastard?" Helena asked archly.

Darrin burst out laughing. "Ah, Hellion. You didn't like admitting you were wrong when we were children and it would seem you like it even less now."

"I'll have you know that I am almost never wrong. You on the other hand..."

"Pfft," he sputtered, "as if there's anyone here that would buy that."

Von lifted his brow but didn't comment. He was used to their antics and knew better than to insert himself in the middle.

Effie just shook her head in amusement, hiding her laughter behind her hand. Sensing that the friendly insults weren't far away from devolving completely, she pointed her head in the direction of the couples dancing. "Care to dance?"

Darrin was torn, enjoying the almost normal moment with his best friend, but also looking forward to the idea of having a beautiful woman in his arms. It was no surprise which of the two won out. With barely a backward glance, Darrin escorted Effie to the center of the room.

Effie spun around and the look on Darrin's face as he watched her was a look Helena recognized. It was the same one Von wore when she'd catch him staring at her. Helena's heart ached as the reality of what was before her took shape.

"He's falling for her," Helena said softly.

"Well, the boy isn't entirely stupid."

Helena's lips lifted in a smile but fell just as quickly. "They can never be together, not while he serves in the Circle."

Von's voice grew serious, "I know and so does he, Helena. He knows where his duty lies."

"But does she?" Helena asked sadly, her voice barely more than a whisper as she noted the joy on Effie's face as Darrin twirled her in his arms again and again. "I don't want to be the reason he has to break her heart, Von. It isn't fair to either of them."

"He knew what he was agreeing to when he made his vows, Helena. All of us do. There are reasons for the rules."

"Now you sound like Timmins," she muttered.

"Hey!" he protested. "Now *you're* just being mean. I am not saying I will enjoy watching this play out as it must, but there can be no hesitation, Helena. If he gets put in a situation where he has to choose between saving her or you, how is he supposed to make that decision? As the Shield, the duty to serve his Kiri must come before everything."

Helena snorted. "As if rules ever stopped anyone from doing anything they knew in their heart to be right. If he loves her, Von, then he will always choose her. Any other vow will be meaningless. I would never fault him for that."

"That is not what it means to serve."

"No, that is what it means to be human."

Von was silent. She was right.

"I would release him from his vows, if he asked me."

"He will never ask."

"Then maybe, when this is over, I will find a way to change the rules so he doesn't have to."

Von stared at her in stunned silence.

"What?"

Von shook his head. "You continue to amaze me, *Mira.*"

"It's the right thing to do. No one should have to deny themselves the chance for love or finding their Mate, just because they also serve. That cannot be what the Mother truly intends for her children."

"Perhaps not," Von agreed.

After a moment of silence where they watched the other couple dance, Helena added, "How hard can it be, really? I mean, I am the one in charge after all. Don't people have to do what I say?"

Von's laughter caused many curious stares to turn their way. "I love how you remember that whenever it's convenient, but you forget it when it truly matters."

Helena shrugged. "As long as everyone else remembers."

They grew silent again, the sounds of laughter and music swelling around them.

After a few heartbeats she spoke again. "It's a stupid rule, and stupid rules should be broken if they cannot be changed."

"As one who has broken every rule ever set in front of him, I must wholeheartedly agree."

"I knew I could count on you."

"Always." He reinforced the promise so that it echoed through their bond.

CHAPTER 14

*I*t was still early, but Helena was already standing on the beach, the sound of the crashing waves and the echoing caw of gulls her only companions. When she'd awoken that morning, the salty tang of the sea was permeating her room, even though no windows had been open, and she'd felt the need to go down and become familiar with the element she'd be trying to control only a few hours later.

The wind still raged, although the Stormbringer's keep sheltered her from the worst of it. She hadn't gone far from the gates, just over to the small beach off of the main entrance. Most were still asleep, so she'd only had to endure a few curious glances, and one barely concealed yawn, as she'd made her way.

At the time, it'd seemed entirely reasonable to introduce herself to the sea but now that she was standing here she felt incredibly foolish. The problem was that she didn't know exactly what she was trying to do. She'd woken with a nameless need to be outside, and so she'd followed it. Now that she was here, she was at a bit of a loss.

She'd already given up trying to control her hair. Every time she'd tie it back the wind would pull it free so that it'd whip around her. As it was, she could barely keep the cloak she'd brought clasped about her shoulders. Helena removed her boots and walked further out on the soft sand until it became wet beneath her feet. It was chilly, but bearable. She forced herself to take the final two steps until the waves began lapping at her feet. She shivered but did not move away.

Yesterday, when they'd been greeted by the storm, and the man that controlled it, there was a sense of threat in the water and air. Not today. The way that the wind was teasing her felt curious and playful. She could feel none of Anduin in it; this was the Mother's magic, wild and free.

Closing her eyes, Helena opened herself up to the power surrounding her. She let her magic bubble up and flow out of her. The reaction was subtle but instantaneous. The wind whipped up, and the waves began to crash with increasing frequency. It was a greeting; the elements here recognized her.

In her own way, Helena recognized them as well. Even though she was standing in the Emerald Ocean, she could feel the icy current of the Mother's Tears. The river nearly bisected Elysia, flowing from Vyruul until it fed the ocean at the southern tip of Daejara. That wasn't the only reason why she recognized the feel of it though. When they'd traveled through Bael, the Mother's Tears had been her source of water for nourishment as well as bathing. She'd been immersed in this water once before.

Helena was feeling fanciful. She imagined that the water she'd drank months before had become a part of her, and that even now its residual energy lived within her. She laughed at her silliness and opened her eyes.

Her power was radiating out of her in glowing waves of energy. She was sure no one else who saw her would see what she could see and was glad for it. Helena caused enough of a stir as it was, no need to add to the gossip fodder. She watched as tendrils of the iridescent power swam through the water and spun through the air. Her power was weaving itself into the elements around them. Each individual strand pulsed in time to her heartbeat.

It was breathtaking.

As her magic moved through the elements, she could feel them accept her presence amongst them. The wind continued to play, twisting around her body and making the loose strands of her hair dance in the breeze. Tentatively, Helena used her power to push the wind out and away from her. Not forcefully; it was a tickle not a shove. She could feel the air around her shiver before it assented to her request and flowed away from her. The sea, in response to the air, grew still. Its churning waves died down until the water was placid and calm around her. There was a sense of expectation, as if they were waiting to see what she would do next. She felt for all the world as if she was playing hide and seek with children.

Not wanting to disappoint them, Helena answered the unspoken request. She called the air back to her, using it to form a massive ball. If not for the swirl of her power within it, she would have looked as if she was holding nothing. Pushing the air out toward the water, she added her energy and strength to the ball. Where the ball met the water, it pushed it aside, dividing the ocean and creating a little path for her to walk through. The water was not high here, perhaps only to her knees, but as she walked forward, she could see the ocean straining against the invisible barrier of air she used to reinforce the divide. Helena had the distinct impression the water was trembling with laughter, loving her antics.

With a startled laugh, she stepped back onto the beach and released her hold on the water and air, letting them return to their natural state. They wasted no time coming back to her, it was like a game of chase; they were not ready for her to leave. Helena laughed again, feeling the joy in the elements around her.

Any doubts she still had vanished, disappearing with the wind. Helena knew these elements and they knew her. More than that, they'd already recognized her authority. Whatever she had to ask of them today, they would grant her. They'd just proven it.

She was going to win.

It was only a couple hours later, but the playfulness from the morning was nowhere to be found. Helena stood on the dock she'd arrived at yesterday, although this time she stood alone. Anduin was also standing alone, although he was on a dock some hundred yards away from her. Before each of them, the maelstrom churned, its inky depths howling with fury.

The Circle and those that traveled with her stood beside the Storm Forged on the rocky cliffs a safe distance away. Apparently, it was just as dangerous to be an observer as a participant in Aegaeon's Challenge given how often a challenger would lose control of their storm.

As if he could feel her looking for him, Von called to her through the bond. *"Are you ready, Mira?"*

"As ready as I can be."

"He is a fool to underestimate you."

Helena considered his words before responding, *"I do not get the impression that he does."*

"What makes you say that?"

"The way he responded to Starshine, and the look in his eyes when we mentioned the prophecy. He wanted to discount it as childish stories, but I sensed the fear in him. I think it is desperation that makes him cling to his beliefs. He is afraid of the alternative."

"I'm not sure if that makes him smart or foolish."

Helena's answering laugh flowed through their bond. *"A man can be both wise and foolish, one does not preclude the other. It is hope for peace that makes him want to bury his head in the sand... or should I say sea?"*

"Both are sure ways to die," Von replied, his own amusement in the words.

"I think we just proved my point with our own silliness."

Growing serious Von said, *"Be careful, Mira. Anduin intends to fight to the death, he does not realize you will try to save him. A man that desperate to deny the truth will not go down easily."*

"I know."

"If you have need of me, I am here."

His words were a balm. Feeling him through the bond and knowing that he was close even if they were not touching, filled her with a sense of calm. She might be standing by herself, but she was not alone.

One of the Storm Forged's priests had briefed her on the challenge. He hadn't told her much more than she'd learned from Joquil the day before, but he'd let her know that the challenge would start once lightning cracked across the sky and would not stop until only one of them was still standing. Shivering, Helena turned her eyes upward, waiting for the sign that the challenge had begun.

She did not have to wait long. The crack of lightning flared bright, illuminating everything around them. As soon as the flash receded, the sky went dark; black clouds rolling in out of nowhere. The sea responded to the shift. The water surged, causing the dock to quake beneath her feet. *Anduin* she realized. He'd already begun and she was still standing here admiring the sky.

Her hair was flying wildly around her in the wind while icy rain pelted her from every direction, but she ignored it. Blocking out everything but the sea, Helena summoned her power as she had that morning. She distantly felt her body react as she released it but was solely focused on the shimmering tendrils that began to weave themselves into the air and sea.

From her place on the dock she could see down into the center of the maelstrom. She funneled her power toward it, feeling the slightest resistance before the water gave way, allowing her power to become part of the massive spiral. As it did, the glowing threads of her magic swirled down and into the center of the maelstrom. They crackled like electricity as the twisting fury of the water helped it gather strength.

While Helena was focused on the maelstrom and building her storm from its depths, Anduin had moved straight toward his cyclone. What had already been an impressive blend of wind and water was now a towering beast that had flashes of lightning shooting out of it. She could see him only peripherally, but his hands were outstretched above him, moving like he was shaping the spinning mass between them. She knew it was only a matter of time before he sent it straight toward her.

The wind and rain continued to beat at her, and she felt herself rocking like a tree in a storm as she withstood the attack. It was time to pull her own tempest from the maelstrom. She started to raise her arms, willing the water to follow. The maelstrom fought back, the intensity of its current unwilling to surrender to her will. Helena pushed more of her power into the churning water. There was a stutter in the spiraling water, as if her power had struck it like a blow, knocking it off course. It was all the opening she needed.

Helena pulled, her teeth baring down until she tasted blood. A twisting ball of water began to form in the center of the maelstrom, growing in strength and size very quickly. In order to overtake Anduin's, Helena knew that it would have to be so much more than an ordinary cyclone, so she continued to feed the storm. She used her power to pull more water from the eye of the maelstrom, while pushing the air to keep it spinning. It was only a matter of a few heartbeats before two cyclones spun on the horizon.

Anduin's storm was a deep pulsing black, the bright flickers of lightning making the water seem to glow the same color as his eyes. Helena's was a smoky gray, the water spinning so fast that its foam diluted the color of the water until it appeared almost entirely white. In size they were evenly matched, but Anduin's seemed deadlier as it began to shoot across the water straight toward her.

Helena threw her hand out, and her storm responded, lurching to intercept the attack. Her sparkling eyes flicked to where Anduin stood, and even with the distance between them she could make out the fierce smile on his face. He was enjoying himself.

Helena had to admit, so was she. Her heart was pounding within her, but the way her power merged with the intensity of the storm was like nothing she'd ever experienced. She felt wholly alive. There was raw power here, and an unmatched ferocity in the elements that was now pulsing through her. Under different circumstances, she might even say she was having fun.

That was when the dueling storms collided. Thunder roared, and the dock trembled but did not break. Helena lurched back, her body reeling from the impact. Anduin fared worse. He was thrown backwards, swept off his feet by the force. She was vibrating like the plucked string of an instrument, the tangle of wind, water and power becoming a tangible barrier pushing against her very fragile body.

Helena couldn't remember ever being quite this aware of her mortality before. Even with the full force of her power unleashed, giving her almost limitless strength, her human body was not immune to the power of the elements that surrounded her. If she lost control, they'd tear her apart.

As Anduin pushed to his feet, she watched his eyes blaze white-hot before his tower of black water flung itself into hers. What her cyclone lacked in speed, it more than made up for in strength. It didn't falter under the repeated blows.

Helena was starting to realize his strategy. He would continue to ram at her storm, and through it her power, weakening both to the point he could blast through and obliterate them. She would not survive the instantaneous loss of control. That kind of attack on her power would be the equivalent of a hammer shattering her mind, thereby severing her body's connection to her innermost self. It was a brilliant strategy, although utterly merciless.

Her initial reaction was to continue to reinforce the storm, but she wouldn't be able to keep that up indefinitely. Eventually Anduin would find a way through. Instead, Helena took a cue she'd learned from Anderson many years ago.

When she'd first learned how to ride a horse, Anderson had warned her that she would eventually fall off. In order to protect herself, he'd taught her that when that day came, she would need to become as limp as her rag doll, so that her body would absorb and not fight the impact. He said it could be the difference between whether or not she survived the fall.

Helena was about to test his theory with these storms. Instead of fighting against the attack, she would release a bit of her hold on it, allowing Anduin's to slip through. Once the storms were fully integrated she would tighten her hold again, trapping his storm within hers. To defeat him, she would then have to use her power to force his into submission. She just hoped he didn't sense the trap.

She would need to time this perfectly. He could not sense the change in resistance, until it was too late for him to pull back. Taking a deep breath, Helena began to pull small tendrils of power back into herself. By the time Anduin struck again, Helena's hold on the cyclone was quite loose and his storm blew a hole through hers.

Even from this distance she could hear the startled gasps and fierce cheers from the crowd. Anduin let out his own battle cry, sensing victory was within his grasp.

Helena waited for two long heartbeats, not wanting to move too quickly. Just as Anduin's storm had the power to destroy her, so too could her storm end him. But unlike Anduin, that was not her goal.

She needed to nullify his power. That was going to require her to absorb it completely. She would have to act fast, once he realized he was caged, he would throw everything he had at trying to escape her hold.

Helena took one last breath just as the second half of Anduin's storm made contact with the far edge of hers. She pumped every bit of power she still had back into the storm, strengthening it to the point that the water nearest to the cyclone began to push away, creating angry waves that moved toward the crowd.

"No!" Anduin screamed, finally realizing what Helena had done, but not ready to give up.

As she predicted, his power lashed out at her. Helena bore down, bearing the attack. Seeing the glowing blue ribbons of Anduin's power spiraling through the water, Helena pushed her own shining strands toward them, willing the power to merge. Where the threads of power touched, lightning sparked and booms of thunder split the sky. With what felt like a shudder, the strands combined, fusing into one glowing beam. Helena had taken full control of both storms.

Anduin dropped to his knees, defeated.

The violence of the storm threatened to overwhelm her, but Helena pushed the water back down into the sea. At the same time, she used the air to send the rain and clouds out and away from the cyclone so that they would stop feeding the storm. Both elements resisted at first, seeming to relish their dance across the ocean, but eventually, layers of the storm were stripped away, floating out across the sky or sliding back into the sea.

With shaking limbs, Helena began to draw her power back into herself, slowly releasing her hold on the cyclone entirely. When she was done, her cyclone, now much diminished in size, was left lazily spinning beside the maelstrom.

Anduin lifted his head, eyes glowing as he stared at her in awe. Helena shrugged sheepishly, before her knees buckled and she staggered. The euphoria she'd felt controlling the storm left along with her hold on it, and all she felt now was a bone-deep weariness.

She made to move toward the beach and the crowd, but her legs didn't want to carry her. They didn't have to. Von was already there, picking her up and spinning her around.

"You did it!"

The rest of her Circle was not far behind, whooping and laughing in celebration.

"Helena Stormbringer!" Darrin crowed, grinning at her.

With a shaky smile, Helena waved away their cheers before burying her face in Von's neck and closing her eyes. She had passed out before he made it off the dock.

CHAPTER 15

*H*elena stretched and rubbed a bit of sleep from her eyes. She'd slept through the night and well into the next day and now her body felt equal parts heavy and weak, almost like she'd spent the night drinking instead of sleeping.

Apparently, there are side effects to playing with storms, she thought with a grimace.

Swinging her feet over the side of the bed, she padded softly to the side table that held a cup of magic-heated tea and a neatly folded letter.

She eyed the note curiously but moved for the tea first. Wasn't Timmins always telling her that establishing priorities was an important part of ruling? Helena was certain tea constituted a priority. The warm liquid did much to ease the sluggishness she was feeling. She sent a thanks to Von for including the healing brew in the drink and lifted the heavy cream parchment.

It was addressed to "The Stormbringer."

"Hmm," she murmured, before taking another sip and setting her cup down.

She unfolded the note and scanned it quickly. The words were simple but formal.

GREETINGS STORMBRINGER,

I WISH TO SPEAK WITH YOU AT YOUR FIRST
    CONVENIENCE. I AM AWAITING YOU IN MY STUDY.

~ A

HELENA RAN a finger over the boldly penned words. The nib had been pressed down hard, leaving deep indents in the paper. She did not need magic to feel the conflict in his looping letters. This was not a man used to making requests, even writing one made him uncomfortable. Helena smirked at that; she had a habit of making strong men uncomfortable.

Not wanting to further delay their trip to the next tribe, Helena quickly finished her tea and got dressed in her traveling clothes. Von walked in just as she laced the last of her boots. Seeing the scrap of paper sitting on the table, he picked it up and scanned the contents.

"Want company?"

Helena shook her head, smiling at his annoyed expression. "Anduin poses no threat."

"Backup is never a bad idea."

"You just want to know what he has to say."

He shrugged, but his lips lifted in the ghost of a grin.

She made for the door. "I'm not the one that needs a babysitter. If you'd like to make yourself truly useful, go ensure the others are ready to leave as soon as I'm finished."

He grasped her arm as she moved past, tugging her back toward him.

At her questioning look he murmured, "You forgot something." He leaned over and pressed a kiss to her lips.

The kiss ended as quickly as it began, but even still Helena felt her insides turn to liquid. She blinked up at him a few times before stepping back. "What was I doing?"

Von laughed. "You're off to salvage what you can of a man's bruised ego."

"Is it Firesday already?" she deadpanned, indicating that such was a normal occurrence.

"Minx," he growled affectionately, before slapping her on the ass and sending her on her way.

She blew him a kiss over her shoulder and left the room. Helena strode toward the central hall, keeping an eye out for one of the Storm Forged. Since she had not received any sort of tour, Helena had absolutely no clue where Anduin's study was located. She was hoping to run into someone that wouldn't mind pointing her in the right direction.

The lack of people about was surprising. Yesterday, the keep had been a flurry of activity, but today it was a ghost town. The silence was unnerving. After fifteen minutes of wandering aimlessly, Helena finally spotted a turquoise-haired woman.

"Excuse me!" Helena called. "Hey!" she shouted in exasperation when the woman pretended to ignore her and continued to scurry down the hall. Helena had wasted enough time; she wasn't about to miss this opportunity. Silently apologizing for what she was about to do, Helena summoned a wall of Air directly in the woman's path.

The woman bounced off it with a startled cry, providing Helena with just enough time to catch up to her. She spun around ready to launch into a verbal attack but realized it was Helena and quickly cast her eyes down.

Summoning her sweetest voice, Helena said, "Sorry for that, I was just hoping you'd be so kind as to give me directions to Anduin's study. He's waiting for me, and I don't want to keep him."

The woman refused to meet her eyes and rubbed her nose before pointing back down the hallway they'd just traveled. "Take a right and follow it all the way down." She didn't even wait for a response before she scurried off.

Helena watched her retreating back before shaking her head and walking away. *What is with everyone today?*

She moved quickly down the arched halls and knew she'd reached the Stormbringer's room when she saw the stunning relief carved into the door. It was a seascape, with men and women brilliantly disguised within the shapes of the rolling waves, almost as if they were made from the water. Wishing she had more time to study the beautiful scene, she allowed herself only a moment to run her fingers over the shape of one woman whose hair curled into tufts of wind. At her touch the image came to life. The tangy scent of the sea and the roar of waves greeted her. She would have sworn she could hear laughter, but the door swung open pulling her attention away from the scene and toward the man standing in the doorway.

Anduin's glowing eyes flashed as he took in the sight of her. "Stormbringer."

Helena just barely resisted the urge to laugh; the sound of the title on his lips was forced and sullen.

"I have no wish for another title, Anduin. These are your people, more so than they will ever be mine."

His eyes widened in surprise, but he remained silent.

"I only want what I asked for: assistance. Those were the terms of our bargain."

"Even so, Kiri, that is not the way of the Storm Forged. You won the challenge, the title is rightfully yours."

Helena rolled her eyes, tired of jumping through political hoops. "Fine, then as your rightful leader, I am telling you that the Storm Forged will be assisting the Chosen in this battle."

Anduin's lips flattened, but he inclined his head. "As you wish."

She sighed. "Anduin. Look at me."

He met her gaze.

"We cannot defeat Rowena without your help. Her victory will be the end of us all. If you would like the Storm Forged to be able to continue on with their way of life, this is the only way."

Fear and anger raged in his eyes like a storm about to break. "She wouldn't dare threaten the Storm Forged."

Laying a gentle hand on his arm Helena replied, "She already has. Will you let her threat go unanswered?"

Anduin straightened his shoulders, pride making him stand tall. "Never."

Helena nodded. "So it's settled. The Storm Forged will ally themselves with the Chosen. Not just because of our bargain, but because they are defending their home and way of life."

She could feel the reaction her words caused. Anduin's answering smile was not forced.

"I have others I need to meet, but I will send word once we're ready."

As she made to leave, Anduin called her name. "Helena."

She glanced over her shoulder, startled only because it was the first time he'd refrained from using a title. "Yes?"

"What happens after?"

Her brows furrowed. "After what?"

"After we defeat her."

The confusion cleared. Anduin wanted to know what would happen to the Storm Forged, or more specifically, to him. She gave him a wide smile. "I already told you. I do not want your title. I have my hands full with one realm as it is; I have no need of another. The Ebon Isle is yours, Anduin."

She watched his shoulders rise as he took a deep breath. When he let it out, it was as if a massive weight had fallen away. He gave her a grateful smile. "Thank you, Kiri."

With a wink she called, "Until next time, Stormbringer."

HELENA WASN'T sure where the others had gone off to but she should have known better than to worry. It would have been impossible to miss the crowd of people and creatures milling about near the docks. Starshine's white fur would have been enough of a beacon on its own. Feeling her mistress, Starshine let out a roar of greeting. Those nearest to the Talyrian jumped, not yet seeing Helena in the distance.

Seeing Starshine made Helena yearn to feel the wind in her hair. Unable to fly, Helena took the only option available to her and set off at a run.

"I think we've caused enough chaos here for the time being."

Darrin turned toward her as she closed the distance between them. "These days you seem to bring chaos with you wherever you go."

Helena frowned. "Not true."

He raised a brow. "It is most definitely true."

"You seem to have forgotten that I'm not a six-year-old girl any longer. I'm strong enough that I can kick your ass, with my fists or with my magic. Do you require a demonstration?"

Titters of laughter met Ronan's murmured, "I can vouch for that."

Darrin tutted. "My my my, aren't you quick to threaten violence these days. How quickly a minor victory goes to your head."

Helena sputtered, ready to defend her honor but Von wrapped an arm around her waist, whispering, "Ignore him."

The urge to stick her tongue out at Darrin was strong. She turned from him instead. "Gladly."

Darrin laughed at her, and Helena was just about to zap him with a little lightning when Timmins drawled, "If you two are quite done…"

"He started it," she muttered defensively, feeling chastised even though she hadn't actually done anything.

"Of course he did," Timmins agreed, making the others laugh.

Joquil stepped forward, and Miranda handed him one of the unused Kaelpas stones. His warm amber eyes met hers. "Are you ready to go, Kiri?"

"Are you?"

It was a loaded question. This would be the first time he'd return to his childhood home in almost thirty years. Who knew what, or who, would be waiting for him.

Joquil nodded, "As much as I can be."

The Circle moved in close, getting into position. Helena looked around, partially to ensure that everyone was accounted for, but also to get one final look at her cyclone which was spinning just off the horizon. She was leaving the Ebon Isle in capable hands, but a part of her would remain behind to stand guard.

"Then let's—"

Before she could finish, the familiar feeling of being turned inside out was upon her. When she was able to open her eyes again they were surrounded by a new kind of sea.

"Welcome to the Forest of Whispers, Kiri."

CHAPTER 16

*T*he forest was both beautiful and ancient. Everywhere Helena looked, she was surrounded by life. Trees towered above them, all but obscuring the sky. Their trunks were as wide as three or four grown men standing shoulder-to-shoulder. She ran a hand along the rough edges of bark, feeling a spark of energy in response to the touch.

Helena opened her mouth to ask Joquil where exactly they were, but the hiss of a blade being drawn had her on full alert. Between one heartbeat and the next, she'd shielded the group and called her power; it hummed beneath her skin ready to be unleashed.

"What—" Effie started, but Helena shook her head and held a finger to her lips. The rest of the group were more attuned to battle and didn't need to ask. They had already slipped into position around her, drawing weapons and summoning their power.

"If they wanted you dead, they would not have let you hear them," Joquil murmured. "That was a warning."

"Friendly folks, are they? Is this how they welcome all visitors?" Helena asked neutrally, eyes still scanning the woods for a sign of where someone might be hiding.

Starshine crouched and began to growl, her bared teeth glistening in the dim sunlight.

"Easy girl," Helena cautioned.

The Daejaran pack took up Starshine's call, angry snarls filling the silence.

Memories of the last time Starshine and she walked in the woods came to mind. Apparently, Ronan also recalled the caebris attack, because when she hazarded a glance at him, his steady ice-blue eyes were locked onto her. She wasn't certain if the look was supposed to be a warning, or if he was checking to make sure she remembered that some beasts were adept at hiding in plain sight. Either way, the result was the same. They were on the lookout for something their eyes could not see. He gave her a slow nod and they both went back to searching for the threat the animals could already sense.

Helena loosened her hold on her power, her senses coming alive with the added magic. The trees were pulsing with magic of their own, which would explain the energy she felt when she touched them, but so far nothing else was revealed.

A blade was flung from above. Helena would have missed it until it smacked into the shield, if not for her magic-enhanced vision. She used air to push the dagger off course, causing it to bury itself in the ground just beside her.

"You say you're visitors and yet you've arrived with an army." The female voice also came to them from above.

"We do not mean you any harm," Helena shouted.

"I have no reason to trust you."

Helena wanted to point out that neither did they, especially given that they were not the ones throwing knives. Leaving her shield up, Helena released her power and motioned for the others to do the same.

Her friends scowled, not appreciating the request, but knowing better than to undermine it. Their weapons were just tools anyway. Helena knew that if they truly needed to defend themselves, any of the men and women around her would be able to wield their magic with deadly precision. And for those that did not have magic, they would need only seconds to attack. The ones with magic would buy them that time. All in all, the move was more of a show than anything.

"No one invited you," a second voice hissed.

Helena tilted her head up, only barely able to make out the hazy edges of a woman perched high in the tree nearest to her.

"Intruders," another voice cried. Others took up the cry and soon the forest was filled with jeering calls.

"Do not listen to their lies!"

"Slit their throats before they take another step."

Helena bristled at the menace she heard in the voices. Lifting a brow, she glanced at Joquil. His face was puzzled, as if this greeting was unexpected to him as well.

"We've had others visit recently. They too showed up without invitation. We do not care to repeat the experience," the first voice said.

There was a barely audible oomph to her right. Helena twisted in time to see Von's elbow lowering and Joquil giving him a narrow-eyed glare.

"Was that necessary?"

"What's the point in having a native as your guide if they aren't going to establish safe entry?"

It was a fair question. Von turned his smoky stare back toward Joquil who nervously cleared his throat before calling out, "I am one of you! My father is Demond Mascura of the Mascura tribe."

"More lies," the second voice hissed.

"Demond has no son," the first voice countered.

"Not anymore, perhaps. His son Joquil was taken from him by a Keeper twenty-eight years ago in order to fulfill his destiny. I have returned."

"A likely story."

"He speaks the truth," Miranda said.

"Why come back now?" The voice was cautious, as if it wasn't sure why it was asking the question but could not help but ask it anyway.

"We have need of the Night Stalkers' expertise to defeat an enemy that threatens all of Elysia."

"Pretty words, but the Night Stalkers are not for sale."

"That's not what I heard," Darrin muttered.

"Mother's tits, Darrin! Could you not keep your damned mouth shut for once?" Helena snapped with exasperation.

The others, even Effie, glared at him. Darrin colored, but did not respond.

Wind whipped through the trees making the leaves rattle like thousands of whispers. One-by-one they somersaulted gracefully from the sky, cloaked in shadows like falling clouds. As they rose from the ground, they took shape, releasing the hold on their camouflage. Helena's people were surrounded.

The woman closest to Helena appeared to be the leader. Her mass of black hair was a tangle of curls and braids. She had swirls of black paint obscuring most of her face. It only made her leaf-green eyes stand out in harsh relief. Her body was covered in leather and weapons, but Helena had the impression they were only window dressing. She was the true weapon. Helena felt a kind of kinship with her in that moment because so was she.

"You are not a daughter of the Forest," the woman commented, studying Helena in kind.

"I am the Mother's daughter," she replied.

"One of the Chosen," a voice from behind her spat.

"The Duskfall tribe is dead because of *their* kind!" another voice shouted.

Helena went still at that. *"What does she mean?"*

Von was slow to respond. *"I'm not sure, but I am getting the impression that someone may have beaten us here."*

"Rowena." Helena's disgust for the woman filled the word.

Von dipped his chin in agreement but did not take his eyes off a man spinning twin daggers in his hands. They glowed a sickly green that could only mean one thing: poison.

"The Kiri and her people have not harmed, nor do they have any reason to harm, any of the Forest tribes," Miranda said, holding up her hands as she took a tentative step toward Helena.

"And yet they call us the Forsaken. Those forgotten by the rest of Elysia, left to fend for themselves." The people encircling them shifted warily, their weapons visibly leveled on each of the Chosen.

"I would not be here if I thought that way," Helena countered.

"It is true!" Nial spoke up, startling both Helena and Von. "The Kiri has already lifted the ban on my people. She seeks to unite Elysia, not continue to divide it."

"We have come to seek your help," Timmins added.

"What could the Mother's spoiled children want from us?" For all that the words were an insult, they were truly curious.

"It is as he said. We are here to ask for your help. I believe we share a common enemy."

Helena spoke calmly. These people were looking for any reason to attack; they had probably intended to attack first but had been surprised by Joquil's revelation. Helena had no doubt he was the only reason the Night Stalkers had stayed their hands.

"We have nothing in common," the man standing before Von said, twisting and spitting at his feet.

Von grinned, malice and danger rolling off him in waves. "Do that again."

Ronan and Serena stepped forward, their expressions each holding the promise of violence.

The man glowered, his black paint smeared down the better part of his face and giving the impression he was still cloaked in darkness.

"Ryder, enough," their leader said. The man bit off a curse but stepped back.

"Not the time," Helena told Von. She felt his desire to return the man's insult, but he remained quiet.

"Reyna, this woman arrives unannounced and with an army at her back, mere days after the attack on Duskfall, and yet you let her live?" The question came from behind them.

"I think I know who may have attacked your people. If you were to take us to the site, I would be able to confirm it." Helena's words caused the others to go still.

"It is a tainted, unholy place. We will not go back there," Reyna said in a cold, hard voice.

"I can help with that, as well," Helena offered.

131

There were murmurs as her words were repeated through the crowd.

Reyna tilted her head, staring at Helena as she considered the offer. "You can help the spirits find peace?"

"I can try."

Silence greeted her response. After another long, measured look, Reyna said, "Very well, let us see what you can do. Ryder, stay here and stand guard with your men. The rest of you, with me."

Ryder looked like he wanted to protest, but only grunted his assent before calling swirling shadows around his body and disappearing back into the trees. A handful of men followed suit, each one seamlessly blending into the shadows of the forest.

Helena found herself wondering how the Night Stalkers were able to do that, and if she would also be able to cloak herself that way.

"Jealous?" Von asked, catching the trail of her thoughts.

Helena smiled. *"Maybe just a little."*

Von's expression didn't change, but she could feel his amusement. *"All that power and yet you still want more."*

"What? It's a useful trick."

"Coming?" Reyna asked, already a good distance away.

Helena nodded and quickly caught up while Von's silent laughter and the others followed close behind her.

SOMETHING WAS DEFINITELY WRONG HERE. Given the animals' whines, they were clearly in agreement with her assessment. They'd been walking for a few hours and with each step the sounds of the forest grew quieter. The air felt thick and oppressive, and Helena's senses were screaming for her to run back in the other direction. She'd even looked up, multiple times, to check and see if the sun had disappeared, but it was still there.

"Do you feel that?" she asked.

"Aye."

The strained tone of Von's voice had Helena pausing to look at him. There was something wild about the look in his eyes, his nostrils flaring as if he could smell something in the air. Helena sniffed delicately, trying to see if she could sense anything, but all she detected was the rich scent of pine. That wasn't to say there wasn't anything there. Von had told her once that the reason he'd been able to defeat so many enemies was that he could sense and counter their magic before they even realized he was upon them. He'd never been a fan of what he could not see or touch, but it'd never stopped him from using it to his advantage.

"What's wrong?"

Von shook his head. *"I'm not sure, but it feels familiar. I would bet my life that we've felt this magic before."*

"If it's Rowena that should not be a surprise."

He hesitated, considering. *"It does not feel like Rowena. Her corruption grates at my senses, and even though I can feel the wrongness in the land, this is different. It feels more sinister. As if death itself is here."*

Helena shuddered.

Reyna halted a few steps ahead of them, her face grim. "This is what remains of the Duskfall village."

Helena glanced around, still seeing only trees. Joquil brushed shaking fingers against her arm, before mutely pointing up. Helena tilted her head back, gasping at the village hidden in the treetops. There was an entire city spanned in the trees above them. At least, there had been.

Huge circular houses were interconnected by spiraling stairways and roped bridges. The wooden structures looked almost untouched in places, and completely demolished in others. It almost made it worse, to see the beauty of what once was beside the horror of what was left.

Parts of the houses were still smoking, as if the fire had only just gone out. Huge holes allowed her to peer into the skeletons of the houses. It was heartbreaking to see the evidence of life; like the soft pink of a child's blanket abandoned beside a half-torn doll. There had been happiness here, but now all she could feel was the joy someone had taken in destroying it. For that was what Helena felt as she looked at the charred remains: joy in destruction and pleasure in others' pain. Rowena had definitely been here.

"Where are the bodies?" she asked in a hollow voice. Because of course there would be bodies, there was always a row of corpses to greet them when they'd come across a village Rowena's Shadows had destroyed.

"There are none."

Heads spun toward Reyna in surprise.

"What do you mean?" Von asked.

"No bodies and no survivors. The Duskfall tribe is gone."

"But you mentioned spirits," Timmins said, horror at her words bleaching the color from his skin.

Reyna closed her eyes, as if pained. "Can you not feel the death here? Just because there were no bodies, does not mean there was no death or suffering. The agony of it still haunts this place."

Helena's blood went cold. If what Reyna said was true, then Rowena had come in and turned an entire village into more of her creatures. Those that had died had probably been the village's defenders, the strongest of the men and women. Once the rest of the tribe, likely elders and children, had come face-to-face with the abominations and seen what they were capable of, it would not have taken long for Rowena to convince them that joining her would be a better option. The Duskfall tribe could not have known what they agreed to, or they would have chosen death.

She swallowed back her revulsion, her own eyes falling closed as the ghost of screams met her ears. This place was indeed haunted. But it was not just the people that had suffered. The trees they'd lived in and drawn power from still held an imprint of the attack. It was a wound that could not heal, not while the forest still held onto all of the pain and fear.

It was too much, she couldn't stand it one second longer. Without a word, Helena let her magic free. She felt it flow out of her and over the land. Pushing it out until it wrapped around each tree branch and all that was left of the village. Then, like a sponge, she began to absorb the corruption into the web created by her magic. Even with her eyes closed, she could see the oily black remains of the power used here, the power that still infected the land. Helena trembled as her power came into contact with the worst of the tainted essence, but she did not stop.

Where the corruption did not want to let go, she demanded. When it tried to get around her tendrils of magic, she snared it and pulled it out anyway. She coaxed. She tricked. She was relentless.

By the time she was done drawing the last of it out, Helena was shaky and sweating. She was also left with a problem. Helena could not simply release her hold on this kind of toxic power; it still had the potential to destroy. She would have to nullify it completely, but the only way to do that was to purify it with her own. That would require her to lower her innermost shields and let the heart of her power come into contact with the writhing mass of corruption.

"*Helena, no,*" Von demanded, completely in tune with her thoughts.

"It's the only way," she replied, her voice spectral and echoing throughout the forest.

"It's too dangerous," he insisted aloud, for the benefit of the others.

Ignoring him, Helena lowered her inner barriers, pushing her essence out. The corrupted echo of power she still held onto shrieked and tried to pull away from the light that was radiating out of her body. Helena held firm. Her power slammed into the mass. Everywhere it made contact, the corruption shrank and recoiled, until all that was left was a speck of darkness that finally winked out.

When Helena opened her eyes, they still glowed with her power. The village was still destroyed, a testament to the people that had lived there, but the land had been healed. It was at peace. But she was not finished yet. There was still one last thing she must do. Helena opened her hands, revealing a small pile of glittering dust in her palms.

There were gasps as the others realized what she held. Not only had she pulled out the corruption, she'd also gathered the souls of those that had died. Helena blew softly, the soul dust blowing up and away from her like a sparkling cloud. It flew high, up and over the trees until it made contact with the sky. The sky flared brightly where it came into contact with the motes, and instead of the light fading completely, a star twinkled in its wake.

"May the spirits of the fallen watch over and guide your people," Helena said in the harmonious voice of her power.

Reyna and the Night Stalkers were on their knees, mouths gaping in awe. Reyna's eyes were wet with tears, smearing the black whirls on her skin. "Th-thank you, Kiri. Whatever you need, the people of the Forest are yours."

The Chosen had remained standing, and yet their expressions were no less awestruck. Feeling raw and over-exposed, Helena walked away from the others, needing time to find her way back to herself.

Von followed. She could feel him at her back, quietly trailing her as she headed deeper into the forest. When she could carry herself no further, her knees buckled and she fell to the floor. She gagged, her body heaving as it purged the remnants of the contaminated magic. For all that she'd destroyed it, some of its taint had still been absorbed into her body and now her magic was forcing it out.

Helena sat back on her heels, a shaking hand wiping at her mouth. Von rubbed her back and brushed a warm hand over her clammy skin.

"Are you all right?" he asked gruffly.

Helena shrugged. There were no words to explain what it had felt like to come into contact with that much corruption. No words to tell him how much it had hurt, both physically and emotionally, or about the bruises that it had left on her heart. Nor could she express what it had been like to hold the fragments of those tortured souls in the palm of her hand. It was beautiful. It was horrifying. It was more than any one person should bear.

She looked up at him with pleading aqua eyes. Nameless emotions swam in his own as he looked at her, assessing the damage and all that she could not say. In silence he wrapped his arms around her, holding her trembling body tight against his own. Von used his strength to provide the comfort his words could not. He held her until she felt strong enough to stand. And then, together, they returned to the others.

CHAPTER 17

*H*elena did not recall much about the walk back to Reyna's village. Like Duskfall, it too was practically a city hidden in the trees. For their quadruped companions, who didn't think much about such things, there were a series of nearby dens where they could make themselves comfortable. Starshine, as usual, took to the sky to find her own sleeping arrangements.

In order to get access to the treetop village of Penumbra, Reyna pressed on a nondescript knot of wood causing golden light to spill forth as a hidden door fell open. Just beyond the door a staircase spiraled up and into the massive trunk of the tree. From what Helena had gathered, it was not the sole means of entrance to the city, but all others were known only to those that called it home.

Once they'd returned to the village, the runners were able to use the Kaelpas stones to bring the remainder of their people from the Ebon Isle to the Forest of Whispers. To say they were worried would have been an understatement. Unfortunately, there hadn't been an opportunity to send anyone back before then, especially in the midst of a potential ambush.

Before she'd wandered off, Reyna had mentioned that dinner would be served in something they affectionately referred to as the crow's nest. It was a communal structure located in the middle of

Penumbra where all the villagers took their meals. As it was the only building that was enclosed by windows on all sides, providing a fully panoramic view of the forest, Reyna said they'd have no trouble finding their way when the bell rang.

There was not much in the way of additional space, at least not for housing forty unexpected people, so Helena found herself sharing rather cramped quarters with Von, Ronan, Darrin, Nial, Serena, and Effie. How the seven of them managed to end up together, Helena could only guess. Perhaps it was the similarity in their ages, or the tangle of shared relationships and history among them. More likely, it was the Mother having a bit of a joke at their expense. While there was no outward hostility amongst any of them, there was an undeniable underlying tension.

Ronan had it the worst. He'd handled Serena and Nial's budding relationship with more grace than she ever would have expected from one who'd shared that kind of intimacy with her. There was no doubt that he certainly handled it better than she would have. The image of Von from her trial, thrusting into another woman while grinning wickedly up at her, was still one she could not manage to unsee, at least not completely. The thought alone was enough to set her blood boiling with jealous anger. How Ronan could manage to stay pleasant around his ex-lover and her new one eluded Helena. But while he was tolerant, it didn't mean he cared to be slapped in the face with their relationship more than was absolutely necessary. Some heartaches were not easily mended, and there was only so much his pride could stand. He'd taken one look at Serena and Nial setting up their joint bedroll and dropped his pack on the floor with a muttered, "I'll be back later."

Shortly thereafter, Effie and Serena had wandered off looking for a place to clean up. Still unsettled from the day's events, Von had wanted to explore their surroundings and establish a watch rotation. Nial had gone with him, still enjoying the freedom his newly healed legs granted, which left Darrin and Helena alone for the first time in weeks.

Helena was slowly unpacking what she needed for the evening when Darrin sat down beside her.

"I'm sorry," he groaned, scrubbing his hands over his face. At the raise of her eyebrow, he elaborated, "For earlier. With my comments. You know how I get..."

Helena sighed. That she did. Darrin's mouth ran without the consent of his brain more often than not. It always had. All things considered, his muttered comment was a non-event, but it could have been the difference between an alliance and an attack. For that reason, she could not simply let it go.

Her voice was weary when she spoke, "There is so much at stake, Darrin. We cannot risk offending potential allies because of hearsay. Where did you even hear such rumors about the Night Stalkers anyway?"

Darrin shrugged uncomfortably, his eyes not meeting hers as he answered, "You know how gossip is. A soldier knows a guy, who knows a guy, who met a Night Stalker once..."

Helena's stare was weighted, but she did not chastise him further. She was not his mother, for all that he still acted like a child.

"Can you at least try to keep your comments to yourself? If only when we are around any that aren't part of the Circle? I value your opinions—" Darrin opened his mouth as if he would disagree, but Helena spoke over him, "even when you see fit to constantly contradict and undermine me. I know that your concern for me stems from love."

His green eyes were warm as he smiled wryly. "It does."

"As does mine," Helena said, squeezing his arm before returning to unpacking.

Darrin took a deep breath. "I know, Hellion. That has never changed."

They shared a smile, their years of friendship apparent in the knowing gazes. It was because of that friendship she broached the other subject between them. "So, when are you going to tell a certain blonde about your feelings for her?"

Darrin went crimson. He protested immediately, sputtering, "There is no blonde. That is, I have no feelings one way or the other about any woman. I took a vow!"

Helena rolled her eyes. "Don't forget who you're talking to, Shield.

I can feel the lie through the Jaka." She scratched at her side where her tattoo faintly buzzed to prove the point. "Not to mention one need only look at you to see it on your face. You are falling for her."

It was not a question.

Darrin's shoulders slumped. "I have tried to fight it. I know that nothing will come of it." He looked so hopeless that her heart ached.

"What if it could?"

His eyes shot to hers. "What are you saying?"

Helena shrugged. "I'm just asking what it would mean to you if you could act on your feelings."

"I have no wish to leave the Circle!" he said with panic.

"Who said anything about that?" she asked, genuinely confused.

"But there is no other way..." he trailed off.

She smirked at him, the impish girl she'd once been evident in the expression. "What's the point of being in charge if you cannot make your own rules?" The question was an echo of one she'd already posed to Von.

Darrin's grin grew as her meaning became clear. "Are you saying—"

"Do not lose hope."

He jumped up, lifting her in his arms and spinning her around. "Hellion... you do not know how happy you've just made me."

She laughed, a pure joyous sound. He set her down, a hand on each of her shoulders. "Helena, truly. Thank you. Just the chance to have something real with her... it is more than I dared hope for."

His hands moved to her cheeks and he pressed a happy, smacking kiss to her forehead before clambering for the door. "I have a need to get clean all of a sudden!" he called.

"But not before you get dirty," she said under her breath, unable to resist.

Popping his head back through the door, he asked: "Did you say something?"

"No!" she lied, smiling brightly.

With a cheery wave, he was off.

Helena had barely retied her pack when Ronan walked back in.

Glancing around he asked, "Where'd everyone go?"

Helena filled him in quickly as she settled on her bedroll and contemplated taking a short nap before dinner. So much had happened in the span of a few days that the extra sleep felt almost like a luxury.

Ronan sat down in a leather armchair, his elbows resting on his knees. He looked around the room, visibly flinching when his eyes found the area Serena and Nial had claimed.

"How are you holding up?" she asked.

His icy eyes moved back to hers and she was struck by how handsome he was. Helena had always thought Ronan was good-looking in a rugged, could probably kill you with his bare hands, kind of way. But without the scar marring the perfect symmetry of his face, Helena could see that he was actually devastatingly handsome. For her part, she greatly preferred inky hair and smoldering silver eyes but that didn't mean she couldn't appreciate his masculine beauty.

The question made his brows dip. "Is it obvious?"

Helena shook her head. "No. Not to the others. You do a good job of hiding it."

He raked a hand through his hair, tugging at the braided strands. Then, like water bursting through a dam, words poured out of him on a tortured groan, "I know she is his, but a part of me cannot help but look at her and think '*mine*.'"

"I know what it is like to lose the one your soul has claimed."

They shared a look only those who were intimately familiar with heartache would recognize.

Her own experience aside, Helena still didn't need to imagine the kind of emotional hell Ronan was going through. Now that her power was continuing to evolve and grow with Von back, she could actually feel snippets of what those connected to her through her Jaka were feeling. It was how she knew Darrin was trying to lie to her. The Jaka granted a sense of knowing or intuition that was often accompanied by a slight burn or tingle beneath her skin. The awareness was nothing like what she shared with Von, as it was only the barest hint of emotion or thought, but it was enough.

Ronan hung his head. "That's the twist isn't it? It's not my soul, but my heart. The damned fool does not want to admit defeat, even though it knows the truth."

"That is the way of hope."

"If what I've been feeling is even a hint of what you went through while he was gone... you're a damned sight stronger than anyone ever gave you credit for."

Helena laughed in surprise. "The last thing I ever felt was strong. Most days I could hardly recognize myself as broken as I felt, but I had friends that did not allow me to break completely. They held me together when it felt like nothing could."

Sad blue eyes met hers, forcing her to admit, "I would not have made it without you pushing me forward."

He smiled at that. "It is no less than you would do for me."

"And here we are." They chuckled.

As the laughter faded, he said, "It gets easier as the days pass. Sometimes it just sneaks up on me. A look or gesture and it's as if nothing has changed, and then I remember." His eyes shuttered and he pulled his emotions back inside, the warrior once more. "Anyway, it will pass." He slapped his hands on his knees, pushing himself out of the chair.

Helena knew better than to mention that there would be another. For one who had loved as wholly as Ronan, it was very likely there never would be. Unless he was lucky enough to find his mate, as Serena had. She would not give him empty platitudes. They were too close for that.

"You once told me that she was your strength, but that is not true, Ronan. Your true strength is in your ability to love and your loyalty to those who are fortunate enough to earn it. Serena was lucky enough to experience both. You loved her so much, you wanted nothing but her happiness. It was why you were able to let her go. It may never feel that way, but you are a better man because of it."

Ronan had already turned away from her, and his body hunched at her words as if they had inflicted a wound but also cradled him. He looked back at her over her shoulder, a sheen in his eyes.

For Ronan, she would pretend that she did not notice the streak of wetness down his smooth cheek. Helena's hand was braced over her Jaka, a silent reminder that she did not forget what his symbol meant, or how its presence there would always connect them.

When he smiled at her, it was a beautifully broken thing. "One lesson I have learned from your Mate, is that a warrior never knows if his next battle will be the last. Life is a gift from the Mother. I will not begrudge anyone their right to happiness during the handful of days the Mother grants them."

"You have a poet's soul, Ronan."

He gave her a disgusted look. "You're lucky no one heard you say such a hateful thing." Then he winked.

Helena sighed and shook her head. She closed her eyes, thanking the Mother for sending her a wonderful friend like Ronan, and asking her to please heal his broken heart. Before she could make good on her wish for a nap there was a light tapping on the door.

Serena strode in with an apologetic smile.

Helena sat up and just stared at the door with an incredulous expression. "Is there a queue out there or something?"

Serena blinked in confusion. "What?"

Helena pointed. "Out there, are people lined up waiting their turn to speak to me? Is there a sign on the wall saying I'm giving out free advice? I only ask because the timing today has been impeccable. It's as if you all planned this."

Serena threw her head back and laughed. "I suppose it could certainly seem that way. Alas, I am merely here to summon you to dinner."

"I didn't hear a bell."

"The mysterious one," Serena paused and made a gesture with her hand to indicate the swirling make-up of the Night Stalkers' leader.

"Reyna?" Helena asked.

"Sure."

Helena snorted. "Aren't you supposed to be observant? I seem to remember something about attention to detail being a highly valued skill for mercenaries and warriors alike."

Serena shrugged. "I forgot a name, bite me. You figured out who I was talking about through my reference to said details."

"Because wiggling fingers in front of your face is a clear detail. I think that speaks more to my skills at deduction than your description."

Unimpressed with Helena's logic, Serena's violet eyes narrowed and she continued, "Anyway, as I was saying. *Reyna* ran into Effie and me on our way back. She let us know food was already being set out. She also said it doesn't last long and we might want to hustle if we prefer our food hot."

With a groan, Helena pushed herself off the bedroll and into a standing position. "Lead the way," she sighed with resignation. Looks like she wouldn't be getting a nap after all.

"Are you sure you trust me to get us there? I may have forgotten some key details and may lead you straight off a bridge."

"If that's the case then you're the one that will have to explain what happened to Von and Ronan. As the ones that trained you, I can't see them reacting very well to the attempted murder of their favorite female."

"Pfft. You sure think highly of yourself. I've known them years longer than you."

"Yes, but they like me better."

The women laughed, their teasing a welcome respite from the intensity of the day.

"Are you feeling a bit better?" Serena asked seriously, weaving her arm through Helena's.

"A bit, although I don't think any of us will rest easy until this is over."

The blonde woman nodded as she said, "That is always the way of war. And yet somehow, we will still sleep, and dream, and live."

Helena smiled, her cheeks flushing as she thought back to Von and their stolen moments together. "Yes, even in times of war, we must also find time to live."

Giving Helena an appraising look, Serena whistled. "From the way you say live, I gather you mean fu—"

"Shhhhh," Helena interjected, slapping a hand over her friend's mouth as the curious gaze of one of the Night Stalkers passed over them. Once they were clear of the man, Helena dropped her hand and added under her breath, "You weren't wrong."

Serena blinked comically and after a moment of surprised silence let out a bark of laughter. The two women walked into the crow's nest laughing hysterically, no longer caring who was looking at them.

THE CROW'S nest was loud, and by loud Helena did not mean just a little noisy. It was positively deafening. Something about a group of people who prided themselves on moving about undetected being responsible for this kind of racket amused Helena greatly. But her smile began to waver as she realized it was because the Night Stalkers felt safe here. Even after what had happened in Duskfall, these people felt untouchable. If she'd learned only one thing in the past year it was that nowhere was truly safe. Not with Rowena and her ghastly minions intent on wreaking havoc.

Von's warm hand curled around hers beneath the table. It was a small gesture but helped anchor her back to the present. She gave him a thankful smile and pushed her plate away. For the most part the meal had been uneventful, but the food was good and the mood relaxed. Actually, maybe not completely relaxed. There was a sense of anticipation buzzing throughout the room, the voices holding an expectant edge. Every now and then she'd catch a sidelong glance from someone who had heard what she'd done in Duskfall. Who was she kidding, everyone in the room knew what had happened.

There was no scraping of the chair against the floor to signal that Reyna was about to stand, but Helena didn't need a signal to realize something was about to happen. The room fell silent instantly. The immediate shift in sound made her head feel as if it was suddenly filled with cotton. She had the urge to clap her hands, or drop something on the floor, anything to prove that her ears still functioned.

Kragen's eyes met hers from across the table. After a cursory glance he lifted his brows as though asking if she needed something.

Her expression must have broadcasted her absurd thoughts. Bemused, Helena shook her head, returning her attention to Reyna.

"For centuries the Night Stalkers have called the Forest of Whispers home. There are few among us that have ever left the beauty of the Forest, fewer still that leave never to return."

The hush in the room was absolute. Everyone was focused on Reyna as she continued, "Our people are born from the first shadows of nightfall. From the time we can walk, we already know how to wrap ourselves in a cloak of darkness to conceal us from our enemies. Our greatest gift is our ability to move through the trees, remaining unseen and unheard until it is time to strike. Many call us assassins because of the secretive nature of our work. What they do not realize is that we are the guardians; the protectors of the Forest and her secrets."

There were a few cheers and Reyna's lips lifted in the slightest semblance of a smile. "In order for us to fulfill our duty, the time has come for us to leave our home. It must be done if we want to keep it safe. This time, it is not enough to remain amongst the trees and wait for our enemies to come to us. This time, we must bring the fight to them. We will fight as one, with the Chosen as our allies, until our enemy has been destroyed."

The roar of approval was immediate. Helena had expected more of a resistance, especially after Reyna's mention that few had ever left the Forest.

Pulling out a small glimmering piece of metal from beneath her shirt, Reyna held it up so that it could catch the light. Gasps filled the room. Helena looked to Joquil, hoping he might have an explanation for the crowd's reaction. His amber eyes were wide and his mouth had fallen open in shock. Feeling the weight of her stare, he turned and whispered, "I always thought it was a myth."

"Long has my family passed this down, each generation gifting it to the eldest daughter when she comes of age. With it comes the reminder to not use it lightly, for it can only ever be used once. Never has one of my line had need to call on the aid of the Watchers. Until now." Reyna raised her voice, speaking over the shocked whispers, "I do not make this choice lightly. Let there be no doubt among you what our failure will mean. There is a fate worse than death, as we have learned from our brothers and sisters in Duskfall. We will take no chances."

The room fell silent again, until a man called out, "A worthy cause indeed!"

"Aye!"

Reyna lifted a hand to halt the cheering of the crowd. "Knowing what is on the line, and that I cannot guarantee you a safe return, I will not force any of you into this decision. There is still time before the battle will begin. It is up to you if you will join me. I will not think less of any that wish to remain." With a final look at the glittering necklace, Reyna let it fall back against her chest and then strode quickly from the room.

Helena peered at the men and women sitting beside her. "What just happened?"

"The stuff of legend," Joquil answered in a hushed voice. "Reyna is going to call in the Watchers' promise."

With a lift of her brow that clearly expressed how little he'd enlightened her, Joquil flushed and continued. "There is a story that the Night Stalkers pass down from generation to generation. When the first of the Night Stalkers began to settle in the Forest, they were faced with the Watchers, who did not want their land polluted by humans. With nowhere left to go after being cast out of Chosen lands, the Night Stalkers vowed their allegiance to the Watchers, promising to be the guardians of the Forest. The Watchers laughed, as they were its true defenders, but they were intrigued by these small men who thought they would be able to protect the Forest, and so they agreed to let them stay."

Joquil cleared his throat, uncomfortable with the attention of the others. "Years passed without any issue, until a new tribe tried to settle in the Forest. The Watchers gave them a choice: make the same vow as the others or leave. The tribe refused and set about burning the Forest down. In the years that they'd been citizens of the Forest, the Night Stalkers learned from the Watchers how to become part of it. They discovered the skill of shadow weaving. Now they put it to use, hiding atop the trees and spying on their would-be attackers. Armed with information, the Night Stalkers and Watchers were able to defeat the tribe."

Joquil was all but vibrating with pride as he spoke about his ancestors, his excitement that the story was true impossible to hide. "As thanks to the humans, who ensured their victory since they were small enough to move about unseen and unheard where the Watchers could not, they made a promise. It was represented by a token, the golden acorn. If ever there was a time of great need, when the Night Stalkers were threatened by an enemy they could not defeat on their own, the Watchers would come to their aid."

The members of the Circle were quiet, until Darrin finally asked. "But what *are* the Watchers?"

Joquil's voice was barely more than a breath. "The oldest denizens of the Forest: the trees themselves."

Helena wasn't sure how one was supposed to respond to that kind of revelation. So she let out a soft, "Oh."

Joquil nodded. "And now you understand."

Helena wasn't sure she did, not entirely, but she was starting to. They'd just gained an ally more powerful than she'd ever thought possible. Not only would they be fighting beside the full force of the Night Stalkers, but the Forest itself would be at their side.

FAR AWAY IN a much smaller room, a man knelt before the shimmering surface of an ancient mirror.

"The Circle is still intact," an icy voice accused.

"Yes, my Queen."

"Why?"

The word hit him like the blow of a lash. The man barely restrained himself from flinching. "The usurper had a stash of Kaelpas stones that allowed her and her party to move about more quickly than anticipated. I was unable to locate her, because I did not have one within their initial ranks."

"And now?"

The man lifted his head and grinned. "And now I do."

There was a thaw in the room, and he would have said his Queen was pleased if he didn't know her better. One didn't become her lover by failing to correctly interpret her moods. Rather, one did not *remain* her lover. The latter was a much more difficult feat to achieve.

"Good. Then there will be no more mistakes."

"No, my Queen," he promised.

"My patience is wearing thin, Thomas. Break the Circle, or I will have no choice but to break you."

Her hazy visage faded from the mirror until all he could see were his own coal eyes staring back at him from a grizzled face. He watched as his lips lifted in a sadistic smile, despite her threat. It was hardly the worst thing she'd ever said to him.

"It will be done."

CHAPTER 18

"*I* need more time!" Helena growled in frustration, her fingers squeezing the bridge of her nose in an attempt to stave off her growing headache. She wasn't sure any longer if this was a strategy meeting or an intervention.

"Time is one thing you can no longer afford," Darrin protested. "You saw what she did to their village. Rowena is still ten steps ahead of you! We need to move. Now."

Helena shot him a venomous look. "We are making the time. This is important, Shield."

"You already have the Storm Forged and the Night Stalkers, not to mention their Watchers. And this is on top of the Chosen forces that already swore their allegiance."

Helena glared at him. "What part of this is important do you not understand?"

"How big of an army do you need?" he asked in exasperation.

"As big as possible," she ground out.

The two stared at each other in silence, neither party wanting to look away first.

"Helena," he tried again in a softer, pleading voice.

"She is taking control of entire villages, Darrin. If you think our army is big, hers is still twice the size, if not larger. We. Need. Allies."

Darrin hung his head in defeat. He recognized that stubborn set of her jaw from a childhood filled with such arguments.

Von's hand lifted to squeeze her shoulder, his indication that he had something to add. "Do you need to make the request personally?"

Helena looked at him in surprise. Von did not often go against her, especially not in front of the others. "What do you mean?"

"You both make solid arguments. We need allies, but we have to move as quickly as possible if we hope to gain the upper hand—"

Helena cut him off, "I'm going as fast as I can. We've already cut out weeks of travel by using the Kaelpas stones. How much faster do you want me to go?"

Von lifted his brows, waiting for her to finish. "I'm not arguing that. I'm merely pointing out that perhaps if we split up, we could make these last two visits in the time it has taken us to visit one. That would give us much-needed time, but still provide you with your allies. So my question for you stands, does it have to be you?"

Helena frowned, considering the question.

"Kiri," Timmins began. Lifting her eyes, Helena focused on her Advisor. He was leaning on a bookcase just beside Miranda and Kragen. "As the Advisor, I could go in your stead. Any of the Circle could. Since it is known that the Circle is bound to you, it would not be unexpected, or even seen as an insult, if we made the request on your behalf."

"I don't know," she murmured. Something about not being there felt wrong.

"For what it is worth, I do not think the Talyrians would tolerate more than you and Von anyway. At least not for an initial visit to their lands. The rest of us could easily represent you in the Broken Vale." Ronan's voice was measured, as if he knew his reasoning would not necessarily be welcome.

"He's right," Von added through the bond. Helena wanted to snarl at him but refrained. She felt cornered.

"It just feels wrong somehow," she said, echoing her earlier thoughts aloud. She took the time to meet each of their eyes, hoping she could express through her gaze what she was failing to explain with her words. While she saw understanding reflected back at her, it was the urgency she felt through her Jaka that truly resonated. The attack on the Night Stalkers hit them harder than she had realized.

Helena's shoulders slumped. She could force them to do it her way, but what would she really gain? She already trusted these men with her life, this task should be easy by comparison. "I just don't want to give them any reason to doubt the importance or sincerity of my request."

"We won't let them," Joquil assured her. Danger glittered in his amber eyes. He took the attack on Duskfall personally. Now that he did not have to hide his ancestry, it was clear he still felt deep ties to the people of the Forest.

With a sigh she relented completely. "What are you proposing?"

"Essentially the plan would not change. Reyna is providing us with one of her Night Stalkers that has ties to the Broken Vale. With their assistance, we will use the Kaelpas stones and seek an audience. Meanwhile, you and Von will travel with Starshine to Talyria. You should be able to make the trip in a couple of days. We will regroup in Etillion in five days' time and meet with our allies to discuss a full assault on Vyruul."

Von looked amused as Ronan spoke. Usually, he was the one laying out the battle plans. "It is unlikely we will find Rowena in Vyruul."

Ronan's answering smile was fierce. "Perhaps not, but Greyspire is. She will not react well to losing her ancestral home."

"You hope to force her hand and make her come out of hiding before she is ready."

Ronan nodded. "What better way to smoke the rat out?"

The other men murmured their approval.

The plan was sound, if simple, but Helena could not shake the feeling that it wouldn't be so straightforward. Rowena had proven that time and again. Instead of saying so, Helena remained silent. They could worry about the details once they knew what resources they truly had. Any plans made before then were likely to be changed anyway.

"I know you do not like the idea of splitting up, Mira. But we will be safe with the Talyrians."

"It's not us I'm worried about."

"Ronan will not let any harm come to your Circle."

Helena frowned at him. *"And who will protect him? With each meeting there has been an obstacle none of us anticipated: Rowena's general, the challenge, the ambush. It has taken our combined strength and my power to see us through, and this time we will be sending them off without it."*

Von wrapped his arm around her and held her close. *"They have fought and won many battles without you, Mira. They are more prepared than you give them credit for."*

Her frown deepened, but she did not argue further. She knew what he said was true, but that didn't make him right. Rowena wasn't just another enemy.

"Fine." She sighed with resignation. "I suppose we should get some sleep then. There's long days ahead for all of us."

ONLY REYNA WAS awake to see them off. Since they were flying rather than traveling via Kaelpas stone, they needed to make an early start of it. She had led them to a small clearing, just outside of the Penumbra camp. It was still protected by the forest, but a break in the trees would allow them to take flight. The sky was clear but dark; the last of the stars still twinkling above them.

"Thank you again, Kiri. What you did for my people…"

Helena held up a hand to stop her. "If either of us should be saying thank you, it is I. Your help in the days to come will be invaluable."

The women smiled at each other, kindred spirits despite a lifetime of different experiences.

Reyna held out her leather clad arm. "Safe travels until we meet again, Kiri."

"Mother's blessings, Reyna," Helena replied, grasping the proffered arm with her hand.

They shared another smile before stepping away from each other. Turning, Helena watched as Von double-checked the bags they'd strapped to Starshine. The Talyrian Queen tolerated the inspection, but only just. From the snicker behind her, Helena knew that Reyna noticed as well.

Von turned toward her with a smile. "Ready?"

Helena nodded and closed the distance between them. Starshine's luminous turquoise eye swiveled as it watched her approach. The Talyrian stood perfectly still while Helena ran a hand along the length of her neck. Starshine lifted her wings as a rumbling purr started deep in her throat.

"I've missed you too, girl," Helena murmured, pressing her forehead into the velvety fur.

"Sneaking off in the middle of the night?" a loud voice called from the edge of the clearing.

Helena and Von turned toward the voice, neither surprised to see Ronan and the rest of the Circle standing there. Ronan was grinning smugly; this was his doing then.

Von shrugged and called out, "We were trying to give you assholes a bit of much-needed beauty sleep."

There were some chuckles as the men moved closer.

"Sleep is overrated. Besides, I'm too pretty by half these days and we couldn't let you go without a proper send off," Ronan said.

Helena laughed as she said, "In that case, you might as well get over here."

Darrin reached her first. He was smiling but his green eyes were tinged with sadness as he pulled her in for a tight hug. "It is only for a few days, everything will be fine. You'll see that this was the right call."

Helena made a face causing him to laugh and roll his eyes.

"Be safe, Hellion."

"You as well, Shield. That's an order," she replied in a thick voice, trying to swallow back the emotion that was threatening to spill forth. Nothing about saying goodbye to these men was sitting right with her.

With a tug of her braid and a wink, Darrin moved aside for Kragen. Her Sword picked her up and spun her around, causing her to sputter with laughter.

"See you soon, Hellion," he rumbled.

She pressed a hand to his cheek. "Stay safe, Kragen."

He grinned, setting her down gently before stepping to the side.

Timmins came next. He reached formally for her hand, moving to bow and press a kiss to the back of it.

"I think we are far past the days of such ceremony, Advisor."

With a laugh, Timmins pulled her in for a quick hug. He rested his head atop hers as he promised, "We will not fail you, Kiri."

"I do not doubt it, Timmins."

His smile was forced as he nodded and turned away, making room for her Master to step forward. Joquil's amber eyes seemed to glow in the darkness. They shared a soft smile and hugged each other tight. "Remember what I've taught you," he whispered.

"As if I could forget."

Joquil chuckled and made to step back, but Helena stopped him, gripping his hand. "Thank you for being brave."

His brows furrowed as he tried to make sense of her words.

"It took much for you to tell us of your past. It is because of you we found such powerful allies. Thank you for trusting me with your secret."

Joquil smiled in surprise and ducked his head. He nodded once more before walking away.

Ronan was the last to come forth. He stared at her for a long moment, his blue eyes dark with emotion. Helena let out a shaky breath as he wrapped his strong arms around her.

"I do not like saying goodbye to you," she admitted in a watery voice.

"Nor I," he replied gruffly.

"Keep them safe for me, Ronan."

"With my dying breath," he promised.

"All right, that's enough of that," Von said, giving Ronan's shoulder a sharp shove.

"You're just afraid she's enjoying my embrace more than yours."

"Actually, I can feel the revulsion your touch causes and am trying to spare her."

The men snickered, grasping hands and pulling each other in for a quick hug.

"Be safe, bastard."

"You as well, brother."

The friends slapped each other on the back and stepped apart.

"Tell the others..." Helena trailed off; what was there to say? But the men nodded anyway, understanding the intent even if there wasn't a clear message.

It was time. Helena let out one last long breath and turned toward Starshine, blindly pulling herself up. Von vaulted up behind her, wrapping his arms around her waist as he settled in.

"Let's go, girl."

With a wave they were off, springing up into the starry sky.

Helena felt tears stinging her eyes as the trees below them disappeared. Whether it was due to the wind, or the pieces of her heart that remained behind, she wasn't sure. One thing was certain, however. The farther away they got from her Circle, the greater her sense of foreboding. Something was coming. She just hoped they would be ready.

CHAPTER 19

They flew for hours, the world below them nothing more than a sea of clouds. The gentle rocking of Starshine's body as she beat her wings was hypnotic, and more than once Helena found herself nodding off. If not for Von's arms banded about her, she was certain she would have toppled off the Talyrian's back entirely.

Shortly after they'd taken off, Helena had created an aural shield, which blocked out most of the roaring wind and allowed her and Von to speak without shouting at each other. Even though they could have relied on their bond to communicate, it was nice to be able to speak freely.

Starshine dipped suddenly, angling her massive body down toward the ground.

"Oh!" Helena gasped, clenching Starshine's mane to remain upright.

"I guess it's time for a rest," Von commented wryly as he tightened his hold on her.

"Apparently so."

"I wouldn't mind a break. I could do with a stretch and something to eat."

Helena nodded her agreement, even though she felt conflicted about stopping so soon. Her desire to make it to Talyria as quickly as possible was urging her to keep going. The trip would take another full day's ride at least. She sighed, knowing there was no point in asking Starshine to continue on for a bit longer. There was absolutely no way she could win an argument with a Talyrian. Create a raging storm out of thin air, absolutely. Make fire rain down from the sky, easy. Change a Talyrian's mind once they've settled on a decision, no fucking way.

As the land below them began to take shape, Helena just kept telling herself that there was little harm to be had in resting for a while. She wasn't sure where exactly they were, but given the shimmering pools streaking across large patches of green, Helena would guess somewhere in Sylverlands.

Starshine continued her dive, beginning to spiral in large swooping circles as she neared the ground. Probably to ensure the area was safe, although that was just Helena's guess. Not exactly like she could ask. When they landed, Helena could feel the diluted reverberation of the trembling earth from where she was still perched atop Starshine. She waited for the tremors to settle before sliding down. Von had already dismounted and was waiting to catch her. His hands were warm where they pressed into her waist.

She smiled up at him in wordless thanks and accepted the soft kiss he pressed against her lips with an appreciative moan. He nipped at her bottom lip playfully, his eyes going silver as he grinned at her.

"Alone at last."

"Was that your plan all along?" she teased.

"No," he admitted aloud, "but it should have been. It's a definite side benefit regardless."

"Mmm, definitely," she agreed, kissing him again. Before they could get carried away, Starshine snorted, silvery plumes of smoke wafting around them.

Helena giggled, her cheeks flushing as if they had been caught doing something inappropriate. Turning toward her feline companion, Helena asked, "Need something?"

Starshine sat down hard, as if to say, I just wanted to remind you that I'm right here. Helena couldn't help but laugh. As she was turning back to Von to comment she overheard the tail end of his bitter mutterings.

"...ck blocked by a Talyrian..."

"What was that?" she snickered.

He shot the feline a darkly annoyed glance. "Nothing."

The stare-down between the two was intense, both wanting to assert their dominance over the other. Helena tried hard to fight the laughter that bubbled up and failed miserably. She only laughed harder when it was Von who looked away first. The sounds of his bitter cursing filled the air. With a satisfied huff, Starshine shook out her mane before standing back up and stretching. As she stretched, her gleaming claws were on full display, which Helena was certain was no coincidence. It was just another way for Starshine to show Von why she was the superior creature.

"I suppose we should find some water?" Helena intervened once her laughter had finally died off.

Von just grunted.

Shoulders shaking with amusement, Helena said, "Come on you two."

As Von came abreast of the Talyrian he muttered, "She is *my* Mate, you know."

Starshine huffed again, not even sparing him a glance.

"Doesn't seem like she thinks much of your title," Helena commented.

"Don't start."

Helena grinned, but let it go.

The trio headed off in the direction of the lakes they had noted during their descent. The nearest of them couldn't have been too far off, but it was hard to tell without the aid of true landmarks. The land was flat and open as far as the eye could see and there were no houses or anything to suggest that the area was inhabited. There were a few scattered trees, but nothing like the dense forest they had occupied only that morning.

All-in-all it was a pleasant walk. The sun was warm, but not overbearing, as it beamed down between fluffy white clouds. The lake was further than they'd originally thought, and all three kept a cautious eye on the horizon, just in case anyone mistook their approach as a threat. But there was no one, and they made their way entirely unchallenged.

She knew they were close when the sounds of water hitting the shore met her ears. It was only another fifteen minutes before they saw the silvery sheen of the lake's reflection. Starshine loped ahead, sniffing at the water before eagerly dipping her head down and lapping it up.

When Von and Helena reached her, she threw her head up and thousands of miniature droplets flew through the air, each shimmering in the sunlight as they fell back down. Helena held out a palm, letting the droplets fall into her hand. She turned toward Von, ready to toss the tiny handful of water at him, but her hands fell when she took in the ashen sight of him. He was staring straight ahead, utterly transfixed. His mouth had fallen slack, and she could tell from the vacant look in his eyes that he was a million miles away. It was then she realized what had happened. Just as Miranda had predicted, his memories of the mist had snared him once more.

Apparently the tiny drops of water falling in the air had been just similar enough to the effect of the mist that it had caught him off guard. Helena moved quickly. She grabbed him, shaking him hard, hoping the movement would be enough to pull his focus. It wasn't.

"Von!" she shouted, echoing the cry through their bond. *"Von!"*

Silence.

Beside her, Starshine began to growl menacingly, as if sensing danger.

"Keep watch girl," Helena murmured, trusting the Talyrian to guard them while she focused solely on her Mate.

Placing a hand on either side of his face, Helena closed her eyes and used her power to send a psychic tendril into his mind. She navigated carefully, searching for any sign of Von's presence. When she didn't sense him, she peeled back another layer continuing on until she found herself just outside of his innermost barriers. She had been here once before, when she had helped him finally breakthrough the *Bellamorte's* hold and face his captors.

As she had the last time, Helena placed a metaphorical hand against the barrier, letting it identify her and give her permission to move past. She filled the touch with all of her love and concern for Von. The barrier rippled pleasantly against her senses, similar to a cool breeze on a warm day. Recognizing her, the barrier grew transparent until it gave way completely. Helena found herself standing within the core of Von's mind.

Images surrounded her. *Memories*, she realized. There were ghostly images of Von and Nial playing as children. There was Ronan, snarling as he slammed his fiery ax into an enemy that was about to strike Von. And there she was, smiling shyly up at him as they spoke in the Palace garden.

Helena wanted to walk through all of the memories, learning everything about the man she loved as she relived his past through them. But they were not her memories to explore, and so she resisted. Instead, Helena wandered through them, careful not to touch or disturb any of the wispy fragments. She wasn't certain what effect her interruption would cause and she didn't want to accidentally cause further harm.

Focusing on the feel of him, strong and steady through their bond, Helena used that as her guide. It did not take long for her to find him, but she was unprepared for what she found.

This was no pale memory. Whatever was happening to the shuddering body sitting and rocking on the ground was real. Her heart wrenched painfully in her chest when she heard his rasping moan.

"No more." He was curled into a ball, his hands drawn up over his head and clenched into tight fists. "No more," he groaned again. His voice was raw, as though he had been screaming for hours without end.

While she may have only been a projection of herself, Helena found herself shaking. Not knowing what else to do, she crouched beside him, holding her hand just above his head, not quite making contact.

"Von," she whispered, not wanting to startle him.

There was no response, no indication that he knew she was there at all. Helena let her hand close the gap between them, touching him as gently as possible. When she made contact, light flared brightly obscuring everything around her and forcing her to close her eyes. As the light faded, and her eyes were finally able to flutter open, she wished they'd stayed closed. Swallowing back a scream, Helena staggered to her feet.

VON'S NIGHTMARE RAGED ON. All around him, the bodies of those he loved were chained and bloody. They were lined up, one after the other, a grisly exhibit of human misery. Strips of skin were torn and hanging down where the whip had sliced through to the bone. He gagged, but made himself swallow back his revulsion, forcing himself not to give in to the emotional torture. Instead, he made himself focus on the need for vengeance which was screaming for him to repay each sadistic blow in kind.

But he couldn't move. He, too, was chained. Von struggled against the bonds, more wild animal than man as he worked to get free. He needed to get out of here. To get them all away from this hellhole of a dungeon. Von gnashed his teeth, biting back a scream as the enchanted metal began to sear through his skin. Unable to bear it any longer, he gave in to the roar of pain that clawed its way out of his throat.

There was a bright flash of light, almost as if a door had been opened. He threw his head to the side, squeezing his eyes shut before the light blinded him.

Then he heard the whimper.

"Von."

His eyes flew open.

"Helena?"

"V-Von," came the hopeful but broken reply. From the restored darkness at the end of the room, Helena limped out of the shadows. She was wearing what only the most optimistic would call a white gown. It was so liberally coated in blood that it was more crimson than white. He could see bits of her bone peering out from some of the gaping wounds. Her skin looked purple because of all the bruises, and her face was swollen almost beyond recognition. Whoever had done this to her had taken their time. If the others were an exhibit, she was the masterpiece.

"What did she do to you?" he snarled, lurching forward until his chains went taut. Von roared, going absolutely mad when he could not get to her.

"It's a lie."

Von blinked, the voice in his mind momentarily pulling him out of the nightmare.

"Do not believe the mist."

The mist... Von went entirely still. Was he still lost in the mist? But no, Helena had saved him. And now she was standing right there, beaten almost within an inch of her life. This was some new fresh hell that they were trapped in. This was real... wasn't it?

"Let me show you," the voice insisted.

Von hesitated, equally afraid and desperate to believe the voice. The doubt was enough to break the nightmare's hold. The world swam in and out of focus, the dark dungeon superimposed over a field of green and silver.

He blinked again, and the dungeon settled back into place. The moans of his brother snagging his attention.

"No!" the voice demanded.

Von felt his face twisting away from the writhing body. Startled that his body was moving against his will, he fought the movement.

"Really?" the voice snapped in exasperation. *"You will fight against me, but not the hallucination?"*

That gave him pause. There was only one person who would dare to use that tone with him, especially when he was in this state. Any that knew him well, or even those that knew of his history on the battlefield would recognize the bloodlust that consumed him. It would not abate until he was the last one standing. To interfere with that was a death wish.

"Helena?" He said her name out loud, confused that she could be speaking in his mind when she was collapsed in a heap at his feet.

"Von, you need to resist it. You have to see the lie to break its hold."

He glanced around, not sure how he was supposed to do that.

He thought he heard a sigh, but before he could respond further, his body began to tingle. Every ache and throb was soon replaced with soothing warmth. He recognized that warmth. It was the feeling he'd associated with Helena ever since he'd healed her after her trial, and in doing so, initiated their bond.

"See the lie."

Von looked around, staring at the nearest body. It was Serena, only it wasn't. There was a fuzziness to the outline of her body that became more apparent the longer he stared. He'd been so overwhelmed by the injuries that he'd been unable to look past them and note the other details. Ronan, or rather what he had believed to be Ronan, was tied up beside her and quietly weeping. Ronan would never weep. Not like that. He would be roaring and fighting, just as Von had been, at least until he passed out or his captors knocked him out.

"That's it."

Glancing down where Helena's body was supposed to be, he noted the color of the eyes that were cracked open, staring at the ceiling. If Helena had been tortured, her eyes would have burned with the iridescence of her power as she fought back. No one who caught her would have lived long enough to cause that level of damage to her body.

Helena's warmth grew in intensity, until he felt like he was on fire. He looked at himself, running his hands over his body to ensure that he wasn't. Then he realized what he'd just done and did a double take. His arms were no longer cast in irons. Glancing up, he noticed that the bodies and dungeon were gone.

He was free.

VON WAS NOW LYING PEACEFULLY beside her. When she'd touched him, she'd been sucked into his nightmare. It had taken her awhile to separate herself from the gruesome images that were playing out in front of her. She'd been trapped in Von's body, experiencing everything as he did. It was when she'd seen herself stumbling toward him that she remembered why she was there and was able to help him fight against the hallucination. Knowing now the kind of assault his mind had been under when he'd been trapped within for so many months, Helena could not believe he was still sane.

She stroked a hand along the length of his back, willing him to return to consciousness. They were still within the innermost barrier of his mind and she would not leave him until she knew that he was safely free of the *Bellamorte*.

Remembering the dark smudges she'd seen the first time she'd treated him, Helena cast her awareness out. At first, all she sensed were the wisps of his memories, which still swirled around them, but then she felt it. The sense of something that didn't belong. Focusing on it, she moved away from the resting form of her Mate. Helena wandered through the corridors of his mind until she came to the very center. There she found a flickering ball of light. It was so beautiful she couldn't decide whether she wanted to cry, or laugh, or grasp it carefully in her hand and cradle it against her chest.

The longer she stared at the ball of light, the happier she became. Sensing her happiness, it grew brighter, spinning about almost playfully. As it spun, Helena finally saw what she had been searching for. Pressed against the perfect brightness of his soul, for that's certainly what Helena had found, there was the tiniest smear. No wonder she had missed it before. It was so miniscule that it had been disguised, but now that she knew what to look for, it could no longer hide.

Helena moved closer, calling her power into the tip of her finger. She could not afford to do something careless like toss a bolt of power at it. One wrong move and her power could destroy more than just the mote. Helena shuddered, not wanting to think overlong on that possibility.

Holding her finger out, she stroked the side of the ball, pulling away the mote of darkness. Von's essence rippled where it had come into contact with her hand. It seemed to want her to keep touching it, moving with her as she pulled her hand away. The reaction was reminiscent of a cat that arched its back to encourage further pettings. The thought made Helena smile.

Looking down at her hand, Helena found the smudge still clinging to her finger. With a shake of her head, she made a small o with her lips and blew, infusing her breath with magic. When it touched the mote, instead of sending it flying into the air, it obliterated it completely. Helena smiled, satisfied that she had been able to get rid of the final lingering piece.

Her work here was done, but it was hard to leave. The sense of peace and joy she felt standing beside the beautiful orb was like nothing she'd ever experienced. That was when the orb began to glow a bright, molten gold. It was the same color as Von's eyes when their power merged.

"Oh," she gasped, her hand moving up to her chest where a sudden heat flared. It continued to grow and swell within her until she could feel it in every part of her body. Helena watched in awe as the orb pulsed in time with her heartbeat.

She stood in silence, filled with a happiness so absolute it eclipsed all else. This was a special kind of magic that had nothing to do with the elements and everything to do with love.

Helena may never know what the final step had been, her whisper of a touch or the small blast of air filled with her power, but she knew without a doubt that their bond was now complete.

CHAPTER 20

*W*hen Helena opened her eyes, she was still standing in front of Von with her hands pressed against his cheeks. Hours must have passed while they had been in his mind, the sun was now a burnt-orange ball, half-hidden by the horizon.

Starshine let out a low whine, which sounded very much like a question.

"We're safe," Helena answered with a whisper, her eyes never leaving Von's face.

Appeased, Starshine moved away to give the couple a bit of privacy. Despite the added distance, she was no less of a guard.

Helena ran her thumbs along the dark slashes of Von's brows, willing him to open his eyes. She repeated the soft stokes until she noticed his eyelids begin to flutter. When his eyes finally opened they were molten gold. Helena's heart began to pound. They stared, twin looks of wonder on each of their faces.

Nothing was overtly different, but something had clearly changed. Their bond was still there, a steady presence burning brightly inside of them. It was just more: more intense, more vibrant, more focused.

Without a word Von slammed his lips down on hers, kissing her fiercely. They were so in tune with one another, that she could feel Von's reaction to her touch as if it was her own. The added awareness created an intensity to their kisses that had her desperate for him after only a few heartbeats.

Her urgency was his. Von moved his lips from hers, kissing down her neck as his hands began to make quick work of her travel clothes, removing only what was needed. They were still in the open, but Helena didn't care. All she wanted was to feel physically what she was already feeling in her heart; the sense of fullness and completion that would come once he slid inside her.

"Helena," he groaned in her mind, his lips never ceasing their teasing. *"I—"*

"I feel it too." She wrapped her arms around his head and back, holding his mouth against her body. *"Please don't stop."*

He didn't. His hands roamed her body, equal parts possessive and reverent. Where her skin was exposed, goosebumps were left in his wake. She shivered, needing more. Before it was even a conscious thought, he was already there, touching her exactly as she needed. It was not just instinct driving their movements; it was absolute knowing. Each touch carried certainty, as though they were reenacting something they'd done a thousand times before. But there was nothing repetitive about the experience. It felt like the first time.

Helena was not conscious of the moment they moved to the ground. Her senses were too overwhelmed by the emotions spiraling within her, his as well as hers.

Von broke away, and her eyes fluttered open, knowing that he needed her to look at him. His hair was tousled, and his eyes heavy-lidded. Dark stubble coated his jaw and his lips were swollen from their hungry kisses. Helena licked her lips, desire pounding through her at the sight of him poised above her.

His hand moved down, spreading her before he entered her in one hard thrust, his eyes never once straying from hers.

Helena gasped, coming apart from just that single motion. But Von wasn't done with her. He continued to move inside her, each thrust causing her climax to extend.

She was panting incoherent fragments of words as he relentlessly loved her. Each drive of his hips set off another explosion of sensation and Helena started to feel like entire universes were being created and destroyed within her. Finally, just as she was certain she would pass out, Von came, growling her name. Helena joined him, the feeling of him throbbing inside her setting off one last tidal wave that surpassed every other.

"I love you."

It was a struggle, but Helena forced her eyes to open. Her body was beyond spent, and the urge to fall asleep was almost impossible to fight.

"I love you more," she teased, her voice hoarse from her cries.

He smirked at her, even as he brushed stray strands of hair from her face. "With an orgasm like that I don't doubt it."

Helena didn't even have the energy to deny it. With a yawn and the lift of a shoulder she asked, "Can you blame me? I'm not sure if it was one continuous one, or hundreds of them back-to-back."

With a satisfied smile, he bent down and pressed a kiss to her forehead. "Rest now so we can try it again."

Between one chuckle and the next she fell asleep in his arms.

WHEN SHE WOKE, they were still curled up in the sweet-smelling grass, although Von had made a point to refasten her clothes while she'd slept. It was full night now, and the sky was blanketed with stars.

"Sleep well?" Von asked, his voice a low rumble.

"Mmm," she murmured, lifting her arms above her head in a sinuous stretch. When she relaxed, she noted Von's appreciative leer.

Completely unapologetic, he grinned when he caught her gaze. "Beautiful."

Helena opened her mouth to respond, and then noticed something that had her quickly sitting up. Startled, Von's body tensed and he immediately began to scan the area for danger. "What is it?"

"Your eyes!"

Confused, he looked back at her. "What about them?"

Helena shook her head, unable to explain.

"Here," she said, scrambling up and pulling him with her. "Look," she demanded, pointing into the glassy reflection of the lake. The stars above provided more than enough illumination for them to see their own shimmering reflections.

Peering into the water, it did not take more than a second for Von to notice what she had. Around each of his pupils was a thin iridescent band, just like in hers.

"I guess we match now," he said after a moment of stunned silence.

Helena smiled. "I guess we do."

"Do you think that means..." Von trailed off, not completing the question.

"That our power has merged?" Helena asked for him.

He nodded, his brows lowering as he contemplated what that could mean.

Helena shrugged. "I'm not sure. Shall we test it?"

"How?"

Helena bit down on her lip as she considered. "What's something I can do that you can't?"

He lifted a brow. "Really? Can we set the bar a little lower, please?"

"Okay, fair point," she laughed. "Um... I guess just try something and we'll see what happens."

He agreed with a nod and took a few steps away from her. Focusing intently on where Starshine dozed across the lake, Von took a deep breath and vanished. Almost instantly he reappeared beside a grumpy Starshine who did not appreciate the unexpected company. So their assumption had been right, at least to an extent. Blinking was something he'd already been able to do, but never across a distance that great before. His power had definitely received a boost as a result of their completed bond.

Helena watched as Starshine sniffed at Von. He stood still, uncertain about what the Talyrian was doing. She looked confused as well, twisting her head from Von to Helena and back again, before dipping down to sniff him once more.

He gave Helena a baffled glance. *"Should I be concerned?"*

"I have no idea," Helena admitted with a shrug.

Von looked back at Starshine who was now pressing her face into him. Tentatively, Von lifted a hand and began to stroke her gleaming fur. Helena let out a snort of laughter when Starshine's purrs were audible even where she was standing.

"I guess that answers that."

Starshine had always tolerated Von, but she had never made any overt signs of affection before. Up until now, those had been exclusively reserved for Helena. Starshine must be sensing Helena's essence in Von. She could only assume this was another unanticipated side effect of their completed bond.

"Do you think this means she'll let me ride her without you now?" Von asked as he ran his hand along the length of Starshine's muzzle. Starshine twisted her head away, playfully swiping at Von with her paw. It was her way of letting him know he'd erred when he'd stopped scratching behind her ears. Von jumped back with a startled shout, narrowly avoiding sharp black claws. Unfortunately, what was playful for a Talyrian was still potentially deadly to a human, especially when said paw was the size of a dinner plate.

"Definitely not," Helena snickered.

"Mother's tits! I don't think I'd trust her even if she did."

"She really is quite easy to understand once you learn her tells."

"It's no wonder. Only a fool would chance repeating a mistake with her."

Helena's laughter rang out, filling the night with her joyful melody.

CHAPTER 21

*S*eeing Talyria for the first time was something Helena knew she would never forget. The air was thick with power. She felt it as soon as they flew across the border. It didn't feel like magic, at least not in the way she understood it; this was ancient and much more primal. She wondered if it was what had kept Talyria separated from the rest of Elysia for centuries; if that ancient energy was, in fact, a powerful barrier that kept everyone else out. Knowing that she was one of the first to see the land of the Talyrians was a privilege she would never take for granted.

The setting sun painted the sky in bright oranges and rosy pinks, and thick red clouds obscured all but the highest mountain peaks. These were not the sloping, snow-capped mountains of Vyruul, but rather sheer-faced cliffs that towered high above the ground. From her vantage point, she started to notice cave-like openings scattered across the cliffs. They were often accompanied by small stretches of rock that could act as landing areas.

As they flew deeper into the heart of Talyria, Starshine dipped beneath the clouds, and the land below came into view. There were a few massive waterfalls that surged off of the cliffs, turning into deep pools that broke up the otherwise reddish-brown land. The pools of water were so clear, Helena could see fish darting below the surface.

They were sprayed by the water as they flew past, and what didn't hit them hung in the air like tiny prisms. Helena risked a glance over her shoulder, grinning when she saw that Von's look of delight was a mirror of her own. If the Ebon Isle was a reminder of the deadly power of the elements, Talyria was a testament to their unending beauty. It was paradise.

They were more than an hour inland before Helena caught her first glimpse at another Talyrian. Massive feline heads tracked their movements, letting out roars of greeting as their queen flew past. A few leapt off the cliffs, joining them in flight. Soon the sky was full of beating wings in a variety of colors. Some were dark like Starshine's, while others were so light they appeared to be smoke moving across the sky.

By the changing angle of Starshine's body, Helena knew that they were about to land in an opening that had emerged between two of the flat-topped mountains. Just as they were about to touch down, Helena noticed two balls of fur rolling and playing in the dusty red earth. She let out a small gasp of wonder; they were baby Talyrians.

One of the cubs was an inky black, its glowing violet eyes narrowing as it prepared to pounce. The other was milky-white with amber eyes and small patches of orange covering its tiny body. The black one leapt, jet-black wings flaring out on either side, holding it airborne for an instant before its paws made contact with its target. The white and orange cub tried to dodge the attack, but wasn't fast enough, and ended up rolling backwards.

It jumped up, shaking off the dust and snarling its challenge at the black one. Helena was certain the little one thought the sound was quite fierce, but the snarl sounded more like a squeak and Helena could not contain her giggle. The cubs were about as ferocious as stuffed toys, but she knew better than to ever say so aloud. Especially with two protective mamas standing watch just behind them. She wondered if she had a chance of snuggling one of them.

Starshine landed, and two Talyrian males immediately approached her. Both of the males were bigger in size than Starshine, but there was no doubt she was the alpha here. The silver one reached her first, rumbling a greeting before bowing his head. The other was the black of a midnight sky. Without the glittering sapphire of its eyes, which were utterly focused on his Queen, he could have easily been mistaken for a rippling shadow. A mistake his enemy would likely never survive to repeat. This one did not bow, but stalked toward her until they were all but touching. There was a growl and he bared razor-sharp teeth. Starshine didn't flinch.

The midnight Talyrian growled again, a sound that had the hair on the back of Helena's neck standing on end. Starshine opened her mouth and roared, plumes of smokes flaring up around her. With a huff, the male sat down, its wings shaking out in what seemed like annoyance.

"What in the Mother's name is going on?" Helena asked.

"Isn't it obvious? The midnight one is letting her know he's displeased with how long she's been gone, and in reply Starshine told him to fuck off."

Helena was only mildly surprised that Von had translated the situation so easily. After replaying the last few seconds with his assessment in place she had to agree it held the definite ring of truth.

"Apparently males of all species like to tell their queens what to do," Helena commented dryly.

Von snickered, *"Only the smart ones."*

"See, that is where we disagree."

Starshine finally sat back, allowing Von and Helena to slide down. The glowing gazes of the nearby Talyrians followed them warily; they must have been the first humans they'd ever seen. Helena could not fault their caution.

The cubs were already being carried away from the strangers. *I guess I won't be playing with the babies anytime soon*, Helena thought a bit dejectedly, watching as they dangled from their mothers' jaws.

Following her train of thought, Von rubbed his hand along her back. When she looked over at him he smiled sympathetically. *"Don't take it personally. How comfortable would we be letting a Talyrian play with one of our young?"*

"I know but..." Helena stopped midsentence when she heard the

whine slip into her psychic tone. She gave Von a rueful smile. *"You wanted to play with them too, didn't you?"*

"There's a reason I'm not allowed near the Daejaran litters anymore."

"Oh?"

"The mamas didn't appreciate having to track their pups down. Usually in my room."

Helena chuckled. *"How do people ever mistake you for a fearsome warrior?"*

Von gave her a dark look paired with a wicked grin.

"Let's just hope none of the cubs go missing while we're here. I have a feeling you might be the first suspect."

Their mirth flowed through the bond, but they focused back on the massive felines before them. Knowing the Talyrians would react to any display of weakness, Helena held her chin up and strode purposefully to Starshine's side. She didn't allow herself to so much as blink while the darker of the two males sniffed her. It was not a threatening act, but it was certainly intimidating.

Beside her Starshine let out a warning growl. She did not need Von to translate this time; Starshine had just declared Helena as hers. By association, that meant that she had just declared Helena as *Pride*. There was a confused whine from the silver male, but Starshine's warning had only made the black one more curious.

"And we thought the Talyrians would be the easiest of the tribes to convince…"

"He just wants to make sure you are not a threat. He's protecting the ones he loves."

"Does he have to be so thorough?" she asked, her voice terse as his sniffed between her legs.

Von let out his own warning growl. Apparently Starshine wasn't the only one that felt the need to claim her. Helena sighed.

Curious about the two-legged creature that would attempt to intimidate him, the black Talyrian shifted focus to her Mate. He unfurled his wings until they were fully extended and blocked out everything but him and his glowing sapphire eyes. Helena stiffened, knowing this was a challenge.

Von crossed his arms and lifted his chin, never once looking away from the sapphire gaze. The Talyrian lowered his head until it was level with Von's. The two males stared at each other silently. After a long moment, the Talyrian opened his mouth and bellowed. Von's hair and cloak blew back, but otherwise he stood still. The Talyrian blinked, surprised that the other male had not cowered.

"Are you done?" Von asked in a slightly bored tone. The tone, if not the words, were clear. The Talyrian huffed. There was a calculating cast to his gaze now, as if a decision was being reached.

Finally, he nudged Von, rubbing him with his head and marking him with his scent. Starshine let out a rumble of approval.

"Looks like I'm not the only one who's been claimed. What will Karma do when you come home with your own Talyrian?"

Von shook his head. *"I'm not sure he's going to have much of a say in the matter."*

Helena wasn't certain any of them did.

Moving slowly, Von extended his hand, stroking the velvety fur of his Talyrian's neck.

"What will you call him?"

Von considered the question for a moment. *"If Starshine was named for the color of her fur, then there's really only one name for him."*

"Midnight," they said together.

"Welcome to the family, Midnight," Helena said aloud.

Midnight did not reply, he was too busy purring as Von scratched him behind the ears.

THEIR TIME in Talyria passed quickly. After the initial meeting, they'd been taken deeper into the heart of the encampment located between the two mountains. There was a central valley with its own pool of water surrounded by a series of caves and tunnels where the Talyrians made their homes. Starshine's cave was the furthest back, whether as a show of respect, or because it was the best protected, Helena wasn't certain. The caves were massive and had clearly been created by the Chosen who had once been welcome here. Soft light glowed, reflecting golden light all along the ebony walls. There were also smaller rooms, more proportioned in size to something one of the Chosen would be comfortable with. Von and Helena had shared one such room in Starshine's cave.

The morning after their arrival, Starshine left the cave early. Catching a glimpse of the brilliant white fur streaking past her room, Helena started to follow her but stopped dead when Starshine turned. With one warning growl the Talyrian made it clear that Helena was not welcome at whatever meeting was about to take place.

Without being present it was impossible to know what transpired, but given their situation, it seemed most likely that Starshine was calling the Talyrians to war. When she did not see the Talyrian Queen for the rest of the day, Helena figured Starshine was spending time with the family she'd had to leave behind when she came to Tigaera. Or perhaps it wasn't her entire family but just one midnight fellow in particular. Either way, Helena couldn't blame the girl.

But now, with the sun just beginning to break through the clouds, it was time to meet the rest of the Circle in Etillion. When they'd left the others, they'd agreed to meet again in five days, and they'd been in Talyria for two, which meant they were already a couple hours behind schedule if they wanted to make it to Etillion by nightfall. Talyrians were fast, but they were not Kaelpas stones.

Helena stepped out of the cave and was stunned by the number of Talyrians that greeted her. At most, she'd come into contact with perhaps fifteen Talyrians in the past few days, and sadly not one of them was a snuggly cub. Now, however, there were well over forty gathered and preparing for flight. Some would surely stay behind to protect the young, but otherwise, they had a greater aerial force than she'd imagined.

Standing in the front of them all was Starshine. She looked more than a little majestic when surrounded by the others. As she made to walk over toward the Talyrian Queen, something unexpected happened.

Starshine tipped her head back and roared, a blast of flame lighting up the early morning sky. As one, every Talyrian responded in kind, their roars deafening. As the roars tapered off, they dropped low, baring their necks in the universal sign of submission. But it was not to Starshine that they made this display; it was to Helena.

Helena trembled, her throat thick with emotion as she watched the beautiful and proud creatures pledge themselves, and their lives, to her. And then Von was there, stepping past her and moving to stand beside Midnight.

"Von," she whispered, her voice quavering as she realized what he was going to do.

His gaze held hers as he joined the Talyrians, dropping to his knee and bowing his head.

"My power, my life, and my love are yours, Mira."

"That's all?" she asked, teasing because anything else would have her in tears. In the end, her levity didn't matter. When Von replied, his words leveled her.

"It's all that I am."

"It is more than I deserve."

His eyes went dark with the same emotion that filled her.

Too overwhelmed to speak, Helena placed her hand over her heart and dipped her head, bowing until she was almost bent in half. It was the Chosen's sign of deepest respect and reverence, one often used in the Mother's temples. As Kiri, there were none that she should ever have to bow to, but it was the only way she could think of to express how deeply their act had touched her.

There was another roar, and the Talyrians stood, moving to stand closer to her. Helena spent the next hour greeting and thanking each of them for their service. After she'd met the last of the Talyrians, Helena moved back to Starshine.

This time, Von would not be riding with her. Midnight had made it clear that he alone would have the privilege of carrying her Mate. Helena felt her heart stutter and then slam against her ribs as she

181

caught sight of Von seated atop the great beast. It was like looking at a painting of her ancestors in the Palace. The sky was a blaze of fiery color while the two warriors were wrapped in darkness. The symbolism was not lost on her.

Von had dressed for battle, his ebony armor glinting in the sun's rays. Below him, Midnight's wings were raised as he prepared to leap into the air. Individually, each male was a force to be reckoned with. Together, they were the promise of a quick and painful death. Helena couldn't help but wonder how many would die with the image of Von astride Midnight being the last thing they ever saw.

Blinking she forced herself to turn away. Using a small burst of Air, Helena quickly got into position on Starshine.

"All right, girl. Let's go meet our friends."

With a final roar, Starshine leapt into the air. Behind her, Helena could hear the echoing roars of the Pride as they followed suit. Helena looked back over her shoulder seeing the sky fill with flapping wings. As Talyria grew smaller, Helena's heart grew heavy. This might be the last time any of them would see their home. The unwelcome thought settled tight and heavy in the bottom of her stomach.

Turning back around, she let out her own battle cry followed by a fiercely whispered promise, "I'm coming for you, you fucking bitch. Too many have already been lost because of your greed. You may have struck the first blow, but mine will be the last."

Helena's words were lost to the wind, but she hoped they found Rowena wherever she was hiding.

*H*elena knew they must be in Etillion even without being able to see the massive wall that notoriously divided it from Endoshan. In the months after the twin territories divided, the wall was erected as a physical reminder of the separation. Flying from Talyria meant that they came into the realm from the Northeast and as such, were on the opposite side of the landmark. Even so, the hills that they'd been riding over had given way to flat land that had become pockmarked with buildings in the last hour or so.

Taking shape on the horizon was a much larger structure that she assumed was the embassy. Helena could just make out the silver tree on the forest green flags flying from each of the building's towers. As a Chosen territory, there was no capital as such. Just the sprawling building that housed the ambassador and her family. The additional bedrooms were for visiting Chosen.

There was comfort in seeing the familiar image, although it did little to ease the tension sitting in her neck and shoulders. While Helena clearly remembered the Etillion scholars that she'd met, she never had caught their names. She grimaced, already anticipating the potentially awkward greeting. Hopefully the others were already here, and Timmins could fill her in before she made an ass out of herself.

Being able to make use of the Kaelpas stones, they should have already arrived, assuming everything had gone according to their plan. She was eager to see her friends and hear about their time in the Broken Vale.

As they descended, Helena scanned the ground for some sign of her people, expecting they'd be on the lookout for her and Von's arrival, but there was none. No one was waiting to greet them. In fact, given the shouts of alarm, it did not seem like anyone was expecting them at all. Helena frowned, her spike of concern shooting like an arrow through her bond.

"They could just be delayed."

The unflappably calm sound of his voice did what nothing else could. Helena let out a breath she was unaware she'd been holding. *"We are already later than we'd planned. I had thought they would have made it by now."*

"As did I, but it is too soon for alarm."

Helena worried at her lower lip, but finally nodded. They still had a handful of hours left in the day. Technically no one was late. Yet.

Using her power to project her voice, she called out to the Etillions standing guard, "I am Kiri Helena Solene. I request the hospitality of my Etillion brothers and sisters."

A woman came running from the front door, waving her arms and shouting up at guards, "Stand down! Let them pass!" Her short brown hair and face were familiar. This was the woman that had come to the Palace.

They landed, the Talyrians spreading out until they all but surrounded the building. Helena could certainly appreciate the guards' hesitation to lower their weapons. Nothing about being surrounded by them felt safe. At least, until you saw them as allies and not a threat.

Helena and Von dismounted, walking quickly to reach the woman who they'd first met in Tigaera.

"Thank the Mother that you're here, Kiri. I did not expect you to arrive so soon!" The woman looked around, as if searching for others. "You did not bring your army?"

It was Helena's turn to look confused. "What do you mean?"

"Aren't you here because of Endoshan?"

"No," Helena said slowly. "What's happened to Endoshan?"

The woman's face went pale, she obviously did not relish the idea of breaking the news. "It has fallen, Kiri. Rowena's army marched through not two days past." Her voice broke as she added, "There were no survivors."

Helena felt like she was going to be sick, it was the Forest all over again. She had not been overly fond of the Endoshan heir, with his intense frowns and barbed comments, but he and the Endoshans were still her people.

"Etillion has been on guard ever since, expecting that we'd be her obvious next stop, but we've seen no sign of her army. It's as if they've entirely disappeared. We sent word to you at the Palace, but I gather you were not there to receive it."

There was a moment of stunned silence before Helena shook her head and replied. "No. I've been traveling throughout Elysia to gather allies. Etillion was to become our base. The rest of our party was supposed to meet us here today so that we could begin preparing for our own assault of Vyruul."

She did not think it was possible, but the woman's face became graver. "You are the first people we've seen since the messenger brought news of Endoshan."

Von frowned, sharing a concerned look with Helena.

To think, when they'd landed Helena's first concern was a forgotten name. The slip deserved to be rectified but there was little time to beat around the bush, so she opted for the direct approach. "I'm so sorry, but I can't seem to remember your name."

"There's no need to apologize, Kiri. There was little time for introductions when we last met. I'm Amara."

Helena smiled gratefully. "Amara, is there anyone here, another scholar perhaps, who is familiar with the Broken Vale?"

Amara frowned. "The Forsaken territory? Why, do you think that's where Rowena is?"

Shaking her head, Helena clarified, "It's where the rest of my

Circle is. I need to get word to them about Endoshan. I thought they would beat us here since they have use of the Kaelpas stones, but something must have delayed them."

Amara looked momentarily impressed, but did not hesitate to answer, "We can ask Xander. He's traveled often as part of his studies. If anyone here would be familiar with such a place, it would be him."

Amara made to move into the stone building and Helena turned before she followed, speaking to Starshine, "Stand guard. Let me know when the others arrive."

Starshine dipped her head in acknowledgement of the order.

Sharing one last worried look with Von, the couple followed Amara into the Embassy.

XANDER, it turned out, was the long-haired man that had accompanied Amara to the Palace. Amara had taken them straight to where he was busy flipping through heavy leather-bound tomes.

He looked up in surprise when they'd entered the study, his gaze suggesting he did not appreciate the interruption. When he realized who it was that interrupted him, he'd done a double take before dropping the book he'd been holding.

"K-Kiri! You made it. Thank the Mother."

Amara was quick to shake her head and cut off his effusive thanks. "They only just heard of Endoshan when they arrived. We need to send word to the Circle in the Broken Vale."

Xander's eyebrows dropped in a frown. "What in the Mother's name is the Circle doing with the Forsaken?"

Helena couldn't help her amusement at the censorious cast of his voice. Von's arms crossed and he lifted a brow as the younger man continued.

"Has everyone forgotten that we're in the middle of a war? A war that they asked *us* to help resolve?"

Amara's cheeks went red and she cleared her throat in warning.

Xander blinked, as he remembered who he was speaking to. He had the grace to look embarrassed, but he did not look away.

"Apologies, Kiri. It's been a stressful few days, well weeks really, ever since the attack at the Palace."

She shook her head, dismissing his apology. "It's been a trying time for us all. No need to apologize."

Von was feeling less forgiving, and just continued to stare although he remained quiet. The lack of words did not make his message any less clear.

Xander, looking flustered, began to shuffle the papers on his desk.

"I think you're making him nervous."

"Good."

"And that's helpful how exactly?" she asked in exasperation.

Relenting, Von lowered his arms and turned the force of his gaze from Xander, back to her.

"Can you help us get a message to the Circle in the Broken Vale?"

Xander's eyes grew distant. "It could be possible to get a message to a specific individual, regardless of the place. Do you have something that belongs to one of them?"

Helena took a mental inventory, working through the list of all that she had packed to take with her to Talyria. Just as she was about the shake her head, she remembered Effie had tucked a heavy cloak in her bag. "It could be cold that far North," she'd said when Helena went to protest the addition. It looked like Effie's foresight might be what saved them all.

"I have a cloak."

"Perfect," Xander murmured. "We will need to borrow it."

Helena nodded her agreement.

"The birds should be able to track the individual through their scent."

"Isn't it a little far for them to pick-up the trail?" Von asked dubiously.

"These are no ordinary birds," Xander said with no little bit of pride.

Von snorted in disbelief. Xander's chest puffed out as his mouth fell open. Helena had no doubt he was about to launch into an extensive defense of his birds. Having no patience, or time, for male posturing, she interjected before Xander could.

"Go grab your birds, please. I will prepare a message and gather the cloak."

Xander shot a parting look at Von who rolled his eyes.

"You can't really believe this is going to work."

"What other choice do we have?"

Von shook his head and turned toward the open window behind him. There were a few long moments of silence as the trio waited for Xander to return.

"Helena!" Von shouted suddenly, just as Starshine bellowed a warning.

Rushing to his side at the window, Helena looked where Von was pointing. It was a little hard to see at first, but she could easily spot the human shape once her eyes adjusted to the dim light. Wasting no time, Helena ran for the door, flying through the halls like the hounds of hell were at her heels. Von and Amara were mere seconds behind her as she stumbled back outside. She didn't stop until she was standing just beside a man she vaguely recognized as one of their runners. The man was covered in dirt and smears of what looked like blood.

Her heart seized at the sight. She already knew what he was about to tell her.

"Kiri?" he rasped.

Dropping to her knees, Helena took his hand and held it tightly in hers. "Yes."

"Thank the Mother I found you," the man said before breaking into wet coughs. Helena ran her palm over his chest, doing what she could to numb his pain. As she opened herself to perform the healing, she found the gaping wound in his back; he'd been stabbed.

"Where are the others?" Helena asked through a tight throat.

His one-word reply was inaudible so she dipped her head, all but pressing her ear to his lips. He repeated himself just as his eyes rolled back into his head and he fell unconscious. Her face bleached of color as she looked back up at the others.

"What'd he say?" Von demanded.

"Attack."

Above them the sky ripped in two as a bolt of lightning shot down. A storm began to rage around them, but it had nothing on the one raging inside of her.

CHAPTER 23

Forest of Whispers
Five Days Earlier

*R*onan watched Helena and Von disappear into the sky, a
ripple of unease running along his spine. He'd felt that
same warning tingle countless times before. Normally it preceded an
attack or battle, but glancing around, there was nothing to indicate any
enemies were lurking in the shadows.

"May the Mother watch over you both," he whispered.

The men standing on either side of him shifted, preparing to head
back. He was the last to turn away and was startled to see that Reyna
had also remained behind.

"You are close to them," she stated after her intense green eyes
scanned his face.

Ronan nodded once, wondering what it was that she'd read there.
Her expression was hard to decipher beneath the black swirls of paint.

"Not used to being left behind?" she guessed.

Ronan lifted his right shoulder in a shrug. "The last time the Circle
was parted was hard on all of us. Some memories do not easily fade."

Her eyes softened. "No, they do not."

The only sound as they walked was the soft crunch of dried leaves beneath their feet. After a long pause she asked, "Are you worried for their safety?"

Ronan's eyes narrowed as he examined the unease that still ate at him. "No," he finally answered. "I do not believe it is their safety that concerns me. Helena is more than capable of handling whatever comes their way and Von would die before he let something happen to his Mate. Nor do I doubt the Talyrians will come to their aid if necessary."

"Your Kiri is quite powerful," Reyna said after a long pause.

Ronan gave her a sidelong glance. "Aye. She is."

"Is it love for her that has you worried then?"

Ronan let out a loud bark of laughter at the absurdity of the question. The subtle pink tinge on Reyna's cheeks had the last of his laughter fading. "No, not like that anyway."

"Oh."

Ronan spared her another curious glance as he moved to lift a branch out of their path. He was struggling to make sense of the Night Stalker's line of questioning. Reyna ducked below the branch and continued without looking back. "What has you worried then, Chosen?"

Ronan let out a frustrated sigh, raking his hands through his unbound hair. The problem was that he had no clue what was causing the itchy feeling just beneath his skin. "Something is coming," he finally answered.

"That is not news," she stated, eying him over her shoulder as he closed the distance between them. "It is why you sought our assistance in the first place."

He scowled at her. "It's not the threat of battle." And it wasn't. Battle made his blood sing, it was why he'd never questioned following Von when he'd went mercenary. "What I'm feeling is different. Darker somehow. I cannot explain it."

Reyna's hand burned where it made contact with his arm. He lifted a brow in question, surprised by the touch. Reyna looked equally confused and slowly moved her hand off his arm. "Do not ignore whatever it is that is trying to warn you." Her voice was low and urgent, her green eyes glittering with intensity.

Ronan nodded once. "I won't."

The Night Stalker let out a slow breath as her village came back into view. "I would go with you now, if I could. But my people aren't ready for the battle to come. We need more time."

"I know."

Reyna gave him one last inscrutable look. "Do not die, Chosen. I would like to see you again." With that she turned and walked away.

"What the fuck does that mean?" he asked himself, rubbing a hand along the back of his neck.

THE CHOSEN WERE ALREADY PACKED and ready to go by the time he returned. Serena and Effie were talking in low voices when he joined them. Sensing his presence, Serena spun around looking furious.

"You didn't think we would also appreciate getting to see them off?"

"You were sleeping."

"So?"

Ronan threw up his hands, not ready to walk through a verbal minefield. "I wasn't the only one that didn't wake you up, why am I the one getting the lecture?"

"Because you know better."

"Oh, for fuck's sake."

Effie was trying to smother a smile, which only infuriated him further.

He stuck a finger in her face. "You gonna give me shit too?"

She pressed her lips together and quickly shook her head, her blue eyes twinkling with suppressed laughter.

"That's a fucking first."

Serena's eyes widened at the hint of his temper. "What crawled up your ass?"

Not about to get into another circular conversation regarding what had him on edge he just shook his head.

"Seriously, Ronan. Is everything okay?" The anger had left her face and Serena was looking at him with concerned violet eyes.

Ronan rubbed at his eyes before pinching the bridge of his nose, squeezing hard to relieve some of the extra tension. When he spoke, he sounded tired but steady, "It's just a feeling I can't shake. Nothing to worry about."

The women studied him but did not push him further.

Surprised they let it go so easily, Ronan glanced at each of them. Both women were standing with the alert stillness of warriors awaiting orders. It was then that Ronan realized they had heard all that he hadn't said. Effie because of her natural insight and Serena because of her years of training and fighting beside him. She'd seen what happened when they ignored his 'feelings' in the past and did not care to repeat that experience ever again. He was glad for it. If there was anyone he trusted to watch his back when Von was gone, it was certainly her.

The knowledge steadied him further. Taking the first easy breath since he'd woken that morning, he gave them each a grateful smile before turning to address the others that had gathered behind him.

Ronan cleared his throat, easily silencing the murmuring voices of the gathered crowd. If the men in the Circle minded that he was speaking for them they did not let on. Of all of them, he was the one most used to speaking to large groups. His sheer size and the carrying boom of his voice made him a natural at it.

"Chosen, it's time to leave. We've been lucky so far, no doubt because of our Kiri's power, but that does not mean our luck will continue. As we move through the Broken Vale, be alert, be watchful, but most importantly, be respectful. We do not know which of our actions may cause offense and we cannot risk a misunderstanding."

The men and women nodded solemnly. Even the wolves seemed to bob their heads in agreement. It was clear that they all understood the seriousness of the task that laid ahead of them.

"Gather with your groups, runners be ready to follow shortly."

The crowd dispersed as they moved into position. The men of the

Circle were already waiting for him, along with Miranda, Effie, Serena, Nial and their runner. They'd gotten lucky when they learned that one of the Night Stalkers had been to the Vale before, and that she was going to help the first group make the trip.

The group took hands, bunching in tight. Ronan took the hand of their runner. As he did, a cold tingle ran in a straight line along the back of his neck, almost as if a finger was brushing against it. He shuddered and twisted his head to catch a look at the woman whose hand he was holding. Her face blurred, the swirls of her make-up slithering like snakes across her face. He blinked rapidly, about to shout out a warning as the woman's green eyes went coal black and her lips twisted into a sinister sneer.

Before he could do anything, she activated the Kaelpas stone and made the jump to the Vale.

WHEN THEY LANDED, Ronan fought the wave of sickness that always accompanied the jump, looking for the runner. She was already gone, which meant that they were stranded here; wherever here was. It was not a place he recognized. There was only fine sand as far as the eye could see.

Ronan roared, the others jumping in surprise at the sound.

"What is it?" Effie asked, reaching for him with concern.

Beside her, Miranda stared just past his shoulder in growing horror. "I have Seen this," she murmured.

Effie spun back toward her grandmother. "What did you See?"

Even Timmins, who usually wore a look of thinly veiled contempt when he looked at the Keeper was staring at her intently as they awaited her answer.

"Darkness and bloodshed," she whispered.

Ronan shielded and reached for his axes, but they had been stored. He settled for clenched fists, ready to swing at the first sign of attack.

"What do you mean?" Timmins demanded. His voice held none of the disbelief it usually did when speaking to the Keeper.

Miranda blinked, appearing to return from wherever her thoughts had wandered. When she spoke, she seemed apologetic. "It is only images, nothing specific."

"Whatever warning your vision could provide may be all the upper-hand we need to change the outcome," Kragen said softly.

Some of the color was beginning to return to her face as she spoke. "There is a mountain, surrounded by a forest of trees. A rock breaks from the mountain and flies away. When the rock comes to rest, it is alone in a sea of sand. Darkness rolls in on every side until the rock drowns in it. When light returns all that remains is a ring of blood."

"Not a ring. A Circle," Effie corrected.

Miranda's midnight eyes flew to her granddaughter, who seemed startled that she'd even spoken. Her cornflower blue eyes were wide and her hands had flown up to cover her mouth.

Haunted by her words, Ronan shuddered. If what the Keeper saw was indeed a warning, it seemed that not all of them would be walking away from whatever came with the darkness. At least not entirely unscathed. He glanced around at the others, wondering if they'd reached the same conclusion.

Each of the men looked grim but determined. Nial wrapped his arm around Serena, who looked shaken.

"So what now?" Darrin asked, his eyes ping-ponging between the Keeper and her granddaughter, as if they held more answers.

The group looked around, finally taking in their surroundings. Not that there was much to see. In every direction it was the same. Sand. Sand on the ground and sand whirling through the air carried by gusts of wind. Above them, the sun beat down, its heat punishing.

"Do you think she brought us to the Vale after all?" Serena asked.

"From everything I was able to find, that must be where we are. It's a broken realm, its buildings predominantly in ruins after the great uprising."

"So where are all the people?" It was Darrin who asked the question, but they'd all been wondering the same thing.

"Underground," Joquil answered.

Ronan's brow lifted in disbelief.

"It's true," Nial said. "After the uprising, none of the buildings were fit for habitation. Instead of rebuilding, believing the spirits of their ancestors would haunt anything built on the land where they'd be killed, they used their power to create a network of caverns and tunnels below ground."

Kragen cursed softly. "How are we supposed to find an entrance to these magical tunnels?"

Nial shrugged. "I don't think we are. They are referred to as the lost tribes for a reason."

"Are they really lost if they know where they are and we are the ones that can't seem to find them?" Darrin mused aloud.

The group chuckled, the philosophical question seeming out of place given the circumstances.

Ronan sighed, lifting his hand to cover his eyes as he squinted into the distance. "I'm sure Helena would have a plan to find them, but I cannot pretend to know it. Let us hope that our presence here disturbed some sort of alarm and they come to us. I cannot think of another way to find help."

"Do you think that the Night Stalkers are behind this betrayal?" Kragen asked, purposefully avoiding Joquil's gaze.

"No," Ronan said without hesitation. "This was another of Rowena's spies. They must have stayed behind after the attack on Duskfall, waiting for an opportunity like this one. No one knows where we are save the runner. It is doubtful help is on the way."

"Should we seek shelter then?" Kragen asked. "It does not seem like a good idea to simply wait here if we are indeed about to be attacked."

Ronan frowned as he considered Miranda's warning and their situation. "Do you think the darkness was literal? Does the threat come with the night?"

Miranda shrugged. "I don't know. It's possible."

He looked up, trying to discern the time based on the sun's position in the sky. "At most we have eight hours before nightfall. We may not find anything in that time, but if there's a chance we should probably take it. If for no other reason than to not be sitting ducks, remaining in the exact place the traitor left us."

The group nodded their agreement.

"So which direction do we go?" Serena asked.

"Fuck if I know," Ronan replied. "Your guess is as good as mine."

"Let's head west," Effie said, surprising the others with her suggestion. It was rare for her to take charge.

"Why west?" Darrin asked.

"Doesn't the Vale share a border with the Forest? Perhaps we are not too far away and can get back there. Or at least close enough that their scouts will see us."

Darrin's eyes shone with approval at her reasoning. Even Ronan had to admit he was impressed; he hadn't even considered the possibility. "It's as good of a reason as any, and probably better than most. If there's a chance we could get word to the Night Stalkers, we should definitely take it."

The others were quick to agree.

"All right," Ronan decided, "to the West it is. Stay alert everyone, we may be out in the open, but that means our enemies will be as well. Keep your shields up, but do not use your power more than you have to. We want to be ready when the strike comes, because there is no doubt one is coming."

CHAPTER 24

*R*onan was wrong. When the attack came, no one saw it coming.

They had trudged through the sand for hours, no closer to finding shelter for the effort. They'd finally ended up making camp for the night right there in the open. Two days passed with more of the same. Then, on the fourth day, just as the sun begun to set, clouds filled the sky. Around them sand whipped up into the air, making it impossible to see much of anything.

Their only warning was one long keening cry before a ball of fire flew through the sky and landed at their feet. Suddenly the air cleared and Ronan could make out the black wave of Rowena's army coming at them. It was twelve against twelve hundred, but it would have to be enough. There had been no way to get word to Helena, no one would be coming to save them.

There was no time for words of inspiration. The sound of weapons being drawn rang around him while the four wolves, Karma and Shepa among them, growled and crouched ready for battle. Ronan's eyes caught Serena's, both were wide with panic but when they met a feeling of calm washed through him. He saw the same peace spread across her face.

The first of the Shadows were already running for them. Nial was murmuring, summoning his considerable power to create a shield around them all. Where the Shadows made impact with the smoky barrier it sizzled, and the Shadows flew back with howls of pain. The magic ate at their skin like acid, not stopping until it reached bone.

But they continued to swarm, undaunted. It was only a matter of time before they got through the barrier. Soon Timmins and Joquil were adding their power to reinforce the barrier. Their goal to try to whittle through the numbers as much as possible before they had to start their own attack. The backlash of power through the barrier was not enough to kill the Shadows, but it was strong enough to eat through limbs, which made many of the abominations less of a threat.

Sweat was dripping down Nial's face as he tried to keep the barrier up. Each blow against its surface reverberated through him and it was taking a toll. At least an hour had passed without any sign of relent. Ronan saw the moment Nial knew he'd have to let it go; the burden was becoming more than he could physically withstand. Ronan nodded at Nial, letting him know that it was okay; they were ready to take up the fight.

Ronan moved into position, and the others followed suit around him. There was no hesitation, no sign of fear. He knew this dance well. Whatever the outcome, he was born for battle. The only way he'd stop fighting was if they killed him, and if that was to be the case, he'd take down as many of the walking corpses as he could before he fell.

Ahead of him, standing on a sand dune was Rowena. She was decked out entirely in black, her dress shining like scales of armor. Her crown was twisted spikes of metal, looking more like a weapon than an ornamental headpiece. Ice filled his veins as she smiled down at him. He knew, despite the distance, that her smile was for him alone. The certainty on her face had his own lips pulling back in a snarl. Let her believe she would win this. It would make their victory that much sweeter.

Rowena made a gesture and one of the men standing beside her peeled away from the others to join the fray. But Ronan didn't have time to be distracted by where he went.

When Nial dropped the barrier, Ronan threw his head back and screamed, pouring his rage into the sound. The others joined him, their voices becoming a bloodthirsty chorus.

The battle had begun.

Ronan soon lost sight of the others. Time lost all meaning. Nothing existed but him and the swing of his axes. Each blow was reinforced with his power, and every strike was true. He knew he was leaving a pile of bodies in his wake, but there was no end to the enemies. His only focus was to clear a path to the she-bitch waiting for him atop the hill.

That was when her general struck. Just as at the Palace, this one had corrupted power. A ball of purple-black flame grew in his hand. He threw it, aiming for Ronan. Grabbing the Shadow that was standing beside him, Ronan tossed the creature in front of him before ducking and rolling to the side. When he stood, he twisted back to see the Shadow who had become a pillar of purple flames. The flames made quick work of the body but were not extinguished once the body had been consumed. Instead they continued to burn, snaking slowly toward him.

Ronan continued to throw as many bodies between himself and the flames as possible. Soon the air was thick with pale purple smoke and there were a number of purple fires raging within the crush of bodies. At least the fire also destroyed the Shadows. It had helped take down a number of them so that Ronan could move about a bit more freely.

"Use the flames!" he shouted.

Darrin had caught up to him and nodded his understanding, ducking and ramming his shoulder into the body of the Shadow that was running at him. The Shadow flipped over him and fell on his back into the fire.

The distraction of watching the other man nearly cost him. Ronan did not see the fist that flew toward his face. He took the blow, his vision going dark as stars burst behind his eyes. Using instinct, Ronan lashed out, listening for the grunt that accompanied his ax's impact to determine how to position his body for the next strike. He was rewarded with the gurgle of blood and the thud of a body. Blinking a few more times his vision finally cleared, although he was not entirely certain what it was he was now seeing.

Outside the swarm of Shadows tall dark shapes were beginning to form. It looked like trees, but that didn't make any sense. There had been nothing but sand for days.

There was a shout behind him. Recognizing the voice, Ronan spun. As Serena's face came into view he saw that it was not a shout of warning but excitement. She noticed the gathering shapes as well but knew what they were. He was too far away to hear her words but could make out well enough what her lips were saying.

It looked like she'd said, "Watchers."

Understanding dawned. If the Watchers were here, that meant the Night Stalkers had found them. They must have been close to the border after all. He was going to make a point to give Effie a proper kiss once this was over. Assuming he lived to see the end of it. That girl had probably saved their lives with her suggestion to head west.

The horizon began to fill with shadowy shapes until it looked like the forest was descending on them. There was a shriek of outrage as Rowena took notice. He watched her face twist in anger before she called forth one of her other four generals.

"Not feeling so good now that it's a fair fight, do you, you stupid bitch?" he murmured gleefully. With a renewed sense of purpose, Ronan moved to intercept him before he could add his twisted magic to the fray.

IT WAS FULL NIGHT NOW, but they had not stopped. The battle had been raging for hours. Darrin could feel his body growing tired but pressed on. He was not sure how much longer he would last, but they had not lost anyone so far, and Darrin did not intend to let that change. He kept his eye on Effie, knowing that she did not have power to aid her as the others did. So far, that had not done much to hamper his girl.

She fought like an alley cat, using her small size to her advantage. She would move and twist faster than the Shadows could anticipate, dancing out of the way of their attacks and striking from behind them. He could not help the surge of pride he felt watching her take down the hulking creatures.

The wolves were coated in black blood, the pack responsible for taking down at least a hundred of the monsters on their own. They fought together, going for the throat or distracting their target so another could attack. It was hard to tell if they'd sustained any injuries, but it appeared as if at least one of them was limping slightly. Even so, it did not slow them down at all.

Joquil, Timmins, Miranda and Nial were grouped together, using their power to take down as many of the Shadows as possible. Balls of Fire would hit a Shadow to be followed by one of Water to try to stop the flames from growing out of control. So far, the Water did not seem to do anything against the purple flames that Rowena's general kept launching. Miranda was using Air to keep the pale purple smoke away from them. Darrin's lungs were still burning from the one breath he accidentally inhaled.

Kragen and Serena were relentless, their blades both dripping with blood. Ronan's had been as well, but Darrin had lost sight of him shortly after his tip about the fire. That had been about the time that the Night Stalkers had arrived. The extra numbers quickly changed the tide. The blurred figures were like nothing Darrin had ever seen. They would appear behind their target, using their weapons and sometimes just their hands to rip off the heads of the creatures and then toss them into the smoking fire, before quickly blurring and moving onto another. It was impossible to anticipate where they would strike next.

The Watchers were just as incredible. Darrin wasn't even sure what he was seeing was real when the first of the colossal tree-men moved into range. He was absolutely massive, each of his movements deliberate and slow. That did not mean they were not powerful. With each lumbering step, the Watcher crushed dozens of their enemies. Darrin had the impression of trees swaying in a storm but did not have the time to spend thinking about it. He'd barely had time to crane his head back and try to find the gnarled face etched into the upper trunk of the tree. Darrin had to force himself to look away; he'd study them later. Once they'd won this battle.

As he continued to fight, Darrin saw more of the Watchers come into focus. They would stoop down, using their branches to pick up and fling a handful of Shadows into the crowd. Often the maneuver would kill a Shadow on impact, their necks snapping with the force. More often, Rowena's minions would pick themselves up and rush back into the fray. Still, the Watcher's had greatly culled her force.

A high-pitched scream pulled Darrin out of his thoughts. He spun, making quick work of the two stumbling Shadows in front of him. Both looked more corpse than human, and it was not hard to remove their heads from their bodies. Once they'd fallen he saw what made Effie scream.

Ronan was battling one of the generals. It was hard to tell Rowena's men apart unless they were using their power, but this one had long stringy hair. Its lips were twisted in some gruesome semblance of a smile and it was lifting its hand as it called on its power. There was a chittering sound coming from its gaping mouth that could have been a taunt or laughter. Darrin was too far away to tell but the sound had Ronan launching himself in the air, throwing his axes one after the other. The general stumbled as the axes made contact. One neatly shearing off an arm, while the other buried itself in its chest.

The general snarled, using its remaining arm to pull the ax free and toss it to the ground. Deep black blood spurted from the wounds, but the general did not falter. Still holding onto his power, the general released it down into the sand. That was when Darrin realized which general this one must be. Earth.

When Ronan landed, he began to sink into the mass of quicksand the Earth general had created. He sank fast, his body more than half obscured by the pit of burbling sand. Darrin started to run, intent on saving him before he was completely submerged.

Darrin was full-on sprinting, his heart thundering in his chest. He wasn't going to make it. He was just too far away.

Beside Ronan, shadows rippled and peeled away. In their place,

Reyna took shape. Her face was hidden behind the swirls of her make-up but that did nothing to obscure the look of murderous rage in her glittering green eyes. She dropped to her knees, using her considerable strength to pull Ronan out of the sand. At the same time, she flung her other arm out. Her dagger burying itself in the general's neck. It was not enough to kill him, but it did knock him down.

With a shriek of outrage, Reyna began to stand, digging her heels into the sand and using the counterbalance to help her pull Ronan free. For a moment it did not appear that she would be successful, his body weight combined with the force of the quicksand more than a match for her. But with another shriek, she tugged again. There was a loud, wet sucking sound and Ronan surged upward before promptly falling onto the sand beside her.

They were both panting, but there was no time for them to catch their breath. As one, they stood and raced for the general, who was already struggling back to his feet. Ronan grabbed his ax as he ran toward the man, using his momentum to swing it into the general's neck. The slice was so clean, it almost appeared as if the blow did not land. The general was still blinking when his head began to slide off of his neck and fall to the floor.

Rowena screamed in outrage as her general fell, and with a swirl of her black cloak she fled the battle. Darrin grinned, knowing that her retreat meant the battle would be theirs. Focusing back on the chaos around him, he began to work his way toward Effie. If he hadn't been looking for her, he never would have seen the swirling ball of purple fire as it left the Fire general's hand heading straight toward her.

"No!" Darrin screamed, rushing toward Effie, intent on pushing her out of harm's way. Darrin ran faster than he'd ever moved before, feeling his power give him an inhuman burst of speed. Effie's eyes went wide and he could see them fill with fear as she watched the fireball race toward her.

It was over in a heartbeat, but it felt as though time had slowed completely. He was aware of each frame as it occurred. The blink of her beautiful blue eyes and the way her lashes tangled together when they closed. The petal pink of her lips as her mouth opened on a scream. The heavy thud of her body as it made contact with the ground.

But more than anything, Darrin was aware of the burst of pain as the fireball hit his back and then consumed him. The corrupted flames made quick work of his shield and armor until nothing stood between them and his skin. The pain was absolute.

Darrin stared into Effie's eyes, wanting the image of the woman he'd fallen in love with be the last thing he ever saw as his knees buckled and hit the ground.

A look of confusion, and then horror, crossed Effie's face as she realized what had happened. "Darrin!" she screamed, scrambling on her hands and knees toward him.

He could see the purple flames licking up his chest and arms. It would not be long before they covered him completely. It was impossible to think, let alone form words, but somehow he did. With what he wanted to say, it was too important not to.

"Effie," he gasped.

"Nonononono!" Effie screamed over and over, tears streaming down her face. She searched for something to extinguish the flames but found nothing except the skirt of her travel dress. Even as she tore the fabric using it to beat at the fire, Darrin knew it was futile. The shadow flames had melted armor on impact, there was little that a piece of cloth could do against it. As predicted, the flimsy fabric easily caught fire, forcing Effie to drop it with a strangled cry.

"I love you." The words were barely audible as they left his mouth. Darrin only knew she'd heard him because her face twisted in pain and she repeated them brokenly as she sobbed.

It was all he needed to let go. As his eyes fell closed, Effie's face blurred and faded away. With it went the pain. In his last coherent moment, Darrin was overcome with peace as he saw the familiar face of his best friend take shape within his mind.

Helena, he thought with a mix of relief and surprise. *At least I am not dying alone.*

CHAPTER 25

It was Effie's scream that pulled Ronan's attention away from the still twitching body of Rowena's general. As he turned toward the sound, he saw the pyre of purple flames she was kneeling beside.

"What the hell does she think she's doing?" he muttered darkly, wondering why she was letting her hand hover so close to the deadly flames. That was when he realized Darrin was missing.

Since the battle had started, hell, since they'd left Tigaera a few weeks ago, he'd barely strayed from her side. He may have been Helena's Shield in name and by vow, but he'd clearly extended that duty to Effie. So why wasn't he the one pulling her out of harm's way now?

The answer came to him as he watched the small woman's body begin to shake with the force of her sobs. It wasn't the flames she was trying to touch; it was what was concealed within them.

"Mother be merciful," he said, taking off at a dead run.

"Where do you think—" Reyna started to shout as she efficiently beheaded another of the Shadows, but he didn't have time to explain.

He covered the distance easily, despite the protesting ache of his body from hours of endless fighting.

"Effie," he said softly, watching her begin to rock back and forth.

She didn't hear him.

Ronan glanced around, ensuring that they would remain safe for the moment, before squatting down beside her. "Come on, *Mira*. Let's get you somewhere safe." The Chosen's term of endearment also had no effect. It wasn't until he touched her shoulder that she looked up, hissing at him like a feral cat. Her eyes were crazed and unseeing.

"Shhh, Effie. It's me."

Effie blinked, her eyes returning to normal as she recognized the man in front of her.

"R-Ronan," she sobbed, launching herself at him.

She may have been small, but her momentum almost knocked him on his ass. He caught and held her with a muffled oomph.

"Da-Darrin," she started.

"Shhh," he whispered, tucking her head into his chest so that she could not look back at the body, or what was left of it.

"We can't leave him here," she hiccupped.

Ronan frowned. Darrin wasn't going anywhere. There was nothing he knew of that would extinguish the flames. The Water the others had summoned to try just that didn't even slow the purple blaze down. Perhaps Helena would have been able to do something, but she wasn't here. And by the time she got here... well, there'd be nothing left to bury.

"I'll take care of it," he promised.

Effie looked up at him from where she was cradled in his arms. She looked like a broken doll, her face smeared with dirt and streaked with tears. The sadness in her big blue eyes made his heart ache. "Thank you," she whispered.

They were the last words Effie said for quite some time. It was as if, with that last task assured, she could retreat into the safety of her thoughts to mourn the future she'd never have. Ronan easily picked her up and carried her through the fray. It would have been a comical sight, the way he had to duck and weave around those that were engaged in battle, if so much wasn't on the line.

He carried her to her grandmother, knowing that Miranda would be able to take over from there. He opened his mouth to explain, but by the look in those ancient midnight eyes, he saw he didn't have to. She already knew. The Keeper had probably known it was going to happen days, or maybe even years, before it did. What a burden that must have been.

As he set Effie down, Ronan pressed a swift kiss to her forehead. "Stay strong, little bird. He would not want to see this break you."

The words breathed new life into her, and Effie looked up nodding her understanding.

It wasn't until he turned to run back to the others that he realized what Darrin's death truly meant. The Circle was broken.

Helena had made him promise he would protect them, and he'd let her down. She was never going to forgive him.

EVEN WITH THE appearance of the Night Stalkers, and the rest of the Chosen who'd shown up shortly thereafter once the runners had been able to reestablish their relay, they fought for several more hours. Eventually though, either due to the Mother's grace or sheer dumb luck, they were able to dispatch the remaining Shadows.

Still, it was by no means quick or easy. They were already exhausted and still very much outnumbered. But by the time the sun began to rise, the body count was high but the Chosen were the last ones standing.

No one saw what happened to Rowena or her four remaining generals. Ronan assumed that they must have fled once they saw Darrin fall. He had a feeling that had been what she was after. Ronan wouldn't rest until they he watched the woman breathe her last. Just because she was out of sight, did not mean she was gone.

The battle might be over, but his work here wasn't finished. He tried not to groan as he forced himself forward. He had a promise to keep.

Around him, others worked through what was left of the bodies checking to make sure there were no survivors. They were also carrying off their dead so that they could be given a proper burial. It was grim work, but important.

Reyna caught his eye and gave him a smile so brief he half-thought he imagined it. He still wasn't sure what to make of the Night Stalker, but he did owe her a heartfelt thank you at some point. If it hadn't been for her, none of them would be alive right now.

He walked deliberately, stepping carefully around the shadowy purple flames and dead bodies. As the fight had continued through the night, the purple glow had illuminated the battlefield with its eerie light. Now that the sun was beginning to shine, the glow was almost black.

The fire had a sentience he couldn't explain. It burned through whatever it touched, moving on in search of a new target once its fuel had been consumed. Judging by the fact that the entire landscape was not a blazing purple inferno, it would seem that if the flames did not find a new fuel source they died out on their own. Nothing else they tried had been able to, but to be fair, they'd also had their hands full with the mindless corpses that were trying to kill them.

Ronan sighed as he returned to the spot he'd found Effie and Darrin. He'd lost men before, good men, but this was different. In the months they'd spent searching for Von, the younger man had become part of his family. This loss cut deep. He could only imagine how much worse it would be for Helena. Especially when Darrin had been the last link to her past. A wave of sadness and guilt washed over him at the thought of having to tell her what had happened.

Kneeling, he took a deep breath. There was nothing left except ash. It would have to be enough. He began to scoop the still-smoking pile into one of his travel sacks and was proud when his hands only trembled slightly as they came into contact of what remained of his friend.

Before he stood, Ronan closed his eyes and offered a prayer to the Mother, asking her to welcome her son home. He was not a devout man by any stretch of the imagination. He'd seen entirely too much death and hatefulness in the world to believe that there was really a deity out there watching over them. If the Mother did exist, how could she allow such tragedies to occur? But as he gently lifted the now full bag in his hands, he desperately needed to believe.

Ronan turned back toward the hill where they'd set up a sort of camp and his breath left him with a whoosh. The lone figure standing sentinel was unexpected. He blinked quickly to ensure she was not some kind of mirage. She wasn't. When his eyes reopened, Helena was still there.

The weight of the bag grew heavier with each step as Ronan closed the distance between them, his eyes never once leaving hers. As he neared her, he could see that Von was standing just to the side of her, ready if she needed him. In his own way, Ronan wanted to lend her his strength as well. So he did it in the only way he could, by bearing witness to the full weight of her pain. He let it wash over him, hoping that by sharing it he could ease some of the burden. Ronan had thought Effie had been grief-stricken, but it was nothing compared to the tortured expression in Helena's aqua eyes.

She stood stiffly, holding herself so tightly that her knuckles were white. It looked like she was physically trying to hold herself together, probably to keep herself from completely falling apart. Ronan swallowed down a wave of emotion as he finally reached her. It wasn't until he was standing just in front of her that she looked down at what he was offering her.

Her face and eyes were dry, but Ronan knew that she was dying inside. He could feel it as surely as if he was standing next to her. Her nostrils flared as her eyes flew back up to his. He watched her struggle to catch her breath as she reached out to accept the bag. A part of him wanted to keep it in hopes that it would spare her, but he knew it was far too late for that. There was no escaping this pain.

Helena took the bag from him and curled herself protectively around it, resting her cheek against the top. She stayed there a long time, just holding what was left of her friend close to her. All the while her lips were moving silently, almost like she was praying, or perhaps whispering words meant for him alone. It wasn't until she was done that he saw the first of her tears or took notice of the rain.

HELENA DIDN'T NEED anyone to tell her what had happened. She'd felt it the instant they'd arrived in the Broken Vale. The pain that exploded through her Jaka was enough to have her fall to her knees and clutch at her side. Its intensity was overwhelming; she could hardly focus enough to make sense of what the pain meant. As she struggled to breathe through the waves of fiery pain, she was finally able to gather herself enough to follow the pain to its source. The emptiness that greeted her there rendered her completely numb. The loss was too much for her brain to process.

Ever since Ronan had given her the Jaka, she'd felt the connection to each of the men that comprised her Circle. She'd grown used to the unique feeling of each individual strand, recognizing the nuances that separated each of them without having to try. It was how she knew with utter certainty that one was missing, and who it was.

"Helena, what is it?" Von shouted, the frantic cast of his voice alerting her to the fact that this wasn't the first time he'd asked.

She looked up at him from where she'd curled up on the ground. "Darrin."

The hollow tone of her voice told him everything. His eyes went dark, and he let out a long breath. "What do you need?"

Helena pushed herself to her feet. "We need to find the others. They might still need our help."

A conflicted look crossed his face. Von knew that she was barely holding on, she knew he could feel it through their bond. He'd also witnessed her rage and grief over losing the man who raised her only weeks ago. There was no way he would believe that she was unaffected by the loss of the man she'd grown up with, no matter what sort of brave face she tried to present. But there was a time and a place to grieve, and this was not it. She knew Von reached the same conclusion when he held out a hand to help her stand up.

There was a soft cough. The runner was staring awkwardly at the ground, waiting for them to take notice of him and the Etillions that had travelled with them.

"Do you know where they are?" she asked in the same hollowed out voice.

The man nodded.

"Take me there."

There was no indication that a battle still raged. The sun was just starting to light up the sky, and the world around them was quiet. They did not have to walk far, just over the crest of a sand dune. Helena's stomach rolled at the sight that greeted her, but she did not let herself look away. This was her fault. She should never have left them to face this alone. Her presence could have made all the difference. It could have been what kept Darrin alive.

"You cannot take on that burden, Mira. This is not your fault."

"You don't know that."

"I do," Von countered firmly. *"Rowena was always going to strike, and there cannot be a battle without casualties. We always knew this would end in bloodshed, in death."*

"But not his." The admission was too much. Her psychic voice broke and she shook her head, indicating that she did not want to speak further. Not even to him.

The chaos before them was hard to make sense of. There were bodies everywhere, randomly interspersed with dark purple flames. Helena did not have to try hard to feel the corruption wafting up from them. Her eyes flew over the scene, looking for someone she recognized. A familiar red head snagged her attention, pulling all of her focus. She watched as Ronan walked through the bodies, looking as though he was searching for something. After a few more steps, he stopped and dropped to the ground. His hands seemed to fumble as they pulled open a travel-worn bag.

Helena's heart squeezed painfully and it hurt to breathe as she watched him carefully begin to scoop what could only be ash into the bag. The seconds dragged as she watched him fill it before slowly standing back up. He saw her instantly, his eyes focused intently on her face. The protective way he carried the bag made her want to sob, but she knew if she started, she wouldn't be able to stop. So instead, she made herself take a breath in time with each of his steps. Right foot, in.

Left foot, out. Right foot, in. Left foot, out. There was room for nothing else.

When he reached her he didn't speak, but his thoughts were written across his face. She watched as he debated handing the bag over and could tell he wanted to spare her. Her heart thanked him for that kindness, even though she couldn't say so.

His eyes bore into hers, begging her to forgive him for causing her more pain with this action. She wished she could comfort him, but as soon as the bag made contact with her hands, there wasn't room to worry about any life except the extinguished one she now carried.

It was lighter than she would have thought, knowing that it contained the man who'd towered over her when he hugged her. She'd always felt so safe in his arms. She wanted, needed, him to feel that now. She clutched the bag close to her chest, holding onto him with all the strength she still possessed.

Resting her cheek on the top of the bag, the way he used to do with her head, she whispered, "Goodbye dearest friend. I am so sorry that I wasn't here to save you. I never thought there would be a day I would have to face without you. I know that we didn't always see eye to eye on, well, hardly anything. But I know that you always wanted what was best for me. I will always love you, Darrin. I am so sorry that you will never have the life that you deserved. I will make sure Effie wants for nothing. You do not need to worry about her, or any of us. Rest now. We will handle it from here."

Closing her eyes, she took a shuddering breath, no longer able to keep the tears at bay. When the drops began to fall down her cheeks, she wasn't sure if it was from the tears, or the rain that poured from the sky.

CHAPTER 26

*V*on had helped keep the others at bay until she was ready to face them. And by ready, she meant numb. There was too much going on for the world to stop and let her process the death of her best friend. In some twisted way, the threat of Rowena's next attack allowed her to shift her focus and compartmentalize her grief. She had a feeling that when the loss truly hit her, she would be completely useless.

Helena stepped out of the makeshift tent and headed toward the familiar faces of her friends. It was actually a minor miracle she found them so easily. There were people scattered everywhere. Chosen, Night Stalkers, Watchers, Etillions, Talyrians, Daejaran wolves; it was a motley crew and a lot to take in.

They'd created a temporary camp of sorts. A place for them to care for the injured, get a few hours of much-needed sleep and perhaps eat, if their stomach could handle it. Once those necessities were seen to, they would regroup in a more appropriate location. Not that Helena knew where that was these days. Rowena had already proven with her attacks that nowhere would remain safe for long.

That was why the animals were currently patrolling the perimeter of the camp. Under other circumstances, she would have been amused by the uneasy truce between the wolves and Talyrians. Or the Talyrians and anyone, really. If the Chosen had been shocked by the appearance of Starshine, they were at a complete loss when they saw Midnight prowling at her side.

Of the Talyrians that had flown to Etillion, only Starshine and Midnight had made the trip to the Vale with them. She'd had to leave the rest behind because the remaining charge of the Kaelpas stone was not enough to transport them as well as the Etillions. Besides, the need to travel immediately outweighed all else.

Most of Reyna's Watchers had returned to the Forest, although a few had stayed behind. Helena had not gotten a very good look at any of the hulking tree men, although she was curious how they communicated with the Night Stalkers. Could they even speak? Perhaps Reyna would fill her in before she had to test it out.

There were also the fifteen Etillions that had come with them to the Vale. The plan had been to see what they were up against and hopefully use additional runners to bring more assistance if needed, but since the fighting was already over by the time they'd arrived, it was a moot point. They, along with the thirty or so remaining Chosen who had initially left with them from Tigaera, plus Reyna's two hundred some odd Night Stalkers, currently comprised their group.

What those numbers really meant was that Helena was surrounded by a lot of unfamiliar faces and she was more than a little uneasy about it. They'd had too many traitors among them as it was; friend and stranger alike. The reminder that she knew little, if anything, about the people she was surrounded by left her restless and feeling like she was being watched.

Helena began to walk faster, no longer content with her solitude. As she made her way toward Von and the rest of her Circle, she noticed Amara speaking to Serena and Kragen, while Xander seemed to be interrogating Reyna. Ronan was standing a bit off to the side speaking with Von and Nial. Timmins and Joquil were listening to a solemn Miranda, and Effie was nowhere to be seen.

Do not look for him, she ordered as soon as her eyes began to search for the familiar golden head. Helena shifted her focus to the ground and headed in the direction of Von. He reached for her hand as soon as she made it to his side. The touch helped steady her frayed nerves.

"Helena," Ronan started.

"You have nothing to apologize for," she said, surprising him.

"I should have—"

"No," she said firmly, but softly. She wasn't ready to talk about it, and she certainly didn't want anyone else carrying the guilt of this death. That burden was hers alone. If she had been here, she could have stopped it.

His eyes softened and he nodded, moving as if to walk away. She stopped him with a hand on his arm. "I do not blame you, and I am ordering you to not blame yourself."

Ronan's eyebrows shot up in surprise. "How, exactly, do you intend to enforce that?"

"You're an honorable man, Ronan. Don't let me down."

"Tricksy female."

Her lips lifted in the barest hint of a smile. Ronan reached out and pulled her into his arms, holding her tightly for one long moment before letting her go and backing away.

Sensing the tidal wave of emotion threatening to overwhelm her, Von stepped forward and redirected the conversation. "Have we decided what our next steps will be?"

"No, not beyond the immediate needs. We will honor the dead, but I would like to take Darrin," her voice quavered as she said his name, "home with us. The Palace is big enough to house all of our new allies, perhaps we should start by gathering there and planning our next steps once everyone is assembled."

Von and Ronan exchanged a look. They weren't thrilled with the idea of creating an easy target for Rowena, but they also understood Helena's rationale.

"What if we gather in Daejara?" Von offered by way of compromise.

"Why would we do that? The Palace is more central."

"But also more obvious."

Helena mulled it over before nodding her agreement. "Fine. We will tell the others to join us there in a few days' time. That will allow us to send word to those that are not already with us."

"How do we avoid sending anything that can be intercepted?" Ronan asked.

Nial cleared his throat, "Leave that to me."

Von lifted a questioning brow.

"I discovered something in a few of the books Timmins lent me. Secrecy should not be a problem."

"All right, if that's settled, then all we need to worry about for the moment is saying goodbye."

Helena was tired of saying goodbye. It felt like she was doing it more and more frequently. They'd been lucky, all things considered, and had only suffered a few losses. Unfortunately, that did not lessen the weight or impact of them. One was too many in that regard.

"Kiri," Reyna's low voice interjected.

"Yes?"

"Due to the fire, there is not much that remains of the fallen. It makes it impossible for us to lay them to rest properly. Do you think..." she cleared her throat, "would you mind, doing for them what you did for those in Duskfall?"

The hesitancy of the strong woman's voice swayed her more than anything else could. Reyna did not want to ask this favor when Helena was so clearly distraught, but her desire to do what was right for her people, both the living and the dead, pushed her to anyway. It was not that Helena would have denied the request, or even that she had not been planning on doing so anyway, but the simple fact that Reyna felt she'd had to ask in the first place. It was a reminder, a call to duty. As the Mother's Vessel, she could not get lost in her own grief. She had to put the needs of the others before her own. At least until this was over.

"Of course."

Relief washed over the other woman's face. "Thank you, Kiri."

Helena took a deep, centering breath before turning to face the wreckage. Calling on her power, Helena called to the spirits of the fallen. All of them. The Shadows had once been Chosen too. She would not leave them here.

As in Duskfall, shimmering dust began to rise up from the ground. The people around her had gone silent, watching her work with varying degrees of awe and reverence. By the time she had finished, thousands of new stars were twinkling in the sky, visible despite the presence of the sun.

Feeling empty and heartbroken, Helena sent a single thought to Von. *"Let's go home."*

CHAPTER 27

*W*hen Effie found her, she was sitting in Anderson's garden, watching the clouds move across the sky. The bag filled with Darrin's ashes sat in her lap.

"H-hi," Effie said in a voice hoarse with disuse. No one had heard her say a word since she'd spoken to Ronan on the battlefield.

Helena took in the girl's dark circles and red-rimmed eyes with a healer's assessing gaze. "Are you ready?"

Effie gave Helena a look. "Can you ever really be ready for something like this?"

"No, I guess not." Standing, she handed the bag out toward Effie. "Here, you should be the one to do it."

Effie's eyes went wide. "Me?"

Helena's smile was kind, even though it wobbled slightly. "You were his choice, Effie. The honor is yours."

Effie's nose went red and her eyes filled with tears. "But his loyalty was always to you first, Helena."

"No one is questioning his loyalty. He was sworn into my service, but he died to protect *you*."

Her lips quavered, and she looked up at Helena with lost blue eyes. "Why? Why did he do that Helena? I am no one. He had a duty, he was part of the Circle. He should have let me—"

Helena cut her off. "Because he loved you, Effie. In his eyes, taking care of you was his only duty. You were everything. Do not dishonor his death by discounting his reasoning."

Effie sniffed back her tears. "How can you even stand to look at me? Don't you hate me for being the reason he is gone?"

"Hate you?" Helena looked shocked by the question. "Effie, Darrin was my best friend. I was thrilled he'd had someone to love and love him in return. Even if it was for too short a time. I will never hold that against you."

The blonde woman still looked uncertain.

"Let me ask you this. Would you have done the same for him?"

"Of course! But—"

"No, there are no buts, Effie. It is what anyone would do for the one that they love."

Effie closed her eyes, more tears rolling down her cheeks. She took one long shuddering breath and then opened them. "Let's do it together," she said.

Helena's heart twisted in her chest, but she bit down on her lip, keeping her emotions in check. "Okay."

The women turned to face the center of garden, each holding one of the looping strands of leather that held the bag closed.

"What should we say?" Effie whispered.

"You don't have to say anything," Helena murmured.

They shared one last look and flung open the bag, tossing the ashes out over the garden. As they did, a gentle gust of wind came, carrying the ashes up toward the sky.

Effie let out a small gasp of surprise as she watched the twirling ashes fly away.

"Welcome home," Helena whispered, her heart feeling as though it was being clenched in a vice.

There was one more gust of wind, its breeze warm and fragrant with the scent of flowers. Helena could have sworn it caressed her cheek, wiping away her tears. Her eyes fluttered closed and she had to focus on breathing before she could speak again. "I'll miss you."

The two women stayed there, staring at the sky for a long while.

Eventually, Helena left Effie alone so that she could say the rest of her goodbyes in private.

THE PALACE WAS QUIET, but it was the quiet of peace, not sadness. Despite everything that had happened in the last handful of weeks, there was a sense of calm that resonated throughout the massive structure. Whether it was because it had been imbued with some residual power of those that built it, or because it held its own kind of magic, Helena wasn't sure. She just knew that it felt easier to breathe when she was surrounded by the safety of its walls.

"Kiri," Alina called.

Helena acknowledged her with a soft smile.

"They are waiting for you in the Chambers."

"Thanks, Alina," she said before sighing. More meetings. She was sorely tired of the politics and strategy. She knew it was necessary, but one would think being in charge meant you got to spend more time doing what you wanted to do. Sadly, that was hardly ever the case. Her childhood self would have been gutted to learn it.

Helena took the spiraling staircase a step at a time, walking slowly even though the men were waiting for her. She wanted to stretch out her last remaining moments of peace as long as possible.

When she stepped in the room, five sets of eyes were staring at her with mixed degrees of concern. She felt Von's phantom caress and struggled not to lean into it. He smirked at her from where he was leaning against the wall.

Kragen and Joquil were already seated at the table, and Ronan was pacing at the far end of the room. Timmins set down the papers he'd been holding.

"Where would you like to start?" she asked without preamble, shutting the door behind her.

"Well the most pressing order of business is what you want to do about the Circle."

"Ronan will take Darrin's place."

Ronan's head snapped around toward her. "What?"

Helena blinked in surprise, looking at the others. "Is that really a question? Is there any doubt that he is the best choice?"

Von was grinning as he asked, "All in favor?"

The four other men all lifted their hands.

Ronan looked shocked. Helena's smile faltered. "You do not have to, Ronan. I know that it is a lot to ask."

Ronan shook his head. "No, it is not that, Helena. I just, I didn't think…" he trailed off, looking at his feet. "You honor me."

Von tossed a book at Ronan's head. Ronan ducked, narrowly dodging the attack. "What was that for?"

"Stop being stupid. There is no one else I would trust more to keep her safe."

"Nor I," Helena murmured with a smile.

Von scowled at her. *"Hey now."*

"I thought that the 'besides you' was implied."

"It better have been."

Helena rolled her eyes.

"Do I take the vow now?" Ronan asked, looking sheepish.

Timmins placed a hand on his shoulder. "There is time for us to do it properly. I will get everything in order so that we can hold the ceremony tonight."

"So what else is there to discuss?" Helena asked.

"The Daejaran ambassador is dead."

"How?" Helena asked. "Rowena?"

Timmins quickly shook his head. "No, not as far as we can tell. It appears to be natural causes. I was thinking that Nial would make a good replacement."

Helena's eyes shifted to Von's, checking to see if he had any objection.

"He will not want to stay behind or be separated from Serena."

"He would not have to be. It is more a position in name, a go between for us and the people of Daejara. Other than yourself, he seems uniquely qualified."

Von nodded his agreement.

"Speaking of Serena," Timmins continued, "She and Nial have placed a formal request for their mating bond to be recognized."

Helena's eyes moved to Ronan, but he was lost in his thoughts.

"They want to have a wedding now?" Kragen asked in disbelief. "Have they forgotten we're sort of in the middle of things?"

It was Ronan who spoke next. "What better time? If Darrin's death has taught us anything it is that tomorrow is not a guarantee. You cannot blame them for wanting to take advantage of the time they do have together, while it's still a possibility."

The room was quiet as they processed his words.

"Of course, if that is what they wish, we will make time to do it right. We can hold the ceremony once we are in Daejara so that both their families can be present."

Von smiled at Helena's suggestion. "My parents will be thrilled."

Helena returned his grin, happy that they would have the chance to celebrate something for once. It was an unexpected and very welcome change.

"Is there anything else?" she asked again.

Timmins glanced at his notes. "Nial has sent word to our allies. They should be joining us in Daejara by week's end. That gives us time to hold the mating ceremony before their arrival."

Just like that, Helena's stress and worry returned in full force. "Can the Holbrooke Estate really hold all those people?" she asked.

Von shook his head. "Not within the Estate itself, but there is more than enough land and abandoned houses that can be utilized. The Estate will house the representatives of each realm, but their forces will need to remain in their own camps until we move out."

She closed her eyes. "Where do we even start? Rowena could be anywhere."

"We will draw her out, make her come to us. It is our turn to start calling the shots," Ronan said with utter confidence.

"Do you know how we intend to do that?"

"Not yet. But we will."

His fierceness and determination were contagious. She could feel the steadying effect it had on the others.

"We will be ready to head out tomorrow," Timmins said.

Helena nodded. She wished they could spend more time here, but she understood why they couldn't. At least they had the night to spend with each other. She would take a page from Nial and Serena's book and make sure to use it wisely. It could very well be the last time they were all together.

"IT WAS DONE?" Rowena's icy voice snapped.

"Aye, my Queen. The Circle has been broken, as promised."

"You are certain?"

"I watched her Shield fall myself. There is no doubt."

"Excellent," Rowena replied, her voice sounding almost warm. "Then we can move ahead with phase two."

"It has already been set in motion, my Queen."

"Come here, Thomas. I think you have earned a reward."

Thomas stood and swiftly closed the distance between them. Rowena smiled at him as he walked up the stone steps to the top of the dais where her throne sat. Her dress was the color of darkness and rustled like dead leaves as she stood. He reached for her, but before he could touch her, Rowena lifted up a hand and summoned her power.

"My dear, *I* am not the reward."

Thomas' dark eyes clouded with confusion. "My Queen?"

Rowena's laugh was cold and brittle. "The impostor was not the only one whose Circle was broken. And that simply cannot stand."

Thomas' eyes widened. "Rowena, no! Please. I've done everything you asked. I've only ever wanted to serve you."

Her hands were already glowing with corrupted power as she smiled. "And you shall, darling. Eternally." When she was done, his once coal-black eyes were now milky-white and snaking with dark lines.

CHAPTER 28

*H*elena had never seen Ronan look so nervous. Actually, Helena had never seen him nervous period. He'd taken special care with his appearance that evening, which for a warrior turned mercenary was saying something.

His red hair had been left down, hanging in cinnamon waves past his shoulders. It was a cross between a lion's mane and a halo, which was fitting, all things considered. He'd even left his leather garb behind, opting for a fitted pair of black trousers with a matching jacket and silky lavender shirt.

"Did you help him dress tonight?" Helena asked, recognizing the style immediately.

"I may have made a few suggestions."

Helena lips twitched in amusement. Poor Ronan. There was no hope he'd escape the notice of any woman dressed like that. Even without the scar bisecting his face, his towering presence and aura of fierce brutality usually kept them at bay. But not tonight. The snug black fabric clung to his muscular build, making him a present any woman would be happy to unwrap. They'd gladly risk his temper in the hopes they could see what came with it.

"You can stop gawking at him any time now."

Helena snickered and sent an appreciative look her Mate's way. *"Jealous, my love?"*

"Please."

She laughed and pressed a lingering kiss against his sculpted lips. *"You have nothing to worry about."*

His eyes were warm and slightly hooded as they met hers. *"I know."* He ran a phantom hand along the length of her back causing her to shiver and flush. It was his turn to grin.

Helena blinked, breaking the seductive spell he'd woven around her, and shifted her focus back to the other men in the room. Her smile widened as she realized they'd all incorporated varying shades of purple into their outfits, in honor of her. She was actually the only one in the room not wearing purple. Alina had worked her own special brand of magic, as usual. Helena had tried to protest, saying there wasn't time for such extravagance, but Alina wouldn't budge.

"Is this not a special occasion?" she'd demanded. Helena couldn't argue that it wasn't. It was incredibly rare to replace anyone in the Circle, especially after less than a year of formal service. It was not something that was done lightly.

Relenting, Helena had allowed Alina to have her way and instead of the traditional purple, Alina had chosen gold. There was nothing special about the cut or shape of the dress. It was fitted from chest to hips before flaring down to the ground. What made it special was how, the dress seemed to shine no matter where she was standing. Helena had become a beacon of light.

The pièce de résistance was actually the crown Alina had placed upon her head. It, too, was golden, but a molten, fiery gold. When she turned, the crown would flash, creating the illusion of sparks flying off of the metal. Alina had given her a crown of embers. It was a warning wrapped in decoration.

"Shall we get started?" Timmins asked.

"Mother yes," Ronan said gruffly, his nerves getting the better of him.

Helena pressed her lips together, trying hard not to laugh.

"Do you remember the words we went over earlier?" Timmins asked Ronan in a low voice.

Ronan glowered at him. "Just because I'm from Daejara doesn't mean I'm a simpleton. I can remember a damn vow."

Von snickered, his hand lifting to cover his mouth. He'd said nearly the same thing when Timmins had prepared him for his own ceremony.

Timmins didn't bat an eye. It was hardly the first time he'd caused one of the Circle to snap at him. It certainly wouldn't be the last. "Then if you are ready, we will begin."

Ronan nodded, moving to stand beside Helena.

Timmins began the ceremony with an invocation of the Mother. "Mother, please recognize the vows that are made here today. Bless them with your acceptance to further strengthen the bonds between your Vessel and her Circle."

With that, each of the men repeated the vows they'd already made to her. As her Mate, Von went first. Followed by Timmins, Joquil and then Kragen. After Kragen's rumbling voice quieted, Ronan's clear blue eyes looked into hers. He remained silent, staring down at her.

"Are you sure this is what you want?" he asked quietly, for her alone.

"Are you?" Helena asked, suddenly worried that he felt forced into the decision.

"There are better men than me to be shackled to for a lifetime."

Helena's worry faded completely. She grinned up at him. "Be that as it may, there is no one else I would rather have watching over me."

His serious gaze searched her face awhile longer before he finally nodded. "Be it on your head then when I fuck it up."

The men laughed.

"You wouldn't be the first," she promised, which only caused them to laugh harder.

Ronan grinned, looking more himself than he had since she'd walked into the room. "In that case," he said kneeling, "let's get this over with." Despite his teasing, he was utterly serious when he spoke the words that would bind them together. "I vow to uphold and obey your beliefs and take them as my own. I will be your shield, protecting your life and light from any that would seek to destroy it. I will spend the rest of my days in service to you and your will, until such a time as the Mother reclaims me or the blade of war strikes me."

Helena's grin wavered as an image of a bowed golden head uttering those same words was superimposed over Ronan's form. She closed her eyes, savoring the reminder even though it hurt. When her eyes opened, Ronan was looking up at her, understanding shining in his eyes.

Pressing her hand to his cheek, Helena made her own vow. She'd improvised the first time she'd made a vow to her Circle; tonight was no different. "I will strive to be worthy of the gift of your service, to remain out of harm's way whenever possible so as to not needlessly place your life in danger."

Ronan smirked at that, knowing it was an impossible promise under the circumstances.

"I vow to never take your service for granted, nor will I ask you to give up more than I am willing to give. May your strength be my shield, and my light your compass, in the days and years to come. Rise, Shield."

Ronan stood, looking equal parts humbled and honored. Helena lifted the chalice, finishing the words of the ceremony. As she did, she made a point to look each man in the eyes, "Blood of my blood these five shall be, my voice, my light, my shield, my sword, and my soul. I take them unto me, as my own, to cherish and protect as I would myself, until such a time as the Mother reclaims me."

She drank deep, adding a final silent request as she did. *Mother watch over these men. I have lost so much already. Please...*

She handed the cup to Von, who took a drink and passed it on. So it went, until all had drank and the cup was empty. Remembering the first time they'd taken the vows, Helena looked around with a smirk. "So now what?"

Ronan looked around at the others. "I don't know about you, but I could use a drink."

"That's as good a plan as any."

There was laughter and murmurs of agreement throughout the

room. Timmins pulled open the door and called for one of the nearby guards.

"Bring some refreshments please."

"And lager! Lots of lager!" Ronan shouted.

Helena threw back her head and laughed. At least this time when she wiped away a tear, it was one of laughter.

EPILOGUE

*H*ours had passed as the group welcomed their newest member officially into the fold, while also remembering the one they'd lost. Helena cherished every second of it. It was a moment of joy in the midst of all the chaos.

Somewhere along the way, Serena, Nial and Miranda had all joined them. They'd tried to get Effie to come as well, but she wasn't quite ready for company.

"Mother's tits! What time is it?" Ronan slurred from the chair he was slouched in.

Von, not in a much better condition, glanced out the window, which was covered, trying to discern the time by the color of the night sky. "Looks like it must be near morning."

Helena traded amused glances with Serena and shook her head. "I think that means it's time to get you to bed."

"What?" Ronan roared, "The party is just getting started."

Von winked at her salaciously, before asking in his own suggestive slur, "Bedtime issit?"

"Boyo, in the shape you're in, you're no good to anyone," Kragen commented dryly. He'd drank every bit as deeply as the others but seemed almost entirely unaffected. If not for the subtle shine in his eyes, Helena would have thought he was completely sober.

Von sneered, "Am too."

"Impressive comeback, darling," Helena snickered.

Von opened his mouth, ready to continue proving his abilities, but Helena put her hand over his mouth and shook her head. Von licked her.

There was a discrete tap on the door. Helena was busy wiping her hand on her dress and laughing at her very drunk Mate. She did not immediately notice Alina waiting for their attention.

Still laughing, Helena asked, "What is it, Alina?"

Alina's face was bleached of color, and she wasn't smiling despite the jovial atmosphere of the room. "A letter just arrived for you, Kiri."

"A letter? At this hour?" Helena asked, already walking toward her.

Alina held the black envelope out with a trembling hand.

All amusement fled. She recognized that seal.

"Rowena."

Everyone went deadly silent, instantly sobered by the name.

Von pushed himself up and stood beside her. His eyes were glassy, but focused.

"Open it," he said in a dangerous voice.

Helena was already ahead of him. The thick black envelope was open, and she pulled out the silvery parchment it had contained. There was nothing on the folded piece of paper to indicate what it would entail.

Her heart was pounding as she unfolded it. *What would it be this time? More taunts?*

"We request the honor of your presence for a masquerade ball in celebration of the Solstice," she read aloud. The words were scrawled with precision, obviously written en mass. Below them, in a more feminine and bold hand, it read:

FEEL FREE TO BRING WHAT'S LEFT OF YOUR CIRCLE.

HELENA CRUMPLED the paper in her fist, already vibrating with anger.

Having been reading over her shoulder, Joquil's amber eyes were wide with fear when he said, "It's a trap, Kiri. You cannot mean to take her up on her invitation."

"Why not?"

"Helena, be serious," Timmins snapped, as he took the ball from her fist and smoothed it out for the others to see. "You know you cannot walk into her trap like that."

"We can make it a trap of our own. The party is not for two weeks. There's time."

"Hellion," Kragen rumbled, "the likelihood we'd be able to manipulate her in her own home is beyond slim."

She turned to face Ronan and Von, waiting for their protests. They had none.

"If this is what you wish to do, we will find a way," Ronan said, his voice steady and eyes clear.

Timmins sputtered, and Joquil and Kragen spun on the Daejarans.

Helena silenced their protests with a shout, "Stop! Let Rowena think she has the upper hand. It only benefits us because it makes her careless."

"Kiri," Timmins tried again.

"No. I am done letting her underestimate me. I am not some bunny that cannot defend myself." She paused, unsheathing her lethal black claws and watching them glimmer in the flickering firelight. "She doesn't realize what she's welcoming into her den with this invitation. Let's take the opportunity to remind her what it means to be the Mother's true Vessel."

As Helena reflected on all Rowena had taken from her, the flames throughout the room began to grow and dance wildly, the wind outside howling and shaking the windows with its intensity.

In a voice filled with deadly promise, Helena lifted her iridescent gaze, "But while the Mother might be merciful, I won't be."

HELENA AND VON'S STORY CONTINUES IN QUEEN OF LIGHT, BOOK 4 IN THE CHOSEN SERIES.

KEEP READING FOR A SNEAK PEEK.

CHAPTER 1

*T*hree towering figures stood facing each other in a loose semi-circle. The ruby red of their robes was the only discernible color in the darkness. From afar the color seemed like a bloody smear against the inky black of the cave's wall. Up close, the splash of color only served to emphasize the seemingly empty space within the recessed area of their hoods.

There was no outward sign that the figures were aware of the storm raging just beyond the cave's entrance. They were unmoving even as a flash of lightning filled the cavern with its blinding glare while an answering crash of thunder echoed along its length.

"The pieces are almost in place."

"It won't be long now."

"She is finally ready to become who she was always meant to be."

"Our salvation."

"Perhaps."

Two of the figures twisted their heads to face the one standing between them.

"But it has been foretold."

"It is but one of two paths."

The leftmost figure's robe rippled, as if the person within was fidgeting restlessly.

"For all that we See, we cannot Know."

"Not until it has come to pass."

"There is always a choice."

The figure in the center dipped its head in a nod. *"And so you understand."*

The wind howled as the storm raged on.

"We will wait."

"And bear witness."

"Where is the Vessel now?"

The central figure's shoulders shook with what might have been laughter. Without waiting to see if the others would follow, he turned and began to make his way deeper into the catacombs.

"She celebrates life before she must greet death."

"SWEET MOTHER, YES!" Helena screamed as Von drove into her with one final, toe-curling thrust.

Von's eyes glittered with wicked satisfaction as he leaned down to kiss her before rolling onto his side and pulling her limp body against his. "We should just stay locked in here tonight and skip the dog and pony show."

Helena let out a snort of amusement as she twisted her head to look at her Mate. "That dog and pony show is your brother's mating ceremony."

"Yes, but I much prefer our *mating* ceremonies." There was no mistaking his innuendo or the sexual promise shining in his silvery gaze.

Despite barely being able to keep her eyes open, Helena's blood quickened at his words. "You're trying to kill me," she finally declared.

"But what a way to go."

They chuckled together, sharing another brief kiss. Von moved to lie on his back, and Helena followed him, curling into his side and resting her head over the still thundering beat of his heart. With her fingers lazily tracing the scrolling lines of his Jaka, she sighed and said, "I should probably go down to check on things. There's not much time left before the guests start to arrive."

Von grunted, holding her tighter.

Knowing better than to try to protest, Helena let her sleepy eyes take in the room. Last time she'd stayed at the Holbrooke Estate, they'd set her up in one of their guest rooms. This time she was sharing Von's childhood room, and it amused her to see the evidence of the boy he'd once been still littered around the chamber.

"So how many women know about your penchant for drawing?" she teased.

Von raised a brow. "My what?"

Helena gestured toward the crudely sketched portrait of what she assumed was a Daejaran wolf.

Von followed her hand before bursting into surprised laughter. "Oh, that. Nial made it for me. When he was four."

"And here I was thinking I finally found something you were terrible at." Helena's words were playful, and her smile grew at the thought of the proud little boy showing his big brother what he'd drawn.

He scoffed. "If I *had* drawn it... hell, if it was just a bunch of stick figures holding swords, and I told you I'd made it especially for you, you'd do the same thing."

"What's your point?"

"That the value is not in the skill."

"Obviously."

Von peered at her curiously. "You wanted to take it, didn't you? When you thought I had drawn it?"

"Maybe."

His chest rumbled with his laughter. "Do you want me to draw you a picture, *Mira*?"

"Only if you use stick figures."

They laughed again.

"And what did you mean *my women*?" he asked once their laughter had faded. "Just how many do you think have been in my room?"

Helena's cheeks grew warm. "Well, I mean... clearly you have a past. You don't learn how to do *that* without experience."

"Helena, look at me." His warm voice grew serious. He didn't continue speaking until her eyes met his. "You are the only woman I've ever allowed into my room, at least in any kind of romantic capacity."

The pleasure and relief that filled her at his admission almost surprised her. "But surely you had conquests..."

"Aye, but never here." At her confused expression, he elaborated. "It saves you from enduring a series of uncomfortable conversations. Not to mention it's a lot harder to leave once you've finished when it's your room."

Helena shook her head with mock disapproval. "Quite the lover even then."

Von gave her a wry smile. "Love had nothing to do with it, and there was never a reason to stay."

"Never?"

"Not until you."

Helena could feel the sincerity of his words filling her through their bond. "Lucky me," she murmured, moving to kiss him.

"No, Helena. Lucky me," he corrected, brushing a stray curl behind her ear before closing the distance between their lips.

Before their tender kisses could go any further, a knock sounded at the door.

"Your brother is looking for you," Ronan called from the other side.

"He probably needs advice about what to do after the ceremony," Von muttered dryly, making no move to get up.

Helena gave him a saccharine smile. "If you've seen the way Serena looks at him when she thinks no one's watching, you'd know he doesn't need any help in that regard."

"How could you possibly know that?"

"It's the same way I look at you."

Von's fingers wove into her hair as he pulled her down for a searing kiss. Ronan had to knock three more times before the lovers finally made it out of their bed to greet him.

"About damn time," he said without any heat. Ronan's blue eyes were twinkling with amusement as Von punched his shoulder by way of greeting.

"Fucker," he said beneath his breath as he walked past the newest member of her Circle.

"Bastard," Ronan returned, saluting Von's retreating back.

"Heard that."

"Meant you to."

"See you down there," Helena told Von, staying behind. She wanted a moment alone with Ronan before the ceremony.

"Don't take too long. You know I can only handle my mother in small doses without you as my buffer."

Helena's answering laugh followed Von down the hall. "Poor Margo."

Ronan lifted an inquiring brow.

"Seeing both of her son's happy and whole is proving to be too much for her. She can't seem to go more than ten minutes without bursting into tears. Von is finding it... trying."

"Only a woman cries because she's too happy."

"Careful, Shield."

"What? It's true."

"I'm starting to think Von didn't hit you hard enough."

Ronan snickered. "He's just lucky I stopped punching back."

"Because you know you'd have to deal with me."

Ronan's answering smile was warm. "Can you think of a better reason?"

Weaving her arm through his, they started walking. Helena considered his question for a moment before replying, "No. Self-preservation is a powerful motivator."

"Indeed, it is." They walked a bit further in companionable silence before Ronan sighed and said, "Just ask. I know you want to."

Not even pretending to misunderstand him, she blurted out, "Are you sure you're okay with this?" Helena had hoped she'd be able to read his feelings through the Jaka, but all she could sense was a tangle of conflicted emotions. Her eyes searched his face, looking for physical signs of how he was doing, but it was a neutral mask. "If this is going to be too much for you, I can find some errand to send you on."

"And leave you unprotected? Not a chance." His words were gruff, but he raised his hand to place it over hers and squeezed. He appreciated her offer, even though he would never take her up on it.

"I am hardly unprotected, and I know several men who would take great offense at the implication."

"Maybe if they'd stop losing all their sparring matches with me, I'd have a little more faith in their abilities."

Helena laughed, remembering how the remaining men in her Circle had all found a reason to take her aside and complain about Ronan's morning practices throughout the course of the week. She knew his words were a cover, Ronan didn't doubt Von's ability to protect her for an instant.

"Are you sure?" she asked again in a softer voice.

Ronan was silent for a long stretch. When he finally spoke, his voice was so soft she barely heard him. "It's time."

Time to really let go. Time to say goodbye. Time to move on. Yes, it was time.

"Then let's go."

THERE WASN'T enough space in the Holbrooke's home to fit all Nial and Serena's guests, so they'd decided to hold the ceremony outside. Even if that hadn't been the case, and had it been her decision to make, Helena would have decided the same. It was beautiful being among the trees and mountainside. The roaring sound of the crashing ocean waves was a perfect soundtrack as the sun began its descent through the sky.

Further decoration was unnecessary, given the vibrant beauty of their natural surroundings, but a small pavilion had been erected and swathed in fresh flowers. The scent of roses and jasmine wafted in the mild breeze.

Ronan had left her once she'd made it outside, citing a need to check on his men. Helena scanned the yard, looking for someone that appeared to be in charge. Technically it should have been her, seeing as how the ceremony was her idea, but frankly she was tired of making decisions and gladly passed all decision making on to the couple. It was their day, after all.

Helena's thoughts began to wander, and she closed her eyes only to find Rowena's icy stare waiting for her. She shuddered and shoved the thought away, forcing herself to take a deep, centering breath. The Circle and their new allies would deal with her soon enough. Today was not a day for worrying about such things. It was a day for celebration, probably the last they'd have until the war was over. Today she would focus on love and life; two of the Mother's most precious gifts.

She sent a caress down the bond, wanting her Mate to know that she was thinking of him. An answering ripple of warmth greeted her, washing away the chill her thoughts of Rowena had caused.

Helena looked back at the pavilion, watching the fragile flower petals flutter in the breeze. In a few short hours, she'd be standing there, speaking the words that formally commemorated what two souls had already acknowledged. It would have been nice to be able to stand on the sidelines and simply be a guest for once. But that was not who she was, or who she was meant to be. Not anymore.

Perhaps it never really was.

"Mira?" Von asked, sensing her disappointment.

"It's nothing."

She felt his curiosity as if it was a tickle up her spine, but he did not question her further.

"Isn't it perfect?" Serena asked, joining her.

"That it is," Helena answered with a smile. "Aren't you supposed to be hidden away until the ceremony starts?"

"Alina just finished helping me get ready and I couldn't stand being cooped up any longer. That woman is truly gifted. I've never felt so feminine in my entire life." Serena laughed as she said the words, the warrior in her appreciating the irony. For years she'd had to pretend that she wasn't soft so that the men around her would take her seriously. Today she could set that instinct aside and embrace the purely female part of herself. Still chuckling, Serena asked, "Isn't this dress divine?" She performed a small twirl, holding her arms out to let her simple lilac gown billow around her.

Helena's smile grew, completely understanding the sentiment. She was no stranger to Alina's ministrations, or her miracles. "You look beautiful," Helena agreed, but it was not because of the dress or her upswept curls that had been held back with a garland of flowers. Serena was glowing with the intensity of her joy. She was a woman in love; one who had been lucky enough to find her mate. It was a rare and beautiful gift that none of the Chosen would take for granted.

"Thank you!" Serena beamed brightly before her lips twisted in a grimace. "I'm just ready to get this over with."

"Don't say that," Helena urged, placing a hand on her friend's arm. "Cherish every second of today."

Serena's jaw clenched and her violet eyes hardened. She heard the words that Helena did not say: they were on borrowed time. Rowena could strike at any minute, although given her less than subtle invitation, it appeared that she was in the process of setting the stage for her next salvo.

The blonde woman took Helena's hand in hers and squeezed, hard. "You're right. It's just my nerves speaking."

"I think that's normal," Helena replied, remembering the way her stomach had felt like it was somersaulting within her the day she and Von made their vows.

"You're probably right."

"Aren't I always?"

"Hardly."

They shared a look before bursting into laughter.

"Now that's what I like to see," Nial said from behind them.

They moved to make room for him, Serena peering at him almost shyly as he took in the sight of her.

"Beautiful," he murmured, his storm-gray eyes shining with a possessive intensity Helena instantly recognized.

Knowing that neither of them remembered she was still standing there, Helena quietly stepped away, giving the couple a few stolen moments of solitude before their ceremony began. She smiled softly as she watched the way that they fussed over the other, their tender caresses and heated looks making her long for something she couldn't name.

FROM THE AUTHOR

If you enjoyed this book, please consider writing a short review and posting it on Amazon, Bookbub, Goodreads and/or anywhere else you share your love of books.

Reviews are very helpful to other readers and are greatly appreciated by authors
(especially this one!)

When you post a review, send me an email and let me know! I might feature part, or all, of it on social media.

XOXO

♡ Meg Anne

meg@megannewrites.com

ACKNOWLEDGMENTS

I think I've proven each time I sit down to write one of these that there is truly a village of people that helped make it possible. You (yes you!) make the words 'thank you' seem inadequate, because there's no way for them to fully encapsulate all that your love and support mean to me.

For my readers, my chosen, my family, my squad, my friends, my person and my Henries… I would never have been able to follow my dream without you. My heart is overflowing today, and every day, because I have been lucky enough to have you in my life.

ALSO BY MEG ANNE

HIGH FANTASY ROMANCE

THE CHOSEN UNIVERSE

THE CHOSEN

MOTHER OF SHADOWS

REIGN OF ASH

CROWN OF EMBERS

QUEEN OF LIGHT

THE KEEPERS

THE DREAMER – A KEEPERS STORY

THE KEEPER'S LEGACY

THE KEEPER'S RETRIBUTION

THE KEEPER'S VOW

PARANORMAL & URBAN FANTASY ROMANCE

THE GYPSY'S CURSE

CO-WRITTEN WITH JESSICA WAYNE

VISIONS OF DEATH

VISIONS OF VENGEANCE

VISIONS OF TRIUMPH

CURSED HEARTS: THE COMPLETE COLLECTION

THE GRIMM BROTHERHOOD

CO-WRITTEN WITH KEL CARPENTER

REAPER'S BLOOD

ABOUT MEG ANNE

USA Today and international bestselling paranormal and fantasy romance author Meg Anne has always had stories running on a loop in her head. They started off as daydreams about how the evil queen (aka Mom) had her slaving away doing chores, and more recently shifted into creating backgrounds about the people stuck beside her during rush hour. The stories have always been there; they were just waiting for her to tell them.

Like any true SoCal native, Meg enjoys staying inside curled up with a good book and her cat, Henry . . . or maybe that's just her. You can convince Meg to buy just about anything if it's covered in glitter or rhinestones, or make her laugh by sharing your favorite bad joke. She also accepts bribes in the form of baked goods and Mexican food.

Meg is best known for her leading men #MenbyMeg, her inevitable cliffhangers, and making her readers laugh out loud, all of which started with the bestselling Chosen series.

Made in the USA
Columbia, SC
11 December 2023

28333041R00159